Rowland Evans Robinson

Uncle Lisha's outing

Rowland Evans Robinson

Uncle Lisha's outing

ISBN/EAN: 9783743372696

Manufactured in Europe, USA, Canada, Australia, Japa

Cover: Foto ©Andreas Hilbeck / pixelio.de

Manufactured and distributed by brebook publishing software (www.brebook.com)

Rowland Evans Robinson

Uncle Lisha's outing

UNCLE LISHA'S OUTING

BY

ROWLAND E. ROBINSON

AUTHOR OF "UNCLE LISHA'S SHOP," "DANVIS FOLKS," ETC.

BOSTON AND NEW YORK
HOUGHTON, MIFFLIN AND COMPANY
The Riverside Press, Cambridge
1897

CONTENTS

UNCLE LISHA'S OUTING.

CHAPTER I.

PLANNING THE CAMPAIGN.

THE company in Uncle Lisha's shop, after discoursing of hunting and lamenting the decrease of game, lapsed into a meditative silence, which was broken at last by Sam Lovel's deep-toned, deliberate voice.

"I tell ye what, I 'm jest a-hankerin' tu go daown tu Leetle Otter Crik, a-duck-huntin'. Don't ye remember, Antwine, what a mess on 'em the' was, a-hengin' raound, that spring we was a-trappin'? The' must be sights on 'em there in the fall, when the wild oats is ripe."

The Canadian grunted emphatic assent without interrupting his energetic pulls at a pipeful of damp tobacco till it was in full blast; then he gave further testimony.

"Yas, seh, dey was great many dauk dat tam, but naow dey was two dauk quarrly for every wil' hoat, an' dey was more as honded taousan' bushil wil' hoat."

"That's ruther more 'n I should ha' sot 'em at," said Uncle Lisha, punching a hole in a patch with a crooked awl and inserting the bristle of a waxed end. "But I 've seen slews on 'em on the ma'shes, an' I do' know 's you 're lyin' much, for you, Ann Twine. Why don't ye go, Samwil, you an' Solen an' Jozeff an' Peltier an' 'mongst ye? Ye might jest as well as not, right arter ye git y'r corn cut up, an' stay a good spell, 'fore tater diggin'."

"Bah gosh! Ah 'll go, me," cried Antoine. "Ah 'll can show you haow for shot de dauk! Ah 'll was be preffick mans for kill dauk, me."

"Me an' yer father an' the women folks c'ld git along wi' the chores, julluck rollin' off 'm a lawg," Uncle Lisha continued without noticing the Canadian's self-invitation, "an' I don't see as there 's nothin' tu hender ye goin'."

Sam pondered the proposition for a considerable time before he replied with a question.

"Why won't you go, Uncle Lisher? The chores hain't no gret, an' I c'ld git Billy Wiggins tu help du 'em."

"Me go?" said Uncle Lisha, casting a quick glance on Sam to see if he meant what he was saying. "Good airth an' seas! I 'm tew ol' tu go skylarkin' raound wi' a passel o' boys! I should jest sp'ile the rest ou ye's fun. Better take yer father, Samwil."

"You could n't snaike him daown there wi' a yoke o' oxen. He 'd a sight druther stay 'long wi' the women folks. You would n't spile no fun, an' if we settle on goin' you got tu go tew."

"Yas, sch, you jes' good leetly boy as we was, Onc' Lasha," Antoine declared for his further encouragement.

The old man sat meditating for some time with idle hands upon his knees before he answered : —

"Wal, the' hain't no denyin' but what I 'd luf tu. I use tu squirmish raound them ma'shes consid'able when I was a ' whippin' the cat ' daown there thirty year ago. An' I sh'ld luf tu see the folks. I p'sume tu say the 's some 'at hain't fergot me yit. But I guess I 'd ortu stay tu hum an' help yer father an' the women folks." He heaved a sigh of resignation and gave the patch a resolute punch with the awl.

"You need n't let that hender ye," said Pelatiah Gove, "for I c'n turn tu an' help 'm if the 's any extry job."

"Why, you 'll go 'long wi' us, Peltier," said Sam.

Pelatiah shook his head in slow but determined negation. "No, I don't want to go — not down there," and they all knew why.

"Wal, you 'll go, Jozeff?" Sam asked.

The first response was a dubious squeak of the rickety chair as Joseph Hill shifted his position in slow perturbation of spirit, and then as he leaned cautiously aside to inspect his unstable seat, assuring himself in an undertone, " I ruther guess 't won't, not yit," he answered : —

" Wal, I s'pose I 'd ortu, an' then agin I s'pose I hedn't ortu. I 'd ortu go an' git rested up, which I hain't hed no chance sence hayin'. Then agin the 's lot tu du 'at I hain't seemed to git raound tu, an' father he 's kinder peaked, do' know but he 's sorter failin', do' know 's I ever see him quite so docyle. An' I do' know as M'ri an' Bub c'ld git along wi' the chores erless they c'n punch that 'ere 'Lige Kellick tu help 'em some, they can't never git him up tu, in the mornin', the lazy shote. But I do' know 's father 'd let me hev his gun, if Bub 'ld spare it. He 's a-whangin' raound wi' 't ev'y chance he gits. But if the ducks is as thick as you tell on, it seem 's 'ough a feller c'ld git feathers 'nough tu fill a tick, an' that 's jest what M'ri wants. I got tu make that the main p'int in talkin' on 't over with M'ri, an' I can't answer fer sartain until I du, but I 'm hopesin' the feathers 'll fetch her."

" An' what du you say, Solen ? " Sam asked.

Solon Briggs heaved a sigh so deep that it served to clear his throat as well as to express regret.

" Well, I 'm obleeged tu say that my goin' on sech a taower has got tu be forewent, because I have heretobefore gin my bonafied promise tu Mis' Briggs, betwixt hoein's, tu take her over tu Adams

to visit her folks, if she 'd wait till after hayin',
which she hevin' done so, I can't intricate myself
aout on, hon'able."

" I s'pose not," Sam admitted, " but I s'pect all
on us 'at goes hev got tu talk aour women folks
raound fust.   They gen'ally hev objections tu stag
parties.   If it hain't the work 'at ortu be done, it 's
your health.   Stag parties is turrible onhealthy."

" Bah gosh," said Antoine, straightening and
swelling himself to his greatest dimensions and
speaking in a big voice, " when Ah 'll took motion
Ah 'll goin' somewhere, mah hwomans make off
hees min' Ah 'll goin', an' ant said not'ing 'f he
ant want hees head slap."

" Wall," Solon said, " my idee is, 'at moral persuasion goes furder 'n rambumptiousness in argyin'
wi' femaline folks."

" Antwine 's got the advantage o' most on us,"
Sam explained, " in hevin' of him a ' he ' wife 'at 's
twicte as big as what he is."

" O Sam, no he ant, too !   Ah tol' you, seh,
Ah 'll took it w'en he was young an' Ah 'll brought
it up for suit me, not hesef.   Ant you see, hein ? "

" Wal, I cal'late the truth on 't is, she 's glad tu
git red on ye as often as she ken," Uncle Lisha
said as he rubbed down the seam with the handle
of the awl.

" It 'pears 'ough aour huntin' party was sim-
mered daown tu Uncle Lisher an' Jozeff an' An-

twine an' me, anyways, for Peltier won't an' Solon can't an' mebby the' can't none on us, not for sartain' 'fore we find aout what aour women folks says. But s'posin' we du go, we want tu borry Peltier's scaow boat — over 't the pond, haint it, Peltier? — for Uncle Lisher an' Jozeff, an' me an' Antwine 'll hev my canew, an' we c'n lwud them an' aour tent ontu a waggin an' drive daown within tew rod o' where we camped when we went fishin', an' git aour team kep' somewher's nigh."

"Why, Samwil, you've got us so nigh there a'ready, I can e'enamost smell the campfire," said Uncle Lisha.

"We don't want tu kerry no gre't v'riety o' pervisions," Sam continued, " jest some pork an' taters an' a leetle smidgin o' bread tu start on — we c'n buy bread o' the folks daown there when we git aout, an', le' me see " —

"An' onion ; Ah 'll drudder not have had any-t'ing as not had onion, me."

"Of course, so 's 't you c'n be strong whilst we suffer," said Sam, and went on enumerating the necessaries of the trip. "An' a slew o' paowder an' shot an' caps an' waddin' an' blankets an' lemme see what else ? "

"Why, Samwil, you goin' tu du julluk t'other feller 'at went a-huntin'? He got already tu start wi' his ammernition lwuded intu his pockets, an' tu make sure he hed n't forgot nothin' he went over 'em all. 'Here's my shot,' says he, a-slappin' his hand on one pocket, ' an' there's my paowder,' a-puttin' his han' on another, ' an' there's my caps.' All right,' an' off he went till he come tu the woods, an' a pa'tridge a-stan'in' on a lawg, not six rod off. ' By thunder!' says he, ' I hev forgot suthin', an' it's my gun.' "

" Yes," Sam said, " guns might be hendy an' we 'll have us some, an' le' me see " —

" We want tu kerry a gre't big bag tu put them 'ere feathers in," said Joseph Hill; " I do' know as sech an almighty gre't bag, but a tol'lable middlin'-sized sort o' bag; but I 've got tu kerry a bag for 'em' if I don't kerry nothin' else, 'cause the heft o' my argyment lays in them feathers. An' Samwil an' Uncle Lisher," he leaned far forward and spoke in a loud, impressive whisper which was emphasized by a prolonged creak of the unstable chair, " you don't want tu say nothin' 'baout it tu your women folks, 'cause they 'd up an' tell M'ri an' then daown 'ould go my shanty." He settled back in his seat with spasmodic chuckles, to which the chair responded with a series of short squeaks, then its legs began to slip and sprawl apart; there was a gathering sound of splitting and breaking wood fibres, till with a final crash and resounding bump chair and occupant went down to the floor together.

" I 'm almighty glad on 't," Uncle Lisha roared,

almost like an echo of the brief sudden uproar. "I wish't it had bruk two year ago, the dumb'd squeakin' thing. Open the stove door, Peltier, an' chuck in the pieces 'fore some tarnal fool sets tu mendin' it. Hurt ye any, Jozeff?"

"Wal, not ra'ly," Joseph answered, looking helpless and foolish as he sat amid the ruins. "I sot daown a little sollider 'an I cal'lated tu, an' it jarred me some, an' I b'lieve I bit my tongue, seems 's 'ough."

"Where was de litlin' struck?" Antoine asked; and Aunt Jerusha, appearing at the door of the kitchen, cried out in a tremor of anxiety: —

"What in the livin' airth! Has the stove fell daown? Lisher Peggs, be you hevin' a fit?"

"It's that dumb'd chair, an' I'm glad on 't."

"It's fort'nate 'at the linter hain't underminded by no suller," said Solon, as he viewed the wreck, "or Jozeff might have been promulgated into the dep's."

"Sam Hill!" Joseph ejaculated, as he began to push aside the wreckage with deliberate hands preparatory to rising. "Ef that wan't a kerwollups! Wal, I guess I'll g' hum an' kinder begin tu hint tu M'ri 'baout the feathers. Don't seem 's 'ough I sot daown on none that time sca'cely." And as he went forth the other visitors departed after him.

CHAPTER II.

A REKINDLED CAMPFIRE.

THE household divinities proved kind, and when Sam's cornfield had lost its semblance to a miniature tropical jungle and had taken on the likeness of a village of aboriginal wigwams, he and his friends set forth for the lowlands in the chill, vaporous stillness of a September dawn.

The silence continued undisturbed save by the echoed rumbling of the wagon over the first mile or two of the road, and from the woodside by the clamorous assault of crows upon some furred or feathered enemy.

At length the travelers began to hear other sounds of life, first the muffled indoor clatter of a stove being made ready for lighting the fire, interrupted by the creaky opening of a door as the half-clad fire-builder peered forth to see who was faring abroad so early and to wonder why, if not to ask. Then the sleepy voice of a cowboy arousing the herd while he was but half awake, and presently the clattering of milk-pails, the clank of bars, and creak of barnyard gates. Next came from kitchens appetizing sounds of breakfast-getting and voices of women, high-pitched above the clatter of tableware, the screech of frying-pans, the songs of kettles, and the punching of reluctant fires. A little later, the voices of children arose, drowsily at first, then breaking forth in all the volubility of refreshed life and action, and the day was fairly begun for every one.

Then people were fallen in with on the highway, faring one way and the other, and men and teams were seen going afield. By and by conchs and horns began to sound at farmsteads far and near, the long-drawn dinner call, that, though not for our travelers, reminded them that they were hungry.

They halted in the first inviting wayside shade to feed their horses and themselves, and unhurried by the sequence of after-dinner chores ate more deliberately even than they did at home, aiding digestion by slowly ruminated mouthfuls, while their eyes wandered over unfamiliar surroundings.

Then they went forward, the course of the day marked by one and another visible or audible sign as the progress of their journey was by the changing landscape, till at mid-afternoon they were in the level lowlands with their own mountains as blue behind them as the nameless peaks of the Adirondacks before them.

" The lay o' the land here is consid'able like the West," Uncle Lisha remarked to his companions as they lumbered between broad fields of pasture, meadow, and stubble land, after crossing Little Otter for the last time at its lower falls. "On'y the 's more woods 'an what the' is where I was. I cal'late this 'ere 's a good enough country for most anybody tu live in, level 'nough so 't you need n't roll off, an' hills an' maountains so 's 'at your eye-sight don't git tired a trav'lin' 't the eend o' the airth. But I d' know but what I 'd hanker arter the smell o' spreuce an' balsam if I lived here."

"Dey ant got no Injin or greasily bear here, prob'ly," Antoine remarked by way of comparison with the West.

"Sho, Ann Twine, the' wan't no Injins tu hurt nob'dy where I was, an' them grizzly bears is way aout furder where the 's buffaloes an' wil' Injins."

"Ah 'll s'pose dey call it greasily bear 'cause it was so fat, ant he, prob'ly?"

"Wal, no, I cal'late they call 'em grizzly 'cause they 're so almighty tough an' chuck full o' grizzle. They say you can shoot 'em so full o' lead 'at they 'll sink in water afore they 'll die."

"Bah gosh, dey more wusser as you hol' sprim gawn bear ant he, Onc' Lasha?"

The sun was low in the west and cows were com-ing home through goldenrod and aster bordered lanes and dusty highways when the travelers jolted over the ruinous Slang bridge. Half an hour later they were at the old campground on the rocky bluff, its place still marked by a russet mat of decaying cedar twigs and the stone fireplace which Antoine was delighted to find in serviceable condition. He at once got the necessary provisions and utensils from the wagon and set about getting supper while the others unloaded the wagon and pitched the tent.

Sam drove away to the nearest farmhouse to find keeping for the horses, and after a while came stumbling out of the gathering gloom into the light of the campfire, to which his nose guided him as well as his eyes, for Antoine's cookery diffused a far-reaching savory odor to direct and hasten the steps of a hungry man.

The camp had already taken on the cheerful aspect of an established abiding-place, blankets and boxes having been stowed inside the tent. In front of it Uncle Lisha and Joseph sat, comfortably smoking their pipes as they quietly watched Antoine prancing around the frying-pan and potato kettle, while his shadow sprawled along the ground and leaped from trunk to branch in ever-varying grotesqueness of form and motion.

"Git a put-uppance fer the hosses, did ye, Samwil?" Uncle Lisha asked, making room for Sam on the fireside log.

"Yes, I got 'em turned aout tu paster arter some coaxin'," Sam answered, seating himself in the proffered place with a sigh of satisfaction. "But

I du hope we c'n keep Antwine away f'm there, fer I 'm afeared if he hears much o' the ol' feller's talk 'at owns the place he 'll larn tu lie. Why, he tol' me, a-lookin' as honest as the cooper's caow, haow 'at he was a-patchin' the ruff of his barn, to-day, an' somehaow er nother he begin tu slip, an' kep' a-slippin', an' could n't stop himself no way, till jest as he went over the eaves, feet fust an' face daown, he ketched a holt o' the aidge o' the shingles with his teeth, an' there he hung till they fetched a ladder, an' he clumb daown."

"What ye think o' that, Ann Twine?" Uncle Lisha asked the Canadian, who was cocking an alert ear while his eyes were intent upon the sputtering frying-pan.

Antoine blew away the smoke with a contemptuous "Pooh, dat ant noting! Ah 'll gat brudder-law in Canada was more strong of his jaw as dat. One tam he run away wid hees hoss an' it broke loose of hees woggin, an' he touch hol' of de line wid hees toof an' hang on de woggin wid bose hees han' of it, an', seh, dat hoss run more as mile 'fore he stop it up. Come, gat ready for heat you suppy. Fetch de bread an' de onion, Sam," and he whisked the frying-pan from the fire to the flat rock that served as table, then poured the water from the potato kettle and set it beside the pan.

"I ruther guess, Samwil," said Uncle Lisha, as he arose and moved toward the supper, " 'at you might let Ann Twine g'wup there if you hain't feared for t' other feller."

As they smoked their after-supper pipes and planned the morrow's campaign, in every lull of conversation they could hear the quacking and splashing of the host of ducks feeding in the marsh, and now and then the pulsing whistle of swift wings as a belated flock came in from the lake, and then the restful sounding splash as the newcomers settled upon the water to join the feasting horde. And when the tired campers fell asleep on the bed of cedar, these sounds still ran through their dreams, a thread of reality woven into the misty fabric.

CHAPTER III.

THE campers were astir betimes in the silver dawn that they counted of greater worth for their use than a golden day. After a hasty breakfast, Sam and Antoine embarked in the canoe at the landing above the Slab Hole, where the boats were unloaded the night before; but Uncle Lisha and Joseph preferred the stable land to the fickle waters, and prowled westward along the lake shore as slowly and almost as stealthily as a couple of aged mud turtles might have gone over the same ground.

Peering out upon the bay through loopholes of the cedar-clad cliff, they saw great flocks of ducks riding safe and far on the glassy water. The nearest were a triple gunshot out of range of this shore, while many were so tantalizingly close to Garden Island that the dusky lines cut the reflected brightness of the island's autumnal splendor.

"Good airth and seas!" Uncle Lisha whispered, as he and Joseph crouched on hands and knees,

peering through the branches with longing eyes at
the distant flocks, " ef we was on'y jest on that
'ere islan'. I wonder if we hed n't better go an'
git the scaow bwut an' go 'way raound an' come
up on t' other side ? "

" Wal, I do' know 'baout it," Joseph whispered
dubiously. " It's a good way off, seem 's 'ough it
was, an' the weather might change consid'able
'fore we could git back. I hain't no gre't appetite
for water, not sech a sight on 't, an' I don't b'lieve
I want tu go aout 'mongst so much on 't, not
sca'cely, anyways, not tu-day."

" Wal, I wish the wind 'ould change an' come
aouten the north, an' blow 'em over here er
suthin'."

" Ef we hed us some corn an' kinder hove it
over the bank, mebby it 'ould call 'em up tu us."
But as they had not the means at hand for trying
this experiment and as no favoring gale blew the
ducks within range, but they on the contrary began
to waddle out by dozens upon the shelving shore
of the island to bask in the sun, the two sportsmen
reluctantly withdrew from their point of observation and pursued their way along the cliff to where
it slopes to the low shore of a shallow bay. Here
grew some hickory - trees bearing a profusion of
nuts as foreign to Danvis as the fruit of a cocoa
palm. As Uncle Lisha and his companion were
filling their pockets with the fallen nuts, they sur-

prised a gray squirrel who was rasping out his breakfast on a lower branch and now retreated to a hiding-place among the topmost leaves. They were at once filled with a desire to secure him as a trophy and a toothsome addition to camp fare, and so with guns at a ready they went slowly around the tree, scanning every branch and intricacy of leafage, often fooled almost to the point of firing at some semblance of the object of their search, but never quite discovering it.

"Wal," said Uncle Lisha at last, grounding the butt of his gun and leaning on the muzzle while he gazed wistfully up into the tree, "the critter's up there somewheres, sartain, fer he hain't got no wings an' the' hain't no tree he could jump off intu. Naow, Jozeff, I b'lieve if you'd go down there tu the lake an' git a han'f'l o' stuns, I c'ld fling 'em up in there an' start the critter aout so's 't we c'ld shoot him. I use 'ter be tol'able hendy flingin' stuns."

Accordingly Joseph set his gun against a tree and made for the shore with all speed, which he did not abate till he had crashed through the fringe of cedars and come out upon the stony beach. Then to his intense disgust a great flock of teal arose almost at his feet in a flurry of alarm at the noise and sudden apparition, and went whistling away far over the bay. Joseph stared after them open - mouthed but speechless, till surprise and

chagrin took audible expression in a long exhaled
" Gosh ! " and then, with eyes following the swiftly
retreating flock : —

" Who in Sam Hill 'spected you was here?
Wal, there goes one lot o' M'ri's feathers."

Heaving another sigh, he turned his back upon
the lake, and picking up an armful of stones returned to his companion, inwardly berating himself
at every step and groaning over the lost opportunity.

Uncle Lisha's arm still possessed enough of the
strength and skill of youth to dislodge the squirrel with a few well-directed missiles, and Joseph
brought it down after a pottering aim of the long
gun.

" You done well, Jozeff, an' your father 'd be'n
praoud on ye if he 'd seen ye," said Uncle Lisha as
he picked up the squirrel and held it forth for the
successful sportsman to feast his eyes upon.

" Father ! " cried Joseph ruefully. " Gosh, ef
he 'd ha' seen what I done er ruther what I did n't
du, he 'd kick me higher 'n Gilderoy's kite, if 't
wan't for the rheumatiz in his laigs. I went a
kerflummuxin' daown yunder through the bushes
right slap ontu a snag o' ducks 'at I might jes' 's'
well crep' up tu an' shot if I 'd on'y 'spected they
was there. I bate ye the' was more 'n ten paound
o' feathers on 'em. But haow easy they did kerry
'em off, though."

Uncle Lisha lamented the chance which had deprived both of distinguishing themselves, but consoled Joseph by assuming an equal portion of the blame. "An' naow, who knows but what the critters 'll come back there arter they git over their scare. What fetched 'em there oncte 'll fetch 'em ag'in. Le' 's go an' sed daown there an' wait."

Joseph readily assented to a plan which required so little exertion, and the two sat down behind the screen of evergreens, where through an opening in the bushes they could command a view of the shore and the rushy border of the bay in front of them, and so for half an hour they sat enjoying their pipes and a whispered conversation no louder than the stir of the breeze among the treetops, the patter of the falling leaves, and the break of the ripples on the beach.. Suddenly these dreamy sounds were overborne by a pulsing, sibilant beat, prolonged in a whistle of set wings, which ended with a resounding, fluttering splash, as a flock of twenty or more teal settled upon the water within forty yards of the ambuscade and swam to and fro in busy inspection of their surroundings.

"Aim int' the thick on' em, an' when I caount three, fire," said Uncle Lisha in a trembling whisper as he and his companion cautiously poked their guns through the bushes and took deliberate aim.

"One — tew — three," Uncle Lisha counted, and with the sharp expiration of the last word his ancient queen's arm belched forth its mighty voice. Joseph Hill pulled lustily at the trigger of his half-cocked piece, shutting both eyes tighter as the pull became more desperate, and bracing his nerves for the inevitable recoil which must follow such a reluctant discharge.

"Sam Hill!" he ejaculated, when at last he desisted and opened his eyes to see a half dozen victims of Uncle Lisha's shot floating belly up and the affrighted survivors scurrying away in wild flight. "It don't seem 's 'ough this plagued ol' gun was use to shootin' ducks. It don't 'pear tu want tu go off at 'em."

"It wants tu be cocked fust, Jozeff," Uncle Lisha remarked, casting an eye upon the unready weapon, as they rushed from cover to secure the game. "Cock her an' let flicker at that waounded one. It 's a-floppin' clean aouten reach."

Joseph stared a moment in chopfallen dismay at the lock of his gun, then cocking it and leveling the long barrel to careful aim, put a merciful end to the struggles of the wounded duck. By the aid of a pole and a favoring breeze the sportsmen were able to gather their booty, — seven plump teal in all, which they ranged side by side and gloated over with as complete satisfaction as if 'the green beauty spots on each wing had been as many emeralds. Then they tied the birds in two bunches, to the smaller of which the squirrel was added, and these Uncle Lisha magnanimously permitted his less successful comrade to carry as if it were his rightful trophy.

So laden, and quite content to try their fortune no further, they set forth toward camp. As they drew near it Joseph broke a long interval of silence.

"I've kinder be'n a-thinkin' on 't over in my mind, Uncle Lisher, 'at like 'nough, mebby, it 'ould be jes' 's well not tu say nothin' 'baout my not cockin' my gun; I do' know but mebby it 'ould be full better not tu, Ann Twine 's so kinder aggervatin'."

"Good airth an' seas, Jozeff, I won't say nothin'! Ef the ol' fuzee hed n't sot back so, I should n't knowed whether it was me or you 'at fired, an' I sh'd thought you hed if you had n't said nothin'. It 's lucky you did n't er we would n't ha' got that 'ere waounded one. Pshaw, I won't say nothin', Jozeff."

The camp was silent and deserted but for a chipmunk that sat clucking contentedly on the rock table after a feast of crumbs. The fireplace gave forth neither smoke nor warmth, but only the faint breath of new-made ashes and freshly-charred wood. The slovenly array of frying-pan, pot, and tin plates stood cold and untouched since breakfast, and it was evident that Sam and Antoine had not returned since the morning departure.

"My sakes!" said Joseph, as he viewed the unhousewifely scene with a kind of a shamefaced satisfaction, "I 'm glad M'ri hain't here to see aour housekeepin'. She 'd have a tantribogus fit, 'most seem 's 'ough she would."

"Wal," said Uncle Lisha, "the' is a diff'ence 'twixt men folkses haousekeepin' an' women folkses, as a gen'al thing. Where the' hain't, the 's suthin' wrong wi' the man er the womern. If it 's a womern a keepin' haouse like a man, she 's a reg'lar sloven, you may depend; an' if it 's a man 'at keeps haouse as a womern ort tu, he 's jest as sartain ter be a he ol' maid. Naow le 's eat a col' bite an' then light up a fire an' heat some water, an' kinder git the thick on 't off 'm these 'ere dishes. It 's tew bad Drive ain't here tu help us."

After fortifying themselves with cold potatoes, raw pork, and onions, they set manfully and unskillfully to the task of dishwashing, which was in a manner accomplished in the hour which intervened before the return of their friends.

CHAPTER IV.

THE DUCKS OF LITTLE OTTER.

WHEN Sam and Antoine paddled out from the landing a thick film of fog lay upon marsh and channel, undulating in the almost imperceptible breath of the morning breeze, but disclosing the dun and green rushes and glassy water the canoe's length away, beyond which color and substance dissolved and vanished in the pearl gray mist. Now a vague form loomed up in the marsh's edge till it shrunk to the solid reality of a muskrat house, then again became unreal in the veil of vapor. To the voyagers' eyes there was nothing substantial but themselves and their canoe and the little circle of glassy water sliding smoothly into the fog before, rippling a widening wake into the fog behind.

Now and then the raucous quack of dusky ducks was heard calling to their befogged mates, and the rustle and splash of some unseen life occasionally stirred in the marsh; but far or near there was no sound telling of human presence save the tinkling drip of the paddles or the scratching of a weed along the canoe's side, or a few whispered words of consultation.

So for half an hour they drove the arrow of their wake through the fog till at a turn of the channel Sam saw the ripple of another wake ruffling the water before him, and following it toward its point discovered five dark objects appearing as if hung in the mist. In two cautious noiseless motions he laid down the paddle and took up his gun, then aimed and fired just as the ducks, now suspicious and restless, were pivoting, on the point of taking flight. As the smoke slowly lifted it disclosed two ducks killed outright and one fluttering toward the marsh with a broken wing, while two drove away . into the fog, uttering wild quacks of terror. Antoine stopped the cripple with a timely shot, and then sent the canoe forward with a few dexterous strokes of his paddle till Sam could recover the dead birds.

The report of the guns was followed so quickly by the roar of myriad wings, as a mighty host of waterfowl uprose from the marshes, that it seemed a part of the echo which rebounded from along the wooded shores and far away among the distant hills, and then for a few moments the air was filled with the whistle of wings as the disturbed flocks circled above the almost invisible intruders or set forth in flight toward the lake.

"Wal, there!" said Sam, after listening till the

confusion of sounds subsided to a faint whisper of retreating flight and the splashing flutter of laggards suddenly alarmed at finding themselves alone, " I guess we started aout the last duck in the hull crik, an' might as well go back tu camp. The' can't be no more, the' hain't no room for 'em."

" Oh, Ah 'll tol' you, Sam, dey was roos' top one 'nudder, an' dey ant honly top one flewed off yet," Antoine answered in a low voice. " Naow we go in de ma'sh for load off aour gaun."

With a few strokes they sent the canoe her length among the wild rice stalks to insure greater steadiness while they stood up to reload their guns. The sun was rising, and the first level beams paved a gilded path and pillared and spanned it with resplendent columns and arches of mist as it lifted and wreathed in the light wafts of the uncertain air, and now through and beneath the rising vapor a stretch of the channel shone in a curving line of silver, still barred with fading ripples of the canoe's wake. Sam's eyes were following it as he capped his gun, when suddenly he crouched upon his knees, whispering hurriedly : —

" Scrooch daown, Antwine, th' 's su'thin' comin'; I 'm goin' tu try 'em if they don't light."

Antoine bent his head low as a flock of teal came stringing down the channel in arrowy flight, and Sam, aiming a little ahead of the leading bird, pulled trigger. The hindmost teal in the line slanted downward, and, striking the water with a resounding splash, lay motionless when the impetus of its fall was spent.

" Wal, if that don't beat all natur'," Sam said with a gasp of surprise. " That 'ere duck was ten foot ahind o' the one I shot at. What sort o' ducks du ye call 'em, Antwine ? "

" He come 'fore you call it dis tam, but w'en he ant, you call heem steal dawk in Angleesh, Ah b'lieved so. He was plumpy leetle feller," Antoine remarked as he picked up the bird, when Sam had reloaded and the canoe was again in mid-channel.

" An' a lively breed they be, tu shoot a-flyin'," Sam commented, as he examined this victim of chance. " 'T ain't no use a-shootin' at 'em. You got to shoot 'way off int' the air ahead on 'em, an' let 'em run ag'in your shot. Naow be we goin' tu poke along er lay low for 'em ? "

" Wal, seh, it bes' was dis tam o' day, we go 'long kan o' slowry. 'Long mos' to evelin' was be de bes' tam for hide in de ma'sh, w'en de dauk come for hees suppy. Naow, you be ready for shoot an' Ah 'll paddle de cannoe, me."

They had not gone far up the channel when the canoe in its stealthy progress came close upon a dusky duck sitting among the wild rice, where she might have remained unseen and unsuspected but for her alarm. As she sprang with a startling splash and flutter clear of the rank marsh growth,

Sam thought to profit by his experience with the teal and fired too far ahead his mark, making a clean miss. He stared at the escaping duck and Antoine offered the consoling comment : " Dat feller ant run ag'in you shot, prob'ly."

Sam repeated his mistake with two or three more rising birds, but got two more in a sitting shot at a flock of wood duck discovered in a nook of the marsh, and then to Antoine's great disgust easily knocked over a coot that stupidly permitted them to paddle within short range.

" Dat feller ant worse you' paouder, Sam. You see he gat mout' mos' lak' hen was, an' hees foots some lak' hen, some lak' dauk, an' he 'll ant t' oddur t'ing or one. Ah 'll 'spee' prob'ly it was hens try for be dauk, or dauk try for be hens, an' he 'll ant mek' up very good. He mek' some good fedder for Zhozeff. Hello, Sam, you 'll know dis place, ant it ? " he asked with eager interest as he came to a narrow tributary channel with fishing stakes set on either side.

" Wal, if it hain't the East Slang, sure as guns," said Sam in joyful recognition of their old trapping ground. " I tell ye what, Antwine, we mus' go an' take a look at aour ol' hum'stead," and Antoine turned the canoe's prow into the narrower waterway and followed its lazy meandering among the broad level of the marsh to where the sluggish current creeps between narrower margins of wild rice, rushes, and sedges flanked by open fields on the east and, at that time, by almost unbroken forest on the west.

At the nearest point of this shore they found an opening to their old landing and pushed the canoe to a berth alongside a clumsy dugout which gave evidence of recent use in a fish-pole and line and a basin of earth in which a few angle-worms were crawling and reaching vainly for a way of escape over the edges of rusty tin.   A well-worn footpath led away through the bushy border and under the hemlocks.

"Prob'ly some more mah rellashin, Ah guess," said Antoine.

"One o' your brother-in-laws.   Mebby we 'll go an' look him up bime by.   I b'lieve I 've heard you tell o' hevin' one or tew.   But le 's gwup tu the ol' shanty," and he led the way to the familiar spot.

It was not hard to find, for the moss-grown slabs were lying in a crushed heap upon the broken ridge-pole, and in front a patch of ashes filmed with moss, nourishing fireweed whose silver-winged seeds were now drifting alee on the light breeze, marked the place of the old campfire.   Beside it was the log seat, softer than it used to be with decay and a cushion of lichens.   They seated themselves upon it, looking around upon the desolation with half melancholy interest while they slowly filled their pipes.

"It looks so as if de folks was all dead gre't many year 'go, an' it seem so we was de folks," said Antoine ruefully. "It mek' me feel lone-sick."

"Yes, it does make a feller sort er lunsome, a mournin' for the feller that was himself oncte."

"Dat true as you livin', Sam. Bah gosh, seh, it ant seem if Ah was me, w'en Ah 'll re'mbler dat leetly boy in Canada wid hees fader an' mudder, young folks dat dance all naght, an' Ah 'll gat honly one brudder-law, an' de summer las' mos' all de year an' de winter ant never too long 'cause Ah 'll happy every day. Oh, Ah 'll ant dat leetly feller. Den w'en Ah 'll growed big mans Ah be naow Ah 'll ant know much an' can' spik Ang-leesh more as frawg ; dat ant de sem' feller Ah was naow, for know much anybody an' spik jus' lak' Yankee. Den Ah 'll faght in de Papineau war more hugly as dev', naow Ah 'll was peaceably mans, honly w'en Ah 'll was get mad, den dey want for look aout, everybody but you, Sam. Oh, Ah 'll was been great many feller, me."

"We 're gen'ally tew folks all the time," said Sam, following a climbing wreath of tobacco smoke with meditative eyes. "One is the feller 'at we know an' t' other 's the feller 'at other folks knows, an' most on us is almighty shy o' showin' the one 'at we know tu other folks. By the great horn spoon ! I das n't hardly look at my Sam, myself, he's got so many mean streaks in him. Hello, there's aour ol' squirrel, er one 'at looks jus' like him, a-snickerin' at your Antwine er my Sam this minute." He pointed with his pipe at a red squirrel that was jerking himself into a frenzy of derision on the trunk of a hemlock.

The sun and the breeze had burned and blown the mist away and the day was bright with the beauty of late September, the clear blue sky, the first autumnal tints of the unthinned foliage bordered with the lesser glory of woodside goldenrod and aster, the marshes with their broad masses of bronze and russet and gold, unbroken, save where the scarlet flame of an outstanding dwarfed maple blazed among the colder tints, and the verdure of the grass lands, as green as in June.

Such sounds as were heard were distinctive of the season and some were conspicuously absent. The flute of the hermit and the bells of the wood thrushes were silent. The booming of the bittern and the chorus of the frogs no longer sounded over the expanse of marshes. Birds that rejoiced melodiously over the earth's fresh luxuriance in June uttered now only brief notes of farewell to the kindling glory of her ripeness. Only the bluebird sang, and with a mournful cadence. The crows cawed lazily, jays squalled apart or in united vociferation, chickadees repeated their own name, nuthatches piped their nasal call, woodpeckers hammered with voiceless industry and never a rattling drum-call; these and the squirrels were the only tenants of the woods who gave audible evidence of their presence.

Across the fields from distant farmsteads came the regular thud of flails, and from one barn the clatter and roar of a new-fangled threshing machine; and there was also the rumble and clatter of farm wagons and the bawling of plowmen, shouting as if their oxen were deaf or a mile from their driver. Piercing through these larger sounds there could be heard the shrill voice of cockerels practicing their yet unlearned challenge, and the yelping of wandering flocks of turkeys harvesting the half torpid grasshoppers and gleaning the grain fields.

Every sound that came to the ears of Sam and his companion, as they unconsciously listened, was as indicative of the season as the visible signs of the year's ripening which met their abstracted eyes.

" Wal, Antwine," said Sam, arousing himself and knocking the ashes of his pipe upon the grave of the old campfire, " Le 's go an' see if you 've got a new lot o' relations settled here," and Antoine, nothing loath to undertake such quest, followed with him the path into the shadow of the hemlocks.

CHAPTER V.

A WAY STATION.

TANGLES of hobble bush sprawled over the russet carpet of hemlock leaves, gayly flecked with variegated rattlesnake plantain, overtopped by yellowing sarsaparilla; and a crowded cluster of scarlet berries, still upheld on their withered stalk, marked the place where the fiery bulb of the Indian turnip was hidden. There were moss-covered cradle-knolls and mouldering trunks of the old trees whose uprooting had formed them, with trees already old growing upon them. Great mats of sphagnum were in the hollows between, and all were the characteristics of the undisturbed floor of the ancient forest.

For all these Sam had a keen eye, noting the difference of forest growth here from that of his own hill country and speaking of it to his companion, but never of the beauties of nature, for, with the deep and tender feeling of the true lover, he could not prate of the charms of his mistress to the common ear.

Antoine enjoyed them with an undefined touch

of the same feeling, but more than the symmetry or majesty of a tree he saw the axe helves in the hickory, the baskets in the ash, the plank in the hemlock and pine, and the medicinal virtues of the prettiest plant were more to him than its beauty.

Ten minutes' leisurely walking brought them to a clearing of a few acres where some young cattle were pastured. They left off grazing on the approach of the strangers, whom they curiously regarded for a moment and then scampered into the woods in a flurry of alarm. A small log house stood in the middle of the clearing with a pole-, fenced garden patch in front wherein some cabbages flourished in the virgin soil in spite of poor tending. A few beanstalks drooped their frostbitten leaves over the clattering remnant of dry pods, and the withered cucumber vines, linking together the dropsical overlooked fruit, showed with what rampant growth and how riotously they had gadded abroad under the summer sun and showers.

A thin wreath of smoke trailed upward from the low chimney, diffusing a pitchy, pungent odor even to windward in the light breeze, and the merry notes of a fiddle, accompanied by the sound of jigging feet, came through the open door.

" Bah gosh, de smell an' de nowse was kan' o' Frenchy, don't it ? " Antoine remarked as they drew nearer ; but he started backward with an exclamation of astonishment when, still unperceived by the inmates, he cautiously peered in at the door. "Oh, dey was too da'ks color mos' for mah rellashin," he whispered as he fell back to Sam's side, "Dey was nigger!"

Sam stole forward and looked inside. Sitting with his back toward the door was a lithe-figured and very black negro, energetically playing a fiddle, which divided his attention with a taller and more strongly built man of the same race, who was putting his whole soul into the elaborate execution of a jig, occasionally exhaling his breath in a gusty puff that was almost a deep-toned whistle, while the fiddler expressed his delight in the performance by frequent squawks of laughter.

Presently the dancer finished with a grand flourish and a final bump of his quivering heels, and slouched across the room to refresh himself with a draught of water from a pail that stood in the corner, while his comrade hugged his instrument under his arm and rocked to and fro in a spasm of delighted laughter.

"Oh, ah, oh, Lord," he gasped, "if that don't knock the spots out 'n all the dancin' ever I ever did see. Oh, oh, yah, yah! oh, Lord!"

"Wal, yas, honey," said the other modestly, as he dropped heavily into a creaking splint-bottomed old chair, "'at's er de way dey wu'ks de heel an' toe down in ol' Firginny. Now, I 'se gwine for to sing ye dat ar' li'l' song ag'in, so 's you can ketch

de chune wid you wiolin," and he began to sing in
a deep sonorous voice, beating time with his palms
upon his knees, while the other felt for the air with
uncertain touches of the fiddlestrings.

> "De coon fas' 'sleep in de holler ob de gum,
>   'Who dar ?   Who dar ? '
>   Brer Fox come a-scratchin' 'roun' de do' ob his home,
>   ' Who dar knockin' at de do' ? '
>   De coon cock he eye an' he listen wid he ear,
>   ' Who dar ?   Who dar ?
>   Who dat a-wantin' ob somebody hyar ?
>   Who dar ?   Who dar a-knockin' at de do' ? '
>   ' Dat 's me, Brer Coon, so prepar' for to die,
>   Who dar ?   Who dar ? '

> "Coon squirt 'bacca juice plum in he eye,
>   ' Who dar ?   Who dar, knockin' at de do' ?
>   'Taters in de ashes, cawn b'ilin' hot,
>   Who dar ?   Who dar ?
>   Come ter yer supper, table all sot,
>   Who dar ?   Who dar, knockin' at de do' ? '
>   Brer Fox run blin', smash he head 'g'in de tree,
>   ' Who dar ?   Who dar ? '
>   ' Oh, you ain't de man I 'se wantin' for to see,
>   'T ain't me, 't ain't me, knockin' at de do'.'

" Yas, sah," the tall negro remarked, when the
song was ended and cordially applauded by his
friend, " w'en dey is 'bout fawty niggahs jes'
a-shoutin' dar ar, yer could jes' set an' listen at
'em all night."

Unwilling longer to play the eavesdropper, and
loath to leave such entertaining company, Sam
stepped forward and knocked on the doorpost.

"Good-mornin'," he said. "'Scuse me for interruptin', but me an' my friend stopped tu see 'f we c'ld git a drink o' water. This 'ere crik water 's p'isen, I b'lieve."

Both negroes had arisen suddenly when Sam knocked, the taller with an alarmed, alert look, as if in quick consideration of a way of escape, the other with an abashed yet half-defiant air. The first seemed assured of no evil intention by a glance at the visitor's quiet, good-humored face, and stepped backward with a questioning smile on his own no less good-humored visage.

"Water? Course you can hev' some water. My stars! haow you did scare me," said the violinist, emphasizing each sentence with a chuckle and a jerk of the head. "Did n't s'pose anybody was in a mild o' here. No, sir. An' me an' my cousin was sort o' keepin' house whilst the ol' woman an' the coon 's gone. My brother hain't been tu see me afore, I do' know the time when, an' we allus hev' to hev' a little fun when he does come. Oh, I forgot you wanted some water. 'T ain't the best water in the world," he apologized, as he brought a brimming dipper of milky-looking water, "but it 's some wet."

Sam sipped with gingerly lips, but found it better than the clearer, weedy-tasting creek water, and gave it as cordial approval as one could who had been accustomed to the crystal springs of the mountains.

"Ha' some, Antwine? It's pooty good water fer the time o' year," but Antoine would not be prevailed on to help him with this excuse for their call.

"This feller an' me," Sam explained, indicating his companion by a sidewise nod, "come up the Slang a duck huntin', an' he kinder wanted tu see the haouse where he faound his father, so we come over. He did n't know but what he'd find some more relations here."

"Wal," said the negro, chuckling as he cast a quick quizzical glance at Antoine, and jerking his head emphatically, "he is kind o' dark complected, but he don't look like any o' aour folks 'at I remember. I don't claim no relationship, but mebby he does."

"Oh sa-cree, cochon noir!" Antoine growled explosively.

"The' hain't nothin' stuck up 'baout me, an' if he c'n prove it I'll own it," continued the negro, giving no evidence if he comprehended that he was called a holy black pig.

Another person now quietly appeared at the door, a placid-faced middle-aged man in red flannel shirt-sleeves that contrasted oddly with his broad-brimmed hat and sober-hued waistcoat of unmistakable Quaker cut. His sudden appearance did not seem to surprise the negroes, whom he accosted pleasantly, while he saluted Sam and his companion with more reserve, regarding them with some wonder.

"Well, James," he said to the master of the house, "so thee's got company, has thee? And who might thy friends be?"

"That's more'n I c'n tell ye, Mr. Bartlett. Only one on em's arter a drink o' water an' t' other's lookin' for his relations."

"I guess you don't remember us, Mr. Bartlett," Sam said, rising from his broken-backed chair and extending his hand as he smiled on the puzzled face of the Quaker. "Me an' this man shantied on your land here one spring, four, five year ago. We was a-trappin' mushrat. Peltier Gove come tu see us an' hired aout tu you. My name's Samwil Lovel, an' this 'ere's Antwine."

"Why, dear me, yes," said Friend Bartlett, his face brightening with recognition as he shook Sam's hand. "I thought I'd seen thee somewhere. And this man too. Why, his father and mother lived in this very house a whole year."

"Oh, yas, yas," cried Antoine. "Ah'll fan' it here, an' Ah'll ant 'spec' more Ah'll was for fin' it in mah soup, me. He live 'long to me naow, an' he smaat lak boy, an' so was mah mudder."

"That's clever," said Friend Bartlett, and then to Sam, "And Peltier, how's he? He an' Lowizy are married, I s'pose."

"Wal, Peltier's abaout so," Sam answered soberly, "but he hain't merried. Lowizy's dead."

" Thee don't say.   Wal, that's sad, to be sure,"
Friend Bartlett said in a grieved voice.   " Poor
child, poor child.   It will grieve my wife to hear
it, for she set great store by Lowizy.   And Peltier
was a stiddy, clever young man, poor boy.   He
must be greatly cast down."

After some further conversation with Sam he
turned to the negroes and his eyes fell upon the
fiddle.   " Well, James, thee has been entertaining
thy visitors with music, has thee ? "   He bent over
the instrument curiously and touched the strings
with one cautious finger, withdrawing it with a
start and an abashed face as they gave forth a
resonant chord.   " Well, it's rather a pleasant
sound to worldly ears, I dare say," he remarked, ·
and then in a low voice to the man whom he called
James, but who was Jim to the world's people,
" thee should be careful about attracting strangers
to thy house, James, while Robert is with thee."

" I had n't no idee the' was a livin' soul within
a mild o' here, Mr. Bartlett ; no, sir, I had n't,"
Jim protested, with many an emphatic jerk of the
head.   " They popped right on tu us as if they'd
riz right aout o' the airth.   I hain't none afeared
o' the tall feller, but I do' know 'bout that gabbin'
Frenchman," and he cast a suspicious glance at
Antoine, who, unconscious of unfriendly scrutiny,
was leisurely whittling a charge of tobacco for the
waiting pipe between his teeth.

"I come down to fix up the fence a little and look at the young cattle," Friend Bartlett explained to the company, as he went to the door and picked up his axe which he had set down there.

"Friend Samwel, I'd like to speak with thee a little about Peltier," hesitating over the untruth of the pretext. "I feel clear to trust thee," he said in a guarded voice when Sam had followed him apart to a comfortable leaning place on the fence, "but I ain't quite so clear in my mind about thy companion." He paused a little, abstractedly hewing the withered leaves off a sunflower stalk. "The fact is, that tall colored man is a fugitive from slavery, and might be in danger if some folks knew he was here."

"I 'spected where the critter come from," said Sam, "but ye need n't be afeared o' me tellin' on him, Mr. Bartlett, an' I don't b'lieve Antwine would either, not tu mean no harm. All 'at ails him is he 's tew full o' his gab."

"Well, Samwel, thee must caution him. It would be sad if anything should happen to hinder this poor man's getting to Canada."

"I guess the' hain't no danger o' that, Mr. Bartlett."

"More than thee thinks, perhaps." Friend Bartlett glanced cautiously toward the house before he added, "I feel free to tell thee that strangers have been seen not many miles off that we mistrust are looking for him."

" Du you b'lieve it ? " Sam asked in surprise. The Quaker nodded. " Wal," Sam drawled out, " I ruther guess they won't ketch none o' their stray black sheep up this way — not if I c'n help it."

" Thank thee, Samwel; but I think if nobody lets out the secret they won't be apt to discover his hiding-place. Try to keep thy companion's tongue bridled for a few days. Now, I won't hinder thee any longer," and the Quaker moved slowly toward the house.

"Come, Antwine," Sam called, " le 's be a-moggin'," and Antoine coming forth, the two began to retrace their way to the landing.

" Farewell," Friend Bartlett called after them, " thee tell Peltier what I told thee and remember me in kindness to him, will thee ? "

CHAPTER VI.

At the edge of the woods Sam turned and took a careful observation of the clearing.

"I s'pose the's a landin' daown there on the crik 'baout as nigh as the one on the Slang, hain't the'?" he asked.

"Wal, Ah do' know, prob'ly. Yas, Ah guess yas. What you wan' know, hein?" Antoine answered and asked.

"Oh, nothin', on'y I was a-thinkin' if the canew was there we c'ld git tu camp quicker. My stomerk's cryin' cupberd if that feller's water is victuals an' drink. Haow is 't wi' your 'n, Antwine? You hain't hed even water tu stay it."

"Bah gosh!" cried the Canadian with hungry zest, "Ah 'll can heat one of dat dauk raw an' hees fedder."

"That 'ould hurt Joe's feelin's; he wants all the feathers for a peace offerin' tu M'ri," said Sam, lengthening his strides till a glimpse of the open sky beyond the landing was seen, when he slackened his pace and peered cautiously out upon the open marsh.

" Hsssh," he whispered, drawing back and slowly sinking upon his haunches, "the 's a hull snag o' ducks a squddlin' raound not four rod f'm the canew. We c'n crawl up an' git a crack at 'em."

Crawling side by side, they wormed their way within short range of at least a dozen wood ducks that were swimming, diving, and bickering over choice morsels in the narrow pathway of water that made from the channel to the landing. Then taking deliberate aim at the thick of the flock, they fired at the word given by Sam. Above the rolling cloud of smoke they saw but five terrified survivors scurrying away in scattered flight, and beneath it when it lifted seven dead and wounded unto death, all of which they speedily secured, even to one poor cripple that skulked among the weeds and was mercifully dispatched by a stroke of a paddle.

"There, Antwine," said Sam, as the canoe floated out upon the channel, " you set for'ad; I done all the shootin' I want tu."

Thus disposed, they paddled down the Slang. As they passed the trim newly built muskrat houses, almost every one of them had a tally stick stuck beside it marked rather conspicuously by a bit of birch bark inserted in a cleft at the top.

" Dat was Injin fashi'n," Antoine commented, " an' Ah bet you head dere was some of it trappin' raoun' here."

" Jest their shifflin' way, ketchin' lots o' half-growed ones. But the' 's plenty o' white folks 'at 's jest as bad. I wonder where the creatur's is campin'. I sh'd like tu run on tu 'em."

" Oh, Sam, you 'll want great many t'ing, ant it ? You 'll fan' two nigger an' one Quakers to-day already, an' naow you 'll want Injin. Say, Sam, what kan o' nigger you call dat beeg one, hein ? "

" I do' know 's anything more 'n a tol'lable black one. Why ? "

" Wal, seh, he 'll gat diff'nt of aour kan' o' nigger. He 'll ant spick Angleesh sem' lak' you was an' me an' dat odder nigger. Oh, Ah tol' you, Sam," he said impressively, and looking over his shoulder at his companion, " Ah 'll b'lieved he was slave runaways nigger from Souse 'Mericay."

" Sho', Antwine, you du git cur'u's ideas int' your noddle."

" Wal, Ah 'll b'lieved dat, me," said Antoine decidedly.

" Wal, s'posin' he is," said Sam carelessly, " let him run ; I shan't stop him."

" Prob'ly de mans dat hown it was willin' for give feefteen, prob'ly twanty-fav' dollar. Haow many you s'pose, prob'ly ? "

" I s'pose," said Sam with impressive earnestness, " if a man was mean 'nough tu du seeh a sneakin' job he 'd ortu be sunk in this 'ere crik, an' I cal'late that 's as mis'able a death as a fellow could die. If you want tu keep friends wi' me,

Antwine, don't you tell nob'dy 'at we seen sech a man — not nob'dy."

"No, no — no, Ah 'll won't tol' mah waf', no, sah;" adding after some reflection, "honly Onc' Lasha an' Zhozeff, prob'ly."

"Wal, if you must tell someb'dy er bu'st, I s'pose they 'd be as safe as anyb'dy. But don't ye open your head tu no strangers. Naow, remember."

"Dat all Ah want. But Ah 'll tol' you, Sam, it mek me felt kan o' mean for keep all Ah 'll know for mahsef."

"Hol' on," said Sam, steering the canoe close to the marsh where a muskrat house stood in a narrow environment of open water, "there 's a poor leetle mushrat not so big as a haouse rat, all wopsed up in a mess o' weeds where he can't draown ner git away."

As the canoe ran alongside, he reached out and carefully disengaged the trap and its struggling captive from the entanglement of marsh weeds, and after a brief inspection pressed the spring till the jaws opened. When the little prisoner found himself free he made off with scrambling splash into the marsh as Sam gave him a parting admonition.

"There, you poor little devil, go your ways an' grow bigger. Naow, Antwine, would n't a feller be meaner 'n pusley tu put that leetle chap back int' the trap ag'in?"

"Yas, prob'ly," said Antoine; "but Ah 'll ant spec' de Injin t'ank you much, prob'ly, ant it?"

"Wal, I wan't ezackly considerin' the Injin's feelin's."

Their way down the Slang and creek was unmarked by even an unsuccessful shot, for the few ducks they saw arose too far out of range to tempt them to the trial of the uncertain chance. Now and then they were startled by the sudden uprising of a heron beating upward with labored strokes of his broad vans in a long slant to level flight over the marshes, or the frightened squawk of a bittern jerking himself into the air and stumbling through it on awkward wings to a safer retreat. A countless dusky swarm of blackbirds rose up from their busy feeding among the rice in a sudden cloud and with a dull roar of innumerable wings, as if a mine had exploded beneath the flock.

When they rounded the last great bend and came in sight of the bay, they saw a large craft with a single square sail coming in toward the mouth of Lewis Creek.

"Hurra' for Canada," cried Antoine joyfully, after regarding it intently for a moment. "Look, Sam, dat was Canada boats."

"What makes you think so?"

"Oh, Ah 'll know it by hees sail jes' easy as you can tol' nigger by hees skin. Yankee boat ant got square sail lak' dat more as he wore botte sauvage or heat pea soup. Prob'ly, he brought some salt for sol' it or come for bought some happle, prob'ly, bose of it, Ah do' know 'f he ant. Ah 'll gat brudder-law was be captain for one of it. Mebby dat was be mah brudder-law, mos' likel'. Ah 'll go see to-naght 'f Ah 'll ant in de morny, me."

"Wal, I 'll go with ye. It 's turrible interestin' tu look at furrin shippin', an' that looks like an ol' buster, nigh 's big 's a canawl boat."

"Oh, dey was beauty boats," said Antoine proudly. "Ah 'll tol' you, dey was mek de water roar lak' One' Lasha w'en he sleep."

Presently they were at the landing among the willows under the bluff, a place made familiar to them in their summer fishing trip of a previous year. Thence, laden with guns and game, they climbed the steep to the camp, where they were loudly welcomed by Uncle Lisha and Joseph, who generously congratulated them on their success, though it abated the pride of their own achievements.

"Wal done, boys." Uncle Lisha slowly counted the ducks, carefully inspecting and observing each and inquiring its kind. "You did du fust rate, sartain. But what sort o' critter 's this 'ere?" he asked, picking up the coot and minutely examining it. "Ann Twine, hev you be'n a-robbin' someb'dy er nuther's henrwust?"

" No, One' Lasha," said the Canadian, one hand busy with the potato kettle and frying-pan, while from the other he snatched hasty mouthfuls of bread to appease the cravings of his fasting stomach, " dat was you good boy Sam, an' Ah 'll tol' it he don't ought for do so weeked. But he want for pracsit for shoot, so he 'll shot de folkses hen. What you t'ink for dat, hein ? "

" No, 't ain't a hen nuther," the old man decided, " but it looks more like one 'an some o' these 'ere patent new-fashion Chinee faowls does. Clapham's got a rwuster 'at come f'm Boston 'at he calls a High-shang er hang-shy er some sech a name, 'at don't look no more like a civilized barndoor faowl 'an you du, Ann Twine, an' when he does what Clapham calls crowin', it scares child'en. I never heard sech a' on'arthly yollopin'."

" Wal, One' Lasha, dis t'ing was kan' o' fool dauk. Dat hees nem of it. We jus' brought it home for de fedders for Zhozeff."

" Wal, me and Jozeff hes picked 'em all off 'm them leetle baby ducks 'at we got, an' don't you b'lieve both on ye 'at he was so savin' 'at he pulled the pin-feathers aout with his teeth, an' we got pooty nigh a piller case full, an' the ducks is dressed, complete. Haow be ye goin' tu cook 'em, Ann Twine ? Rwust 'em, er bile 'em, er fry 'em ? I 'm kinder hankerin' for some hot victuals."

" Wal, Ah 'll b'lieve Ah 'll goin' for fry it, for

be quickes' way for our hongry," said Antoine, laying the split teal in the frying-pan with a generous lump of Danvis butter from the Lovel dairy. "Come, Sam, ponch de fire. Zhozeff, pull up you stump an' chaup off some hwood. Hoorah."

The fire was properly replenished, the potatoes boiled merrily, the frying-pan screeched, and Antoine pranced around them fully impressed with the importance of his office, while the others sat on the fireside log hungrily watching him with their backs to the world.

"I do' know as ary one on us told ye 'at we hed comp'ny whilst you was gone," Joseph said. Antoine held an attentive ear above the crackling of the fire and the turmoil of cookery, upon which he kept his intent eyes, shielded by one protecting hand, while the other, armed with a fork, urged the process of cooking with frequent prods and shakes of the contents of the pan.

"Wal, sorter comp'ny er vis'ters er callers, mebby you might call 'em. Tew fellers they was 'at come a-saunderin' up an' sod daown an' smoked a spell an' peared turrible sociable. Hed guns, they did, kinder huntin', but was inquirin' if the' was colored man livin' anywher's raound here, o' the name o' Jeems suthin' er nuther. What was 't, Uncle Lisha?"

"I do' know," Uncle Lisha replied, "I tol' 'em 'at we hed n't had time tu git 'quainted wi' the white folks, let alone the niggers."

"Color' man," cried Antoine, lifting his voice above the roar and crackle of the fire, the walloping of the pot and the sizzle of the pan, and making it very audible though his back was turned to his hearers. "Bah gosh, me an' Sam was visit some black color' mans an' hear of some red color' mans. An', seh, de black color' mans leeve raght over dere behin' de hwood, pooty clos' neighbor of us, seh. He gat for stay wid heem one slave nigger dat was run 'way wid hese'f all de ways from Sous 'Meriky, an' oh, he would dance you never see to beat it w'en t'udder nigger was fi'le more better as dat leetly humpy Palmer feller. An' dat beeg slave run'way nigger was sing jus' lak' black yallerbird, sem as de gros riche lady gat in leetly wire coop. Oh, Ah 'll tol' you 'f Ah 'll hown dat nigger, Ah 'll ant took more 's feety dollar for it, no, seh."

As Antoine ceased, Joseph slowly turned in his seat to reach a stick of wood and was confronted by two men standing close behind the unconscious group.

"Sam Hill!" he ejaculated. "Here they be naow! Where in tunket did you come from? Dumbed if you did n't skeer me, anyway!"

The other members of the camp household were as much surprised as Joseph, but Sam was most disturbed, for he felt almost certain that much of Antoine's disclosures must have been overheard by the intruders, whom he suspected were hunting larger game than ducks.

" Beg pardon, gentlemen," said one of the new-comers, a brisk, wiry little man with a sharp face and a business-like, official air. " Don't wanter intrude, but we 'd jes' like to light aour pipes 't your fire. Can't scare up a match betwixt us. Got a flint an' steel, but lost aour punk," and without waiting ·for permission he stepped to the fire and thrust a dry twig of cedar into it, wherewith when ablaze he lit his pipe and then offered it to his companion, a tall, sallow man all of whose movements were deliberate if not indolent, except those of his restless, searching eyes.

" Here, Clark, light up. This 'ere 's better 'n punk or a match."

But Clark had just begun to whittle a charge from a huge plug of peculiar light-colored tobacco, very different, as Sam noticed, from the black nail rod and twist to which he was accustomed, and he also noticed that the stranger's pronunciation of the few words he spoke bore a marked similitude to that of Jim's guest. When he had generously offered his " raal ol' Firginny leaf " to each and lighted his own pipeful, so fragrant that those who refused regretted having done so, the visitors seemed in a hurry to go, but he who was the spokesman returned, after they had gone a little way, to ask in Yankee fashion for the loan of the scow.

" I s'pose you could n't let us take you scaow boat a spell to go aout an' see 'f we could n't git tew three ducks, could ye?   We hate to go hum 'thaout a feather.   They 'll make fun on us so. We can't git a thing huntin' 'long the shore."

Sam shook his head.   " I 'm turrible sorry, but we got tu use aour boat jest as soon as we git some grub."

" We 'd fetch it back in a couple o' hours," urged the man whom his comrade called Baker. " Guess you c'n let us have it as long as that, can't you?"

" No, got tu use it right off," said Sam.   " Come, Antwine, hain't ye got the victuals 'most ready? We want tu be off tu rights."

Reluctantly relinquishing the design of borrowing the boat, Baker and his comrade hurried away up the bank of the creek.   Sam watched them with unfriendly eyes till they disappeared among the trees beyond the landing, saying to himself as much as to his companions : —

" Consarn 'em!   They won't git no boat o' aourn tu hunt niggers."

Uncle Lisha and Joseph stared at him in puzzled inquiry, and Antoine, with an abashed face, devoted himself to his cookery.

" What is 't, Samwil?" the old shoemaker asked at last.   " I can't make head nor tail on 't."

" Why, you know what they ast you, an' you

heard what Antwine said 'baout the darkies an' so did they, a-sneaking up behind of us at just that onlucky minute ; heard all they wanted tu er they 'd ha' ast me some questions. They 're arter that 'ere runaway chap, an' I don't cal'late we 're a-goin' tu help 'em much, be we ? "

Uncle Lisha snorted a contemptuous negative, and Joseph Hill said : —

" It don't seem 's 'ough that was what we come here for, not ezac'ly."

" Prob'ly Ah 'll s'pose, Sam, you blem me all up, but Ah tol' you, seh, Ah 'll ant to blem. Ah 'll ant s'pose dere was anybody but wese'f goin' for heard me tol' Onc' Lasha an' Zhozeff de new, an' Ah mus' tol' dat," Antoine said in deep dejection, as he set the dinner on the table and the hungry crew gathered about it.

" Oh, I do' know 's I blame you none. The' hain't no use in cryin' over spilt milk, an' we 'll jest tend tu aour business an' let other folks tend tu their 'n, if it hain't the pooticst 'at ever was. Say," he continued, as if dismissing the subject, " when we git done eatin' le 's take the scaow boat an' all go over an' see that 'ere boat f'm Canady."

CHAPTER VII.

THE CANADA BOAT.

WHEN the dinner of one course was finished, the simple service of iron and tinware was left unwashed without fear of disparaging feminine comment, and the voyagers embarked, Sam and Antoine at the oars, Uncle Lisha steering with a paddle, and Joseph as passenger and general observer. In these capacities he took his ease so far as he could with a hand on either gunwale and hitching from side to side at every slight lurch of the stanch craft. This he continued to do after the black depths of the creek were passed and they voyaged across the shallow head of the bay, where the oars grated on the sandy bottom and the golden mesh of reflected sunshine twisted and tangled its elusive threads among the caddis worms and mussels, a half arm's-length beneath the rippled surface. One of the rowers leaned over the side to watch a shoal of minnows, and slightly careened the boat, when Joseph frantically pulled on that gunwale and hitched toward the other side.

"Good airth an' seas! I du b'lieve if you was

sot in the middle of a' islan' you 'd be afeared o' tippin' over, Jozeff. Du, for massy sake, set still, erless lay daown in the bottom."

" I tell ye what, Uncle Lisher," and Joseph let out a long-held breath, " sech a mess o' water makes me kinder skeery. I do' know as it 's skeery ezactly, but kinder narvous. I don't seem tu hev no use for no more water 'n what I wanter drink an' wash me in, an' that hain't sech a turrible sight. But it does look dreffle neat," and his eye dwelt with satisfaction on reflections of the painted shores flickering downward on the rippled lake like many colored inverted flames blazing into a nether sky.

Over among the red maples of Lewis Creek could be seen the naked mast of the Canadian craft, its gay pennon lost in the brilliant foliage that it flaunted against. But the incessant gabble of the crew and their snatches of French songs would have guided our voyagers to the vessel without any visible indication of its whereabouts, and following it up the stream a little way beyond its last bend, they came to the boat at its moorings.

The jolly little captain was very polite, and welcomed them as possible apple sellers in English quite as good as Antoine's, if somewhat different from it, having evidently been drawn from a well not entirely undefiled with h's.

" Mek youse'f welcome, mah frien'," he cried,

with his shoulders lifted to his ears and his palms hospitably spread. "Go hall hover mah boats. He was you boats, han' 'e was good boats, hif Hah say hit mahse'f. Oh, 'e good sloops. Han' if you gat happle for sol' Hah ready for bought she han' paid you ten cen' pour baskeet 'f she was mos' hall red happle, han' medjy him mah baskeet, hant' ol' more as t'ree peck," and he gave a contemptuous kick to a basket which could hold at least a bushel and a half.

The visitors gave the odd-looking and not very cleanly craft as complete inspection and as unstinted praise as would satisfy their curiosity and her captain's pride, smothering themselves in the garlic-reeking cabin as long as they could hold their breath and then stumbling forth into the fresh outer air.

"I hain't got no apples tu sell myself," said Sam to the little captain, "but I do' know but what I c'ld send you a man 'at has. Come aout this way a minute, won't ye? Say, captain," he continued when they had got beyond the hearing of the others, "haow long afore you 're a-goin' back to Canady?" Sam picked up a stick and began whittling it, wherefrom the shrewd Canadian, having had some experience of Yankees, augured that a trade was impending.

"Wal, Hah don't mos' know, me. Mos' likel' Hah go day hafter nex' day hif de peop' brought

dey happle. But," he continued, curiously watching the shavings curl slowly away from the keen
knife, " hif you can sen' it me some very good red
happle, Hah could waits hanodder one day."

" No, guess I don't want tu keep you waitin',"
said Sam. " Be you goin' stret hum? Goin' tu
stop anywhere on the way? "

" Ah, no, no, no, bien no. Hah han' goin' let
mah happle rot 'fore Hah cood sol' she. Hah go
fas' Hah cood."

" S'pose you c'ld take 'long a passenger tol'lable
cheap? "

" Wal, seh, mah fren'," said the captain after
some consideration of the proposal, " hif de mans
was clever for behave hese'f, han' paid me one
dollah 'fore 'e go, Hah will took it, me, han' dat
was more sheaps 'e can go hin stimboat, yas, bah
t'under! yas, more sheaps 'e can go 'foots."

" Yes, if you feed him, that 's reasonable 'nough,"
Sam assented.

" Oh, no, no, no," cried the captain, " for dat 'e
mus' heat 'ese'f. Hif Hah heat 'im, Hah mus'
hask more as dat."

" Wal, then, we 'll hev him eat himself," Sam
agreed with a chuckle. " I sh'd wanter be tol'lable
well paid myself if I 'd got tu eat him. All right,
captain, I guess he 'll be here 'baout the time you
start," and having concluded the negotiation he
threw away the neatly whittled stick and pocketed
his knife.

" Mos' likul your frien' was be goin' on Canada for 'ees 'ealthy," said the captain, shrugging his shoulders and winking at Sam.

" He 's a-goin' there tu extend the ary of freedom," Sam answered with an imperturbable countenance.

" Oh, yas, yas," and the little captain tried to cover his pockmarked visage with a mask of profound wisdom as he inwardly phrased the words, " send de hary freedom," and mentally inquired of himself, " What says the holy tall Bostonais?"

Sam and the captain returned to the boat, where Antoine and his compatriots — who, though not old acquaintances, had mutual knowledge of some — were swimming with violent gesticulations in a babbling torrent of gossip, on whose brink Uncle Lisha and Joseph sat in gaping, wondering silence, now turning their puzzled faces upon the Canadians, now slowly upon each other. Their amazement increased when the captain also plunged in and contributed his full share to the confusion of tongues.

" Good airth an' seas! " Uncle Lisha gasped in a loud whisper to Sam, " it hain't no' more like talk 'an a passel o' hens hevin' a cacklin' bee in the mornin', an' I can't pick nothin' aout on 't on'y now an' then a ' wee ' an' a ' sackcree.' I b'lieve the dumbed critters is jest pertendin' they 're a-talkin' an' don't understan' one 'nother no more 'n they would if they was a-whirlin' hoss fiddles at one 'nother.''

" Wal, they 'pear tu git ahead wi' the' vis'tin' some way," said Sam, regarding the animated group with an amused smile.

"I do' know fer sartain," Joseph remarked, after deliberate consideration, "but I kinder cal'-late the heft o' the conversin' is done by signs, an' the gab is jest hove in for sort o' fillin'. Seems 's 'ough that was the way on 't, but mebby 't hain't.''

" Wal, they beat ten women tu a quiltin'," said Uncle Lisha, "an' I give it up. Say, Samwil, you be'n a-buyin' the boat? "

" Wal, no; on'y a sheer on 't. Cal'lated it 'ould be handy for Joseph to go huntin' an' fishin' in.''

Their attention was attracted to a heavily laden wagon that came jolting over the rough pasture, announcing its approach with a rumble and creak that began now to be heard above the voices of the Canadians, till at last their interested attention was called to the fact that a customer was arriving.

" Wal, if there hain't a load of apples comin' a'ready," said Sam. " I guess this feller sent on word ahead 'at he was a-comin'. We 'll wait an' git a pocketful an' then be off.''

While the captain and his customer were pitting Canuck and Yankee shrewdness against each other in sharp bargaining, Sam and his comrades tasted, and selected their pocketsful of the mellowest and least sour of the common fruit, that but for the advent of the Canada boat would have gone to the cider mill, and they then departed. Antoine went most reluctantly, for he was still oppressed by unspoken words.

As they fared forth on their return voyage, Joseph, slowly withdrawing his lingering gaze from the alien craft, remarked : —

"So that 'ere 's a he boat, is 't? Wal, I swan I can't make aout haow on airth a feller 's a-goin' tu tell which f'm t' other. I ruther guess 'at boats is julluk fish ; the he ones an' the she ones looks jest alike tu the onedicated, or'nary eyes ; seems 's 'ough that must be the way on 't."

When they were at home again — for so they at once began to call their temporary abiding-place — they fell to picking their ducks — a task whereof many hands made light work — beguiled by Sam's and Antoine's relation of the circumstances of the day's incidents.

"Naow," said Sam, laying apart a couple of the finest ducks, " if the' hain't no objection, I b'lieve I 'll take them 'ere up tu Mr. Bartlett. There 's more 'n we c'n use anyway. Mebby it 'll be kinder late afore I git back, but you need n't tew, if it 's dark fust, on'y jest set aout the lantern tu one o' the landin's." There being no demur, he embarked at once on this mission.

CHAPTER VIII.

THE shadows of the trees that skirted the west shore stretched far across the marsh and channel as Sam drove the canoe up the creek with quick, strong strokes, quite regardless of the throngs of incoming waterfowl that swept past him or those already arrived that arose from the marsh on either hand and the open water before him, for he had left the temptation of the gun behind him. When he entered the East Slang all lesser shadows were dissolved in the overwhelming shadow of the Adirondacks, and when he stepped on shore at the old camp landing the twilight was thickening into gloom in the woods, through which he took the now dimly-defined path and hastened toward the log house of the negro.

When he came in sight of it, it was a dark blotch in the clearing against the faint light of the afterglow, with one spot of light in it, where a candle shone from its single front window. As he approached he heard the voices and frequent laughter of his acquaintances of the morning, with

the softer voice of a woman sometimes breaking in.
He knocked at the door and the voices were suddenly hushed, and in the stillness he heard the
puff that blew out the candle, followed by excited
whispers and cautious steps across the floor.   He
knocked again, and the woman's voice demanded:

"Who's there?"

"It's me! Sam Lovel! the man 'at was here
this mornin'.   I want tu speak tu the man they
call James."

There was more whispering before Jim asked,
jerking out the words with the characteristic nervous twitches of the head that Sam could almost
see in spite of the intervening door: —

"What d' you want?   Be you alone?   Can't
you talk through the door?"

"I don't want tu holler," said Sam in a low
voice, answering the last question first.   "It's
suthin' 'baout the man 'at you call your brother er
cousin.   He wants tu be makin' himself sca'ce
raoun' here.   I'm all alone, an' you need n't be
afeard tu open the door."

After more whispering inside, the door was un-
fastened and cautiously opened far enough for Jim
to thrust his head outside and assure himself of
Sam's identity and that he was alone.   Then the
door was held wide open and the visitor invited to
enter by a jerk of the head and motion of the hand.
The door was closed so quickly behind Sam that it

nearly caught the skirts of his coat. By the glimmer of light from the stove he saw the lilting, dancing negro of the morning transformed into a stern, threatening giant confronting him with an axe uplifted above his shoulder. The figure of a woman shrank behind the stove, with a child, wide-eyed with fright and wonder, clinging to her gown.

"You need n't be afeared tu light your light an' see who I be," said Sam. "The' hain't nob'dy else."

While Jim relighted the candle with a splinter the others looked intently at Sam, as his features grew distinct in the increasing glow, when being assured that his honest face masked no evil purpose, the tall negro lowered his axe, and the woman, a handsome mulatto, sat down and took the child upon her knee.

Sam told them of his suspicion that the visitors at camp were in search of Jim's guest, " and naow," he said in conclusion, "the chances is they 'll be here arter you to-morrow. I 've laid in with a feller tu take ye tu Canerdy on his boat, but he won't go afore to-morrow night or nex' day, an' you 'll hafter lay low either in the woods or up tu Mr. Bartlett's. I cal'late his haouse is the best place, an' I come tu take ye up there an' tell him abaout gittin' on ye off, an' if that suits ye we 'll be a-moggin' soon as you c'n git ready."

"I 'se ready," said Bob, snatching his hat and coat from a peg on the log wall and moving toward the door.

"It don't take Bob long tu pack his trunk, no sir," Jim said with a nervous laugh. "Lord, haow you did scare me when you knocked. Twice in one day is 'baout often 'nough to scare a man in one day, yes, sir! But naow you 're putty nigh scarin' of me ag'in. You s'pose them fellers r'ally was huntin' arter Bob?"

"I 'se ready," Bob repeated as he drew a small pistol from his coat pocket, and turning stooped to the candle light to examine the cap. Replacing it in his pocket, he turned to Sam and said:—

"I s'pec 's you 're gwine ter sot me 'cross de run, Marse Lovel?"

"The run? Oh, the Slang; yes, I was cal'latin' tu, an' tu go up tu Mr. Bartlett's with ye. I want tu see him. My canew 's up there tu the landin'."

"What! you did n't never come clean raound to the Slang to-night? You might ha' come right acrost the crik no time."

"I did n't know who might be a-watchin'," Sam answered. "The longest way raoun' 's the surest. Come, le' 's be a-moggin'."

"I 'se done b'en ready," said Bob. "Goo'-by, Nancy; goo'-by, little Jimmy. De good Lawd bress ye an' ta' keer on ye."

He shook hands with the woman and laid his

huge hand on the child's curly head, and then stretched it out to Jim.

" Goo'-by, Jeems, er is you gwine 'long ? "

" You stay along wi' me, Jim," said the woman anxiously.

" I guess mebby you 'd better," said Sam.

The two negroes looked at him suspiciously, and exchanged questioning glances.

" I guess I 'll go a piece," Jim said, with an emphatic jerk of the head.

" All right, suit yourself. I only cal'lated it 'ould look better if anybody come. S'posin' you put the light oaut ag'in, so the' can't nob'dy see us goin' aout."

Jim blew out the candle and the three went out into the night, now lighted only by the stars and the flicker of the northern lights.

They took their way across the clearing at a brisk pace, Jim taking the lead as being most familiar with the path, Sam next, and the runaway in the rear. The latter cast frequent glances behind and started nervously when an alarmed bird fluttered suddenly from a bush, or some night prowler scurried among the fallen leaves and dry twigs, while Sam and Jim held steadily on, quite regardless of such harmless sounds. Feeling their way more slowly along the unseen wood path, they came to where they saw the stars again, then saw them repeated in the still water of the channel, and

then were at the landing.   There was a soft splash
in the channel like the cautious dip of an oar.

"Fo' de Lawd," Bob gasped, starting back and
thrusting his hand in his pocket, "dem fellers out
dar layin' fo' me. My Gawd, Marse Lovel, you
ain't de man to fool a pore niggah what's bein'
hunted to de eends of de airth!" and he tried to
scan Sam's face in the dim starlight, but holding
aloof in a half-crouching attitude that might be a
preparation for either a fight or a run.

"I guess it hain't nothin' but a mushrat or a
duck," Sam whispered, looking intently in the direction of the sound, "but mebby Jim hed better
shove aout there in his canew an' see."

Jim pushed his dugout to the edge of the channel and presently jerked back a loud disjointed
whisper.

"Everything's all right. Jist as clear's a Chris-
tian's eye. Yes, sir, jist egzackly."

With this assurance Bob took his place in the
canoe where Sam had already kneeled, with his
paddle in his hand, and he now pushed out and
laid his craft alongside of Jim's.

"I do' know jest where I'm a goin' tu land,"
he said with a questioning inflection.

"You go up 'baout fifty rod an' you'll come tu
the John Clark place, where ol' John Clark allus
used tu fish. You can run right up to the hard
bank there. Mr. Bartlett's is the furdest north

in that string o' lights. You put right straight for it an' you 'll strike a big holler where a brook runs, which you cross it an' follow up the north bank an' you 'll hit the secont road right by his haouse. I guess I won't go no furder an' I 'll bid you good-by, Bob, an' good luck to ye."

" Goo'-by, Jeems; ta' keer yo'se'f, boy."

They shook hands across the gunwales and the bark canoe slid silently up the channel, breaking the smooth surface with wake and paddle strokes that set the mirrored stars a-dancing and startled the sleeping ducks to sudden, noisy flight. Without greater incident the brief voyage was made, and the two men set forth across the fields, guided by the house light and the deep-cut watercourse to which they presently came. They approached the first road with scarcely a precaution of secrecy, for there was not a house upon it nearer than the tavern at the corner, where the bar-room lights shone out with hospitable gleam.

They were beginning to climb the fence when they heard the sound of a wagon and voices in low but earnest conversation close at hand and drawing nearer. Then they saw the intermittent glow of a pipe, and as they sank back and crouched in a weed-grown fence corner they caught a whiff of its odor.

" Fo' de Lawd," Bob whispered, sniffing it eagerly, " I hain't felt de smell o' no terbacca lak dat sence I done lef' Ol' Firginny."

Sam laid a cautionary hand on his arm. " What be they talkin' 'baout ? "

The wagon stopped almost in front of them, and as its clatter and the footfalls of the horse ceased, the guarded voices of the occupants were distinctly heard.

" I tell you the rwud cross lots is consid'able furder on," said one. " The' hain't no gap ner barway here, fer I c'n see stakes an' caps tu ev'ry corner."

Sam held his breath while he knew that two pairs of eyes were closely scanning the fence and the very corner where he crouched beside his companion, whose hand he could hear stealthily creeping to the pocket that held the pistol.

" I reckon yo' ah right," the other occupant of the wagon said at last, and Sam recognized the smooth voice of the quiet visitor at camp; " but 'pears like we 'd come fah enough."

" No, sir," the other rejoined emphatically, " the 's a reg'lar rwud when we come tu it, an' it runs through a paster. This 'ere 's a medder; I can see a stack a-loomin' up."

" All right," the other conceded, " go ahade and hurry up yo' cakes, foh I 'll be bound Baker and his man 's thah with the boat foh now."

The driver spoke sharply to his horse, and the wagon went rattling down the road at a rapid pace.

"Wal," said Sam, rising and letting out his long-held breath, "I cal'late you stayed to Jim's 'baout as long as was healthy for ye."

".Sho's yo' bawn, Marse Lovel! Dat 'ar man saoun' des lak Cap'n Clahk," Bob whispered excitedly. "De shaapes' man faw huntin' niggahs dey is in all dem pahts. Lawd, if I did n't t'ink he was lookin' right squaar' at me."

"Wal, he hain't a-huntin' on his own groun', an' that makes lots o' odds. My sakes, won't they hev fun a-hoofin' on 't raound the head o' the Slang in the dark! It would be tew all-killin' bad if they should break the' necks a-tumblin' through the woods."

When the two came to the broad stage road, no one was astir in the quiet neighborhood, and leaving Bob hidden in an adjacent fence corner, Sam went to Friend Bartlett's kitchen door and knocked. He heard the familiar sound of a pipe rapped on the stove hearth, then stockinged feet bumping across the floor, and the door was opened by a shock-headed Irishman.

"Good evenin'," said Sam. "Is Mr. Bartlett tu hum?"

"Noa thin," the man answered. "He 's gahn to the village beyant t' a timperance matin'. It 's a moral reformed droonkard they calls him, bes lacter'n'."

"Wal, I sh'ld like tu see Mis' Bartlett, then."

" Is it the misthres ? Thin it 's herself that
wint wid him. Divil the wan o' thim in it but the
daughter an' mesilf an' the gyrl."

" When do you think they 'll be back ? "

" Divil a know I know. I 'll hould yez the price
of a quart, the moral reformed crather 'll be afther
blatherin' till nine o'clock, yis tin, be gob, an'
they 'll be to hear the last wurrud."

Sam's heart sank at the poor prospect of com-
municating with Friend Bartlett. " You was
sayin' suthin' about his darter. Is she a growed-
up woman or a leetle gal ? " he asked.

" It 's a fine lump of a wummun she is, thin ;
nearly as big as the mother, an' it 's herself has
the l'arnin'. She been to schule to all the Nine
Partners." [1]

" Wal, then," said Sam, " I can't du no better 'n
to see her if you 'll ask her tu step tu the door a
minute."

The Irishman, going to the door of another
room, spoke to some one therein, and presently a
handsome young woman came forth. Her plain
dress wore some un-Quakerly adornments, but her
face was so kindly that Sam felt sure she must be
in full sympathy with her parents in all benevolent
work.

" Good evenin', Miss Bartlett ; I fetched up a

---

[1] A celebrated Qnaker boarding-school situated in the township
of Nine Partners in the State of New York.

couple o' ducks tu your father, an' I wanted tu speak tu him abaout a little business."

"Yes," she said, with a questioning affirmative, as she took the proffered ducks. "Thee may leave any message for father with me. Why, these ducks are very nice, and I 'm sure he 'll be very much obliged to thee. What is it thee wants me to tell him?"

"It 's a kinder private business," said Sam, looking past her at the Irishman, who stood near the stove with an attentive ear turned toward them. "An' if you 'd jest step aout an' shet the door a minute."

"Michael, won't thee please take these ducks down cellar and hang them up? Are n't they nice ones?" Margaret Bartlett said, and then to Sam, as Michael, taking the ducks and a candle, disappeared in the cellarway, "Won't thee come in?"

Sam declined and she stepped out, closing the door behind her.

"You tell your father," Sam hastened to say in a low voice, "'at ther' 's som'b'dy arter that nigger an' they 've faound aout where he was hid, so I fetched him up here."

"The colored man at James's? Where is he?" Margaret asked anxiously. "Thee must n't let Michael see him. Father does n't think he can be trusted in such matters."

"No, somehaow paddies hates niggers. I do'

know why. I don't hanker arter 'em myself, but I hain't no grudge ag'in 'em. I did n't cal'late tu hev nob'dy see him but your father, an' hid him in the fence aout here. But he can't stay there all night, an' what be I goin' tu du with him?"

"Thee must put him in the barn, in the bay on the west side of the barn floor. No one will go there, and I 'll tell father when he comes."

"All right, an' you tell your father 'at I 've laid in wi' a Canuck 'at 's a-buyin' apples tu take the nigger tu Canerdy in a day or two. Your father 'll want tu take daown a lwud to-morrer an' find aout when, an' we 'll git the nigger there tu rights."

"I wish thee would n't call colored people niggers," said Margaret.

"Why," said Sam, "that 's what he calls himself, an' I rather guess from his looks he is one. Good-night. I 'll mow him away all right."

Groping his way into the unknown interior of the barn, guided only by feeling and a knowledge of the common internal arrangement of barns in general, Sam led his charge to this safe retreat, and bidding him good-by departed on his devious, dark, and solitary way back to camp.

As he silently passed the landing where Jim's dugout lay he saw the light of a lantern glimmering unsteadily along the wood path and heard the hunters returning in bad humor from their unsuccessful quest, stumbling and grumbling over the rough trail.

" Wal," said Sam to himself, as he listened to their floundering progress up the wooded bank of the Slang, " you faound the holler tree, but the coon wan't in it. By the gre't horn spoon! I'd ha gi'n a fo'pence tu ha' be'n there an' seen 'em an' seen Jim shake that head o' his 'n."

When he reached the mouth of the Slang he heard the regular sound of oars and saw another light steadily advancing up the channel of the creek, shining far along the quiet water before it, while glittering reflections flickered out like floating sparks where the wake stirred the rushes.

Sam ran his canoe into the weeds till the other boat had passed. The lantern shining on the face of the man in the stern revealed the features of Baker, the other visitor at the camp.

" You planned it fust-rate," Sam soliloquized again, " but it 's a dre'f'l poor night for huntin' niggers. Oh, you cussed slinks! I don't lay it up so much ag'in that other feller, for that 's the way he was brought up; but you — V'monters — huntin' niggers! Damn ye! I 'd lufter sink ye in the mud! "

So, by turns boiling with wrath and chuckling over the discomfiture of the slave-hunters, Sam pursued his way to where the candle was burning low in the socket of the tin lantern which was hung out to beacon him to the upper landing.

CHAPTER IX.

LE FEU FOLLET.

THE northern horizon was glowing with the pulsating flame of the aurora, and the dark forest of the eastern shore echoed at intervals with the solemn challenges of the horned owls, remotely answered by their brethren who held sway over the sombre realm of the Porterboro woods that stretched their dark expanse along the west bank of the South Slang and beyond the sluggish rivulets of its source.

" 'Cordin' tu the signs we 're a-goin' tu git some sort o' fallin' weather," Uncle Lisha remarked as he gave an eye and ear to these prognostics of a storm.

" The north'n lights is shinin' tol'lable bright," said Joseph, peeping through the trees at the celestial display. " If the sun hain't crawled raoun' an' sot back side o' Canerdy. ' Roarer Borer Alice,' Solon calls it."

Antoine rolled himself off his seat on to all fours, and in that position intently regarded such glimpses of the flickering arch as could be seen between the tree trunks that stood in black relief against it.

"Wal, Ah 'll ant hear it roar, me, but Ah 'll can see it bore some in de sky. Dat was what Solon prob'ly call it de borer Alice for, ant he? But Ah do' know what for he 'll call it roarer, hein."

"Wal, the fact on 't is, Solon val'es words 'cordin' tu the bigness more 'n the meanin', seems 's 'ough," Joseph explained, while Antoine, turning his searching gaze to the creek, descried a light moving about in the black shadows of the farther shore.

"Look, see dar!" he said in a suppressed tone of alarm, as he pointed to the moving light. "Dat was de feu follet!"

"Few follies is better 'n many, Ann Twine," said Uncle Lisha; "but that 'ere hain't nothin' but someb'dy nuther wi' a lantern."

"Oh, no, no, no, One' Lasha, dat ant be lamprin, sah; dat was feu follet! Ah, do' know haow you call it in Angleesh, but he was very bat t'ing, Ah tol' you."

"What is 't, Antwine?" Joseph inquired; "sort of a one-eyed lew grew critter sech as you was a-tellin' us on onete?"

The Canadian watched the light till it vanished in fitful gleams among the woods, and then, heaving a sigh of relief, he turned and stooped to the campfire to rekindle his neglected pipe before he answered.

"No, seh, Zhozeff, he'll ant so hugly for keel someboddy lak de loup garou; he more kan o' funny for foolish somebody. Ah'll had some experiments of it mahse'f, an' Ah'll goin' tol' you of it, me."

Before seating himself at the fire he looked again in the direction where the light had disappeared. If he had been given the vision of an owl he might have seen a boat with two figures in it stealthily landing at the farther shore; but the faint light of the aurora, that barely defined in dimmed silver the course of the channel, revealed nothing to him.

"W'en Ah'll was leeve in Canada," he began, as his pipe responded satisfactorily to his energetic drafts, each ending in a smack like the stroke of a paddle blade upon the water, "one tam, w'en Ah'll han't more hol' as twenty year an' was goin' for see de gal one naght — he ant Ursule, but nudder one dat Ah tink more of as evry'body dat tam," he paused a moment in dreamy retrospect of long past days when eyes were bright and cheeks were rosy that now were dim and faded, and then resumed, "wal, seh, Ah'll was rode 'long on mah leetly mare. Oh, he was good one, Ah'll tol' you, for draw, for rode, for go fas' — ev'ryt'ing 'cep' t'rashin' machine, dey ant gat it den, an' it was kan' o' daks in de naght, an'

Ah 'll see lit over in mah fader hees farm where
dey was be some swamp side of de meader.
Ah 'll ant know if he was somebody steal de hay
or what he was do, but Ah 'll t'ink he ant gat
some beesiness dar, an' Ah 'll go see what he was
do. So Ah hitch mah hoss — dat was, mah mare
— on de fence an' gat on de lot for see what Ah 'll
see.

"Ah 'll go very softle as leetly maouses, but
more furder Ah 'll go de more furder de lit was
go. Den Ah 'll beegin for run fas', but he run
more faster as Ah was, an' den Ah 'll gat mad an'
run more an' more faster, an' de more Ah run de
more Ah 'll gat mad, an' de more Ah 'll gat mad
de more Ah 'll run an' holler sco'ndrel name to
it an' tol' it for stop, an' what beesiness he got,
go to diab' for see his one' — ev'ryt'ing Ah can
tink, me, but he jus' jomp raoun' dis way, dat
way, on de swamp an' say not'ing, only mek notion,
an' dat mek me so mad Ah 'll run on de swamp
at it.

"Ah 'll fregit Ah 'll gat on all mah bes' clos'.
Ah 'll gat mah new moccasin, mah bes' tow traowser, mah han'some shirt mah mudder weave prup-
pus, an', seh, fus, Ah 'll stubble mah toe an' sloop!
Ah 'll go all over, raght on de black mud an'
water. Den Ah peek up mahse'f careful, an' w'en
Ah scoop de mud off mah heye, Ah 'll see de lit go
dance 'way off 'cross de swamp where somebody

can' never go, an' den Ah 'll know it was de feu follet, an' Ah feel 'f Ah 'll ant wort much, me.

"Wal, Ah go back where mah mare was, spluck, spluck, in my wet moccasin, an' seh, mah mare he ant dar. He gat scare an' run home, an' Ah gat for go 'foot all de way ; spluck, spluck, all de way. My clos' all sp'ile up so Ah 'll can' go for see de gal dat naght, an' som naght nudder feller go an' see it an' cut me all off, so Ah 'll lose it. Dat was pooty bad lucky for me, but not so very bad, for den Ah 'll go marry Ursule, an' she more as feefty paoun' bigger as dat gal."

"Why, man alive, what you was a skivin' raoun' in the ma'sh arter wan't nothin' but a jack o' lantern. I s'pose it 's fox-fire 'at 's broke loose from rotten wood an' sich, an' goes fluripin' an' driftin' raoun'. But what you seen over yonder was jest someb'dy wi' a lantern, Samwil's niggers a-fishin', like 's not. I wonder what 's come o' Samwil," and Uncle Lisha got up and moved restlessly about, peering out upon the creek and toward the landing. "Good airth an' seas! I don't see what in tunket he wants to be a rarin' raoun' nights for, when honest folks ort tu be abed. I would n't never ha' come here with him 'f I 'd s'posed he was goin' tu cut up so. I 'm a dum good min' tu go tu bed an' let him go tu thunder, I snum I be!"

Preparatory to the execution of this threat he

retired into the tent and spread his blankets, but presently came forth, sat down by the fire and lighted his pipe, emitting snorts of impatience between silent intervals of listening. The owls had quit their dismal calling, and not a sound was to be heard from the woods or waters save the occasional splash of a fish or a waterfowl or a muskrat busy with its nightly labors.

"What ye s'pose has become o' that 'ere tormented boy?" Uncle Lisha demanded sharply, after some inward fuming at the apparent apathy of his companions, "or don' ye car' whether he 's draownded or lost in the ma'sh? Why don't ye say suthin'?"

"Wal, Ah guess Sam gat hol' 'nough for took care heese'f of it, prob'ly," Antoine answered with some sharpness. "He 'll ant leetly boy, ant it?"

"I was kinder meditatin' it over in my mind," Joseph said apologetically, "an' I don't seem tu feel r'al'y oneasy 'baout Samwil, ner yet ezackly easy, it don't seem 's 'ough. It 's a-gittin' consid'able kinder late, an' then ag'in it hain't so late as it might be."

"I wish 't I hed a rope hitched raoun' his neck, I 'd fetch him, almighty quick. I don't see what in tunket 's come o' him," and Uncle Lisha stumped about, making the circuit of the fire, and gazed out into the surrounding darkness. "Wal, it 's high time honest folks was abed, and I 'm a-goin' right stret off."

Again he retired within the tent, where he could be heard laboriously pulling off his boots, and with deep-drawn sighs disposing his stout form upon his low couch. But not many moments elapsed before he reappeared in his stockings.

"Wal, One' Lasha, you ant so hones' you t'ink you was, ant it?"

Uncle Lisha deigned no reply to the Canadian but asked anxiously, "Hain't that 'ere tarnal boy come back yit? Wal, I swan." Then after a moment of intent listening, "Wal, I 'm a dumbed good min' to holler, anyway. I c'n make him hear if he 's alive within a mild o' here."

As he drew in his breath for a mighty shout they heard disturbed waterfowl, one after another, nearer and nearer, taking sudden flight, the flutter of uprising and cries of alarm continually drawing nearer, till at last the thump of a paddle was heard at the landing, and then the lantern began to sway and undulate, now hidden behind a tree or knoll, now shining brighter till its sprinkled light disclosed Sam's illuminated legs quite close at hand.

"Wal, folks, here I be," he announced as he let the full light of the candle upon his face through the open door and then extinguished it with a puff.

"An' high time 'at you was," and Uncle Lisha spent his hoarded breath in a growl. "What ye be'n shoolin' raound these 'ere ma'shes for, a

ketchin' the fever 'n' aig an' freezin' tu death?
I 'm a tarnal good min' ter shake ye, so I be. Sed
daown there by the fire an' warm ye whilst I put
on some more wood. An' say, Ann Twine, hain't
ye got a col' duck for him an' a hunk o' bread?
I know he 's hungry."

"I hain't a mite hungry, ner cold nuther," Sam
declared, seating himself by the fire and preparing
for a restful smoke. "On'y a leetle mite tired.
I stayed tu Mr. Bartlett's longer 'n what I meant
tu an' it 's kinder slow poky work a-keepin' the
channel in the dark 'specherly in the Slang. I 'm
sorry you got worried."

"Sho, I wan't worryin' none, but I was a leetle
riled," said the old man as he ran his hand down
Sam's long shank. "Why, your laigs is kinder
damp. You want to dry 'em good 'fore you go tu
bed! I 'm a goin' naow, tu stay."

"Ho! ant worry!" Antoine scoffed. "Bah
gosh, seh, he was be fusster, fusster raoun' more as
one hol' sheekin wid one hen."

"Yah, if you ever tol' the truth folks 'ould
b'lieve you oncte in a while," Uncle Lisha growled
back from the depths of the tent, where, after a
prelude of sighs and yawns, there came a regular
succession of sounds wherewith he was wont to pro-
claim his presence in dreamland.

"Wal," said Joseph sleepily, "I s'pose if I
don't never go tu bed I shan't never git up, an'

it's the wust o' goin' tu bed 'at you du hafter git up some time er nuther," and he went to join Uncle Lisha.

"Say, Sam," Antoine whispered cautiously, "Where you was, hein?"

Sam cast a scrutinizing glance upon him as he answered, "Why, up to Mr. Bartlett's. Where d' ye s'pose. Le' 's go tu bed."

CHAPTER X.

THE CANADA BOAT DEPARTS.

IN prompt fulfillment of the night's prophecies, the morning, dawning dully through a thick veil of clouds, brought a drizzle of rain. This fell with such a drowsy patter on the canvas roof that the inmates of the camp felt little inclination to bestir themselves till impelled to do so by hunger.

Then Sam and Antoine crept out and after inspecting the lowering sky set about building a fire and making other preparations for breakfast, though Uncle Lisha advised a cold bite in the shelter of the tent.

"No, sah," Antoine objected as he moved around the fire, quite regardless of the slow drizzle of rain except when the drip of an overhanging bough aroused a spiteful sputter of the pan wherein two split ducks were frying. "We 'll ant goin' for discourage de inside of us wid col' victual w'en de rine comin' on de aoutside. Ah tol' you, if mans wan' have hees heart warm he 'll gat for had hees stommack warm. Ah 'll can' faght wort' four cen' 'fore Ah 'll gat good breakfis' wen Ah 'll was in Papineau war."

" Ner arter, nuther, I guess," Uncle Lisha commented, but Antoine took no notice of this imputation of a lack of valor.

" But w'en Ah gat good big hot breakfis' behin' mah gaun, den Ah tol' you, dey gat for ta' careful if dey ant wan' me for hurt it."

" Sho, Ann Twine! I cal'late," said Uncle Lisha in sentences interrupted by the labor of drawing on his boots, " 'at it 's a dum foolish business — ugh! I got tu grease these 'ere boots — a fillin' up wi' good victuals — m-m-mugh! They 're stiffer 'n sap troughs — afore a feller goes aout a-fightin' an' run the resk on 't bein' wasted s'posin' he gits killed. Then again, s'posin' a feller hed tu run, he 'd stan' a better chance if he was light-loaded. There! you be on, an' ye don't come off ag'in till you 're 'iled, if I hafter rub ye with a fat duck!"

" Ah, Onc' Lasha, you ant know not'ing 'baout war," cried Antoine, lifting the potato kettle off the fire and emptying the water from it. " Fetch de dauk in de coop, Sam. We 'll can't sit aour table in de rine," and he swung the kettle over Uncle Lisha's imperiled legs to a place inside the tent and Sam bestowed the sizzling frying-pan beside it.

Peering under his glasses, Uncle Lisha forked a potato on to his plate as he snorted contemptuously, " Honh! do' known nothin' 'baout wars!

Why, you poor ig'n'ant infant, I was a sojerin' wi'in a mild o' here afore you was borned. Yes, sir, the Hawley place hain't a mild f'm here, where we was posted, a-watchin' for the British, an' abaout a mild furder is Fort Casin, where they come an' fit an' got licked tew. I 'm a-goin' tu take Jozeff over there an' show it tu him some day. An' wan't I tu Plattsburgh? Sho, Ann Twine, your leetle Poppynew muss wan't the jab of a paigin' awl tu what we hed them times. Lord, if you c'ld ha' seen them ships arter they fit. The mas's an' sails an' riggin' all tore tu rags an' kin'lin' wood, an' the decks kivered wi' blood wus 'n a slotter haouse. An' the poor waounded critters, aour 'n an' their 'n. It wan't no putty sight tu look at. It made me praoud 'nough tu bu'st tu see the stars an' stripes a-flyin' over all them ships, but when I see them 'ere poor Britishers waounded an' dyin' fur from hum an' their women folks, it took all the spite ag'in 'em clean aouten on me."

"You t'ink prob'ly dey heat too much breakfis', ant it, One' Lasha? so he can' run."

"I do' know haow 't was wi' them, but we hed n't hed none tew much, I c'n tell ye," Uncle Lisha answered as he sawed laboriously on the thigh of a duck with a dull knife, and was reminded to remark, "I tell ye what it is, boys, it was a terrible good idee they useter hev when I was young, o' cuttin' up the' meat victuals intu maouthfuls 'fore

it was put ontu the table, an' then let ev'b'dy fork
for hisself aouten one dish. It saved lots o' time
an' rastlin' wi' tough meat when folks was in a
hurry tu git aout tu the' work."

" Ah 'll ant want for chaup more as de meat
for mahse'f, bah gosh," Antoine declared.

" The' uster be some tol'lable lively hustlin',
tusslin' for ch'ice pieces," the old man continued,
reminiscently. " Father uster tell of a neighbor
o' his 'n 'at said haow he 'd broke his child'en's
temper wi' maple sugar. One mornin' father happened in of an arrant, when they was eatin' the'
breakfas', all a-fishin' the fried meat aouten one
dish, an' the ol' man hed got him the best and biggest maou'ful in the hul lot ontu his fork, when one
o' the boys up an' flipped it off an' hed his fork into
't an' into his own maouth with 't quicker 'n scat.
Father 'lowed the maple sugar hed worked fust
rate. Wal, I b'lieve I 've hed enough for onete.
Ann Twine, be you a-goin' tu eat all day ? "

" Ah 'll was been lis'lin' to you, One' Lasha,"
Antoine answered, settling himself to his work.
" Naow Ah 'll was goin' for heat. Dat was de
bes' t'ing we can do w'en it was rine, 'cep' go
feeshin'."

" An' I cal'late tu stick right by ye, Antwine,"
said Joseph from behind a duck's wing that he was
gnawing, holding it with both hands. " I hain't
the kind er man tu desart a friend in no sech

scrape, don't seem 's 'ough I was, not as I feel naow."

Uncle Lisha filled his pipe and went out to enjoy it by the fireside under shelter of his blue umbrella, and Sam, after providing a present supply of firewood with a few axe-strokes, wandered out to the bluff overlooking the creek.

Through the windows of the woods, mullioned with gray trunks and curtained with gay branches, there could be gained narrow glimpses of the nearer marsh, tinted with many blended colors and dotted with green islands of button-bush; then the broad channel, leaden gray under the sunless sky and drizzling rain, the dull expanse broken here and there by ducks reveling apart or in companies, enjoying the weather that set all the rest of the world a-moping.

Beyond was the farther border of marsh and then the sheer wall of forest, making the horizon against the low sky that enveloped far mountains and nearer hills in common obscurity.

The yellow poplars and the scarlet pepperidges shone through the veil of rain as if yesterday's sunshine was still held in them to brighten to-day's sombre monotony of gray.

Like outlooks on the lakeward side revealed only the dull expanse of gray water receding into the gray mist toward unseen shores, except where Garden Island loomed, blurred and undefined, between shrouded water and low sky, with one yellow-leafed birch flaring like a beacon half quenched on the western point, and off the eastern point a black rock, like a fast-anchored buoy.

Farther away, Long Point lay like a fallen cloud afloat on the water, moored to the stable earth by nearer drawing shores of rock and sandy beach and the willow-clad bar of Little Otter.

Here and there were dots and lines of swimming waterfowl on the unreflecting surface of the bay, and occasionally a flying flock faring out to safety of wide waters or into the abundance of the marshes, dissolving in the mist or materializing out of it as they went or came.

A scattered company of crows straggled in slow flight athwart the screen of rain and mist; a kingfisher hung in stationary poise against it, then plunged like a plummet into the water, and far out on the shallows a heron stood waiting in statuesque patience for breakfast to swim to him.

Far or near there was no visible sign of human life, nor amid the continuous purr of the rain, the contented gabble of the ducks, the whistle of passing wings, the raucous call of some estray or laggard, and the metallic clatter of the kingfisher, was there any sound of it except from the quarter where the Canadian boat was taking in its cargo.

Thence through the heavy vaporous atmosphere came the lumbering of laden wagons, the rumble of their discharging freight, and then the brisk rattle of departing empty wagons, all mingled with the shouts of teamsters and the vociferous jabber of captain and crew.

For one who had no apparent reason for being interested in fruit trade, Sam was uncommonly well pleased that the rainy day was not hindering it, and having assured himself of the fact he returned to camp.

Uncle Lisha still sat by the fire, the staff of his umbrella resting across his shoulder while he diligently greased his boots with the tallow in the bottom of the lantern, the accumulated drip of many candles, Joseph and Antoine looking on with interest from the tent door.

" You don't want tu burn your boots, Uncle Lisher," said Sam, standing by the fire and letting the water from his hat brim drip into it. " There 's more profit tu you in hevin' other folks burn up their 'n. I do b'lieve I smell burnt luther."

" I guess they hain't gittin' tew hot," said Uncle Lisha, running his finger over the soles. " Makes me think o' the feller 'at went tu a neighbor's a-visitin' wi' a pair o' bran' new boots on, which for all he spread 'em aout on the stove ha'th, an' stuck 'em top o' chairs, the' would n't nob'dy notice 'em, an' so when he see they wan't a-goin' tu say nothin' abaout 'em, he up an' says, says he, ' Ye need n't think strange if ye smell new luther.' Wal, Samwil, what ye diskivered ? "

" Nothin' but water an' ma'sh an' woods, lookin' lunsomer 'n they did a hundred year ago, fer there hain't even an Injun in sight.   I heard the French- man lwudin' his boat, though." .

" Wal," sighed Antoine, " Ah wish Ah 'll was be apples, me, so he was bought me an' took it to Canada.   But so as Ah can' do dat, Ah guess Ah 'll do nex' bes' an' go feesh some bull pawt. You 'll goin' 'long to me, Zhozeff?   We go on de scaow, an' took some funs."

Joseph looked out upon the dismal drizzle with a rueful countenance and answered, " Wal, I don't sca'cely seem tu feel like goin', not ezackly.   It 's kinder oncomf'table an' sorter exposin' a-fishin' in the rain, an' I 'm mortal afeared o' ketchin' a eel. I like tu eat 'em, but I swan I don't lufter ketch 'em."

" Oh, come, Zhozeff," Antoine urged in a persua- sive tone.   " If you ant want for ketch it, Ah 'll ketch it, an' you can ketch de udder leetly feller. Come, Zhozeff."

" Wal, I ruther guess I won't, I 'm 'bleeged tu ye," and Joseph settled himself more comfortably in his seat.   " I don't 'pear tu hanker much fer fishin' tu-day.   Mebby Uncle Lisha 'll go, er Sam- wil, mebby."

But Sam shook his head in decided negative, and Uncle Lisha audibly declined : " Good airth an' seas ! You don't ketch me goin' fishin' fer seeh fish in seeh weather; I hain't a loon er a shell duck."

"Den, bah gosh, all Ah 'll ketch Ah 'll heat all," Antoine declared and went out to grub for worms in the adjacent pasture. After a while he returned from a successful quest, and getting a hook and line from among his stores he cut a cedar pole and set forth. Presently his camp mates heard the creak and splash of his departing oars, then a hollow clank as they were dropped in board, and then the rattle of the chain being wound about the nearest fishing stake, and then they imagined that they heard the whistle of his line and the spang of his heavy sinker as he made the first vigorous cast. Two hours later he appeared, dripping but happy, bringing a number of dressed bull pouts which, fried to a turn, he did not devour alone as he had threatened, but shared with his companions.

The afternoon was spent in the tent. Uncle Lisha discoursed of the past and Antoine of various men in Canada who were always the heroes of his tales, while in the breaks of conversation Sam several times went out for the ostensible purpose of a general inspection of the weather, though the examination was mostly confined to the direction of Lewis Creek.

Late in the afternoon the wind freshened from the northeast, the tossed branches dropped sudden showers upon the canvas with a startling, ripping sound, and amid the sullen murmur of the wind-swept woods and the louder patter of the driven rain could be heard the regular wash of the rising waves and the shrill whistle of frequent flocks scudding in from the lake.

Then Sam saw the Canada boat gliding down the unseen channel, the great square sail stalking between the trees like a gigantic ghost, till at last it walked forth upon the vexed lake amid the taller phantoms of mist and vanished in the thronging host.

Sam reëntered the tent with a satisfied visage and remarked : —

"Wal, that 'ere Frenchman's got started fer Canerdy with his apples."

"An' like 'nough a blackbary," Uncle Lisha added, with a significant twinkle in his eye.

CHAPTER XI.

During the night the rain ceased, and the morning broke through rifted clouds which slowly scattered in white-fleeced flocks and drifted away across the azure field. Though the storm had partially stripped the trees of their ripened leaves, they seemed none the less brilliant when the unveiled splendor of the sun fell upon them, for each unfallen leaf had gained more intense color, and like every branch and twig sparkled with innumerable drops of liquid crystal.

Leaving their companions to the pursuit of sport on shore, Sam and Antoine took their guns and went down to the upper landing, where they were surprised to find a couple of blanket-coated swarthy men, just landed from a bark canoe, bending intently over the dew-beaded bottom of Sam's upturned canoe and conversing in unintelligible, low, and musical tones.

"Dar was you Injin, jes' Ah tol' you," said Antoine triumphantly.

At their approach the Indians turned toward

them without any manifestation of surprise, and one of them, a good-looking man of middle age, greeted Sam with a pleasant smile of recognition.

"How do, Lovel? Know me? Me Joe Tocksoose. Make um dat canoe five, six year 'go."

"Why, yes ; so you be," said Sam, giving him a cordial hand ; "but I never s'posed I'd run ag'in ye here. Trappin', be ye?"

"Yaas, ketch um moosquas, some."

His companion ignored the presence of the white men after the first glance at them, and turned his back upon them and pottered lazily over a useless rearrangement of the traps and muskrats in the bow of his canoe. His low-browed face was sullen, his little eyes as cruel as a snake's, and he looked as if he might be a savage brother rather than a civilized descendant of his barbarian ancestors.

"You no trap um musquas?" Tocksoose asked.

"No, hunting ducks. Shot many, hev ye?"

"No, rather have musquas. Better for eat. Better for skin. Shoot um plenty duck?"

"Wal, some. Hain't hunted a turrible sight. Where be you a-campin'?"

"Up dar," the Indian answered, pointing toward the Slang. "Make 'em good canoe. Very good bark. Come see some day."

"Nawah, Tocksoose," the other Indian growled with gruff impatience as he shoved the canoe afloat and stepped into it.

"Onh-ouh, me come," Tocksoose answered, and followed his companion. "Goo'-by, Lovet, come see canoe," and getting clear of the weeds they paddled away as silently as if they were ghosts of their long-departed progenitors haunting the changed scenes of their earthly life. The Indians went across and down stream, examining and re-setting their traps in houses along the border of the marsh.

Sam and Antoine shaped their course up stream, finding no game on the ground which the trappers had just passed over, but after passing the South Slang ducks arose, singly and in flocks, frequently enough to give them all the shooting they could wish. But they missed much oftener than they killed, for Sam had not acquired the knack of cutting down his birds in the moment that they labored upward from the rushy covert before they began to climb the air in a swift ascending slant, or scurrying away in swifter level flight, when he continually made the mistake of shooting behind his mark.

Antoine always dwelt long on his aim, and when he attempted a shot at a single flying bird, poked after it till it was out of range and then lowered his wabbling muzzle or blazed away into empty space. Now and then a duck succumbed to Sam's shot and came down with a headlong, surging splash into the marsh, perhaps to be lost in the even sameness of the sedgy level, perhaps to be retrieved after a groping search in the maze of wild rice stalks or denser tangle of more diversified marsh growth. Achieving such indifferent success, they came to the East Slang and entered the narrow channel, when a dusky duck arose from the weeds on their left with a prodigious flutter and outcry of alarm. Sam caught aim and fired in the instant during which she hung almost stationary after the upward spring. Confident of the correctness of his aim, he was surprised and disgusted beyond measure to see the heavy bird continue her flight, climbing the air almost perpendicularly and with continually increasing speed to a height at which she looked no bigger than a swallow.

"Wal, by the gre't horn spoon!" was all he could say, and Antoine ·offered such soothing condolence as one is apt to receive when he has made an unsuccessful shot.

"Wal, Ah 'll was spec' for see it tombly, he was ·so beeg lak geese an' so close Ah can mos' stroke it wid mah paddle. Prob'ly you 'll was hit it, but he was fool dauk an' ant know de way for fall, so he fall up, prob'ly, 'less prob'ly he was gat tire of dis wicked worl' an' goin' look for de angel. Bah gosh, he mos' gat where dey was."

They were still watching the towering bird when suddenly her wings closed spasmodically and she came down like a plummet, striking the water so near them that the canoe was sprinkled with the upbursting shower of spray, while in the centre of the circling wavelets the inert, lifeless bird rose and sank like a balancing scale.

Again Sam ejaculated, " Wal, by the gre't horn spoon ! " and Antoine was surprised into an expression of astonishment. ‹ A close examination proved that the bird had been hit by a single shot, which had bored the brain.

" Jes' Ah tol' you," said Antoine complacently ; " you 'll was mek him crazy in hees head of it, so he 'll ant know de way for fall. Ah 'll know what hail it jes' soon Ah 'll see him fall up dat way, me."

Sam's gun was reloaded, and they were again moving forward when a small, dusky-hued waterfowl swam boldly into the channel before them within short range.

" Hol' on. Don' shot," Antoine said in a low but intensely earnest tone as Sam leveled his gun on the easy mark ; but as the words were spoken the trigger was pulled, and out of the cloud of smoke the shot rained upon the spot from which the daring fowl had instantaneously vanished.

" Dar," cried Antoine in supreme disgust, as the rebounding echoes came rolling back from hill and woodland, " Ant Ah 'll tol' you ? What for you shot at dat mis'bly lectly hell-davver ? You can't keel it more as hit litlin', an' if you 'll was gat it, he ant wors more as not'ing 't all. Naow he gone daown for see his fader, de dev', an' in minute he come back for laft at you. Dar." And there indeed the uncanny, keen-eyed, sharp-billed head popped just above the surface two gunshots away, swimming for the marsh, where it presently disappeared.

Then they were startled by a rush of multitudinous swift wings, and a great flock of teal swept past, following every turn of the channel in their arrowy flight till they alighted with a long, resounding splash fifty rods farther up stream. Standing up and peering cautiously over the marsh, Sam saw the flock swimming in the channel opposite to a clump of low-branched trees on the eastern bank.

"They hain't six rod from a good place to crawl up tu 'em," he whispered, as he settled back on to his knees and took up a paddle. "Le 's run int' the brook here an' land an' tackle 'em from the bank. If we git a good lick at 'em we won't want tu hunt no more to-day."

They landed on the bank of the brook and held across the field till the clump of trees were in range with the place where the teal had alighted. Turning at a right angle, they advanced cautiously in this direction and were soon close behind a screen of low-hanging oak branches, looking between which they saw at least a hundred unsuspecting teal swimming and feeding within easy range, the blue wings gleaming in the sunlight in brilliant contrast to the dull color of the general plumage.

"You pour it int' the thick on 'em a-settin'," Sam whispered, as they silently cocked their guns, " an' I 'll let 'em hev when they rise."

Antoine nodded and poked his gun through an opening to what he imagined to be a perfect aim on the thickest huddle of the flock. Sam felt a pang of contrition for the impending slaughter of the innocents, but held his gun ready to do his part in it. The roar of Antoine's gun was prolonged by the roar of a hundred pairs of wings starting to simultaneous flight, and quickly echoed by Sam's discharge. Rushing forward to the verge of the marsh, the shooters peered eagerly under the lifting cloud of smoke and saw one solitary wing-tipped teal struggling toward the cover of the marsh through the frost-blackened lily-pads. Antoine had quite overshot the sitting birds, and Sam, aiming at the whole flock, had missed all but the chance-struck victim.

As far up stream as there was water enough to float one, it must have been alive with ducks, for now the air was swarming with them, a disturbed congregation, uttering cries of alarm, some circling about in confused flight, some making straight away over the woods to the two creeks, and some following the course of the stream, passing overhead and before the chopfallen gunners.

"Sam, bah-a-gosh!" Antoine ejaculated in most abject self-disgust. "Le 's we load off aour gaun an' shot one 'nudder. We gat too fool for leeve some more."

"By the gre't horn spoon, Antwine," Sam replied in utter contempt of their performance, "we could n't hit one 'nuther erless we helt the muzzles o' aour guns in aour maouths. We might 's well go an' git the canew an' see if we c'n find that 'ere waounded duck," and he began carefully reloading his gun.

"Dat dauk? You maght jes' well hunt for haystack wid needle as hunt dat dauk. Nobody fan' him but mink or prob'ly de hawk. What for you load off you gaun? Bah gosh! Ah 'll ant load off mah gaun some more. He ant so good as stick hwood. Ah, sacre hol' damnashin' gaun!" Antoine growled at his musket and handled it as if with an intention of smashing it on the nearest tree, but at last shouldered it. Sam finished reloading and remarked as he set a cap on the nipple: —

"It hain't no use o' blamin' it ont' the guns, Antwine."

They took the shortest way to the canoe, each engaged in the unprofitable silent self-communion which is a common but not happy experience of sportsmen. To what one of the brotherhood does not the missing of a lost opportunity come like a ghost to haunt his waking hours and trouble his dreams?

Their moody silence was continued as they paddled down the Slang, each plying the paddle industriously, quite regardless of every chance of a shot offered by rising or passing birds. Of the last there were not a few, for a boat was coming down the creek, disturbing the waterfowl with more frequent shots than Sam had ever heard except at a general muster of the militia, or had Antoine since the Papineau war.

"It was prob'ly some boy jes' shot for mek nowse," Antoine commented.

The heads of the two occupants of the approaching boat could now be seen above the wild rice that hid craft and channel. Presently a pair of wood ducks sprang into the air a few rods in advance of the moving heads, one flying to the right, the other to the left, and in the same instant the polished barrels of a gun flashed upward in the sunlight, a jet of smoke puffed out, followed by another as quick as a finger could shift triggers, and as the double report rolled up wind to their ears the two canoe-men saw the ducks tumble limp and lifeless back into the marsh. Three more ducks, alarmed by the echoes that rebounded from the wooded shore beside which they were resting, got up together at long range, but the alert sportsman picked up a second gun and brought

down two with the first barrel and with the second
hit the last of three so hard that it came down
with a long slant in front of the canoe now emerging from the Slang.   Sam finished the wounded
fowl with a charge from his long single-barrel and
exclaimed in reply to Antoine : —

"Boys ! I cal'late that feller 's a man, an' one
'at understan's his business.   By mighty ! don't
he jest clear the sky o' ducks ?   Le 's let him go
ahead, for I 'd a dumb'd sight druther see him shoot
'an tu shoot myself, leastways as I 'pear tu shoot
tu-day."

CHAPTER XII.

A SPORTSMAN.

The wild duck, as he scuds along,
　Seeth thine eye of black,
And cries with shrill, despairing tone,
"Don't shoot, old boy, I 'm coming down ;
　I know you, Cousin Jack ! "

E. J. Phelps.

"Here 's another duck o' your 'n," Sam addressed the stranger as the other boat drew near. "You 'pear tu git ev'y bird 'at you p'int at."

"No, not quite," said the gentleman, for such he was, and a handsome one too, with keen black eyes and finely cut features and an easy graceful bearing. "I 've heard of men who did that and heard them tell of doing it, but I never saw them do it. But you 'd better take this bird, you 're quite welcome to it."

"No, thank ye," said Sam, " me an' this man 's a-gittin' more shots 'an we c'n 'tend tu. My, you 'd ortu seen us make the feathers fly up the East Slang." Sam felt that open confession might ease his soul.

" Don' you tol' him, Sam," Antoine whispered

hoarsely. "Ant we shem 'nough for had we an' de dauk know it?"

"Wal, go ahead, mister," said Sam, and the other boat took the lead.

"He hain't got him no gre't of a paddler," Sam remarked as he watched the clumsy propelling of the larger craft, paddled now on one side, now on the other. "I sh'd like tu put him raound a spell."

There were ducks enough scattered among the wild rice to afford fair shooting, though the great flocks had returned to their daytime haunts, the dusky ducks to float on the wide waters of the lake or to bask on its rocky shores, whither the teal accompanied them, while the wood ducks congregated in the embowered lagoons of Lewis Creek, the South Slang, and Goose Creek. There, in listless enjoyment of seclusion, they swam lazily in the shallow pools, checkering the green scum of floating duck weed with a network of water paths, or sat in sleepy rows along the mossy trunks of fallen trees, oftener disturbed by a swooping hawk or prowling fox or mink than by man, the enemy and destroyer of nature.

Sam marveled at the celerity with which his rival made his shots, only missing often enough to prove that there was no magic in the skill which Sam expressed admiration of, in spite of the humiliation of seeing himself so far outdone.

“By the gre’t horn spoon, he’s a buster!” he exclaimed, as two ducks, rising at once on either side of the channel, responded to a double shot with folded wings and a downright fall. “But I sh’ld like tu try him a hack with a rifle.”

“Oh, t’undur, Ah’ll tol’ you it was jes’ he’s gaun,” growled Antoine contemptuously. “’F Ah’ll had gaun sem lak dat Ah’ll show you, me.”

“I s’pose his gun does ha’ suthin’ tu du with it, but I swan I b’lieve arter the ducks git him l’arnt, they’d jest faint away and tumble daown if he p’inted a stick at ’em.”

Sam and Ántoine ran the canoe among the rushes under the willows of the lower landing alongside the craft of the sportsman, who had preceded them by twenty minutes and was now at the foot of the cliff with his boatman making preparation for dinner, the first plucking a fat young wood duck, the other gathering dry fuel out of the abundance of driftwood.

“Naow, mister,” said Sam, as he fed his admiring eyes on the handsome English guns whose like he had never seen before and his fingers itched to lay hold of, “why don’t ye come up tu aour fire an’ cook your dinner? It’ll save ye a lot o’ fussin’, an’ Joseff’ll be mighty glad o’ them feathers you’re a-wastin’. He come a-feather huntin’, leastways he’s a-savin’ of ’em for tu keep his wife good-natur’d. Fetch your stuff right up where it’s handy cookin' an' we 'll put a couple o' extry taters in the kittle for ye."

The stranger was drawn to Sam by the attraction of one honest sportsman to another, and therefore nothing loath to accept the invitation. Carrying the half-plucked duck in one hand and one of the guns in the other, and followed by his man carrying a covered basket, he climbed the steep path with his host in the lead.

They found the camp untenanted, for Uncle Lisha and Joseph had not yet returned from a land expedition along the shore in the direction of the Slang bridge, upon which they had set forth with the intention of stalking ducks in the pond holes of the marsh or lying in wait for incoming flocks.

Antoine soon had a fire blazing on the stone hearth, which he shared with the guest in the preparation of the two dinners. The gentleman now proved himself a thoroughly accomplished sportsman, for when his end of the fire sank to a glowing bed of coals he broiled his neatly dressed duck as skillfully as he had killed it, and its delicate aroma asserted itself above the grosser odor of Antoine's cookery. When the double meal was served he made twofold return for the acceptable potatoes in dainties from his basket, and when all were so well fed that necessity of providing another meal seemed too distant to be worth thinking of, he passed around cigars that were more fragrant than roses. While all but he smoked them with the awkwardness of unaccustomed use, he half won Sam's heart with well-told tales of his shooting adventures in all parts of the country, and completed the conquest ·by interested listening to Sam's stories.

When Sam hinted he would like to paddle him up the South Slang the offer was gladly accepted. So the two set forth in the sportsman's boat, leaving his boatman and Antoine to amuse themselves as they would, an arrangement to the liking of both, as it gave Antoine an opportunity to ask many questions, he being tormented with an itching curiosity as much as any Yankee ever was, and the boatman, a lazy fellow, would as lief be paid for doing nothing as for earning his money.

Sam plied his noiseless paddle with right good will up the narrow channel, whose brown waters here and there turned sharply in its almost currentless course to long curved or straight reaches that ended in other turns among the rice and sedges. Now there would be a stillness that was absolute but for far-removed sounds of farm life or the skyward scream of a hawk, a mote of bronze slowly circling as if adrift in an eddy of the upper air; or, nearer, some unseen stir of life among the rushes, the slow scratch of a weed against the boat's side, or the smothered gulp of a disturbed mud fish beneath the prow. Then the silence was broken suddenly enough to startle the steadiest nerves when, splashing and fluttering, squeaking or quacking in wild alarm, wood duck or dusky duck tore its way upward through its tent of sedge or rice-stalks. Then the ready gun made its quick selection, puffed out its smoke and thunder, answered itself like an echo with a second report, and two ducks dropped back limp and lifeless within the circling wavelets of their own uprising, while the echoes rebounded between the wooded shores, and far and near frightened ducks arose, bitterns took wing with guttural squawks, rails set up a clamorous cackle, and for a few moments the marshes were alive with noisy commotion. Then, while the echoes died in the distance, the ducks settled again in the marsh before or behind the boat, the babble of the rails ceased, the last wads were driven home with a diminuendo of hollow thuds, and after the sharp click of the recapped locks, the silent boat moved on into a new silence, again and again to break it. Now it slid under the low span of a bridge, now came to the mouth of Goose Creek, almost closed between its jams of floating bog that undulated with the boat's wake with a faint rustle of sedgy swells. As the craft squeezed its way up this narrow water path, here, closed by a movable island of bog that was swung aside like a gate to give them passage, there, crowded by a tangled jungle of button-bush, the hunters saw in trodden ooze and the windrows of shed plumage evidence of the throngs of waterfowl that made this natural fastness their nightly resting-place.   There were now only a few stragglers — early to bed or late to rise — one of whom, cut down at long range, they had infinite trouble to retrieve by wading over the treacherous bog.

In one place a woodcock had bored the muddy margin with his long bill and chalked it with his sign, which was scarcely noted before he sprang with a twittering whistle and was cut down with a snap shot of the alert sportsman. Then for the first time Sam had an opportunity to admire and closely inspect what had until now been but an elusive, vanishing myth, and wondered why his new friend should gloat more over this little bird than over a great duck. Yet he himself had just declared that he would be prouder to kill a wild goose than to kill a bear, as much to the astonishment of the other.

They followed the crooked labyrinth of Goose Creek till it forked into two branches, both too narrow to give passage to anything bulkier than a duck or muskrat. They made their way back to the Slang, which from this point to its source was the eastern boundary of a large tract of primeval forest, a level sameness of gloomy evergreen woods.

Where the channel parted in two unboatable

tributaries, one coming out of the cold heart of the forest, the other from the sunny bosom of the fields, the Indians had made their camp. A number of stretched muskrat skins were hung about it, the thin smoke of the spent ·fire drifted up among the hemlock boughs, the canoe was drawn up to the bank with its two paddles stuck in the mud beside it, and the two Waubanakees, full heirs of their wild forefathers' laziness, were pottering indolently over some piece of handicraft.

"They 're a-makin' a canew," Sam said, after watching them a little ; " want tu go an' see haow they du it ? " and his companion assenting, he turned the boat inshore.

The Indians were aware of the approach of visitors, but gave no sign of it when the boat ran alongside the canoe and the occupants stepped ashore, nor did they till the duck-hunters had come close to them, where they were kneeling on a patch of hard-trodden bare earth. Then Sam's old acquaintance turned his good-humored face. to them a moment and greeted them with a low-spoken " Quiee," but his sullen companion did not lift.his eyes from his work.

The top frame and gunwales and cross bars of a canoe lay on the leveled piece of ground, and the Indians were driving stakes at the ends and at the intersections of the cross bars. Having accomplished this, they filled and lighted their pipes and deliberated upon the next step to be taken in the task, conversing in the soft, low tones of their own language. At last he of the sour visage picked up a hatchet and went into the woods, which enfolded him out of sight in their shadowy embrace as if he belonged to them. It did not seem likely that the white men were to see more of the art of canoe building to-day. So Sam's friend bought a couple of bows and a half a dozen arrows for his two boys ; waiting till Tocksoose finished the last with a crooked knife which he held with his palm up and drew towards him, and the dexterous use of which was worth seeing. Then they reëmbarked and set forth down stream as the shadows of the hemlocks were crawling up the eastern bank.

"Now, Lovel," said the sportsman, "I want to show you that I can handle a paddle too, so give it to me and you take my gun and see how it suits you."

Sam was as happy with the beautiful gun in his hands as a lover with his sweetheart, and fondled it with as much delight, sighting it on various inanimate objects and trying again and again the smooth elastic movement of the locks. An awkward splash of the paddle, that was for the most part fairly well handled, startled a duck to flight at long range, and Sam, pottering a little over his aim, made a clean miss. At the report, one nearer, but dozing over his crop full of wild rice, floundered to flight through the rent bower of sedges. Sam covered him neatly, but his finger found the wrong trigger and there was only a hollow snap of the empty barrel. Yet he kept his wits enough to make a second trial, and the big dusky drake came down with a downright splash that told of sudden and merciful death.

"A good shot," was the sportsman's commendation as he turned the boat's prow into the weeds, but Sam was not very proud of it after a bad miss and a worse blunder.

"The's a'most tew many trickers for my fingers," he said as he retrieved the dead bird with an oar. "The gun can't du it all, if it is an almighty good one. It wants the right man behind it."

"It's got a very good one there," the gentleman said. "All the trouble with him is he has learned to shoot a rifle too well to cut loose without half taking sight, as we shotgun fellows do."

So few ducks had come in since the up stream passage of the hunters that it was scarcely worth while to be on the watch for them, and they both paddled leisurely down the channel, chatting as they went, while the one smoked his fragrant cigar, the other his satisfying pipe.

"How would you like the life of our red brethren back there?" the sportsman asked.

"Wal, they don't appear tu be fretted much," said Sam.

" No, they 're contented; food enough for to-
day and a few pipefuls of tobacco; rich with a
hundred muskrat skins. Perhaps it 's the happiest
life a man can lead, and perhaps the happiest is
the best."

" Wal, no," Sam dissented. " It 'll du well
'nough for a play spell naow an' ag'in; but it
hain't jest the sort o' life for a stiddy business,
leastways not for white men. Oh, I d' know, if a
man had n't nob'dy but himself and things had n't
gone jest right with him, but not if the' 's anyb'dy
'at he cares for. I hev wished I was an Injin,
but I don't naow. An' I 've tried it tew, for a
fortni't runnin', up t' other Slang. An' it beats all
haow easy a man settles daown tu that way o' livin',
an' I b'lieve a man 's consid'able like a tame fox —
oncte he gits loose he gits wild ag'in mighty easy.
I feel it a-comin' on every time I git int' the woods,
some sight or some smell 'at you can't sca'cely see
ner smell, a-wakin' up suthin' that 's b'en asleep
sence the Lord knows when. 'T wan't in my father, an' I do' know 's it was in my gran'ther, only
as he hed tu hunt some for a livin'. 'T ain't no
wonder 'at you can't tame an Injin so 't he 'll stay
tame, wi' a hundered generations o' wild blood
a-r'arin' up in him wus 'n we c'n guess. An'
't ain't none tew easy for us tu quit livin' that way
arter bein' in 't a spell. Why, it 's jelluk leavin'
the hum 'at I was born in an' reared in, tu clear

aout from a camp 'at I 've stayed in a week, an' if I come acrost it arterwards it makes me feel sort o' lunsome." He blushed through his sunburns and laughed a little bashfully at his confession of weakness, but the smile on his companion's face was sympathetic.

"Yes, we 've got a drop of the old wild blood in us," the latter said, "and for my part I 'm thankful for it, and I don't take greatly to folks who have n't got it or are ashamed of it. Of course it won't do to let it get the better of us all the time, for there is n't much bread and butter in it, but it is n't best to smother it out. It 's good sauce for the bread and butter."

"No, it won't du," Sam said with a sigh of resignation. "A man 'at don't du nothin' much but hunt an' fish an' trap is lierble tu be a pooty shif'less creetur'; clever an' good-natur'd mebby, but turrible shif'less. Like 's not I 'd ha' be'n one of 'em myself if it had n't ha' be'n fer hevin' a good woman, not tew sot, but reason'ble in goin' ag'n it. As a gin'al thing women folks 'pears tu be kinder onfavorable tu huntin' an' haoun' dawgs an' sech, an' I d' know but they was made so a puppus tu keep us kinder in baounds. Then ag'in the' 's women 'at it 's enough tu drive a man off int' the woods tu git red o' their everlastin' hetchelin'."

His companion laughed and began to speak, but stopped with a sudden cautionary "Sh-h —there comes a flock of teal," as he bent low and turned the boat close behind a tall bunch of weeds. "Give me my gun," he whispered, and just as he got it in his hands the swift-winged little ducks came like a flash, following the channel as if it was a road, till at sight of the boat they swerved away and upward from it. The ready gun sprang as quickly to the shooter's shoulder, and as it touched it spat out its double report and six dead and wounded birds tumbled out of the thinned ranks into marsh and channel in a rapid succession of splashes.

When the game was picked up the hunters went on to the mouth of the Slang, where the boat was run into the tall weeds to await the evening incoming of the ducks. The flight was already begun, giving as frequent shots as a reasonable man could desire, and much more difficult for an unpracticed hand than when the birds were flushed from the marshes.

From the moment when a flock first became visible, like a dark thread drifting up from the horizon of wooded shores beyond the Bay of the Vessels, then became a chain of motes, and the first faint sibilation of hurrying wings dawned on the hearing, till it grew loud and emphatic, and every advancing form became a distinct bird, there was time enough for nerves to be steadied and gun to be ready, but not to find an easy mark in the strong-winged fowl, sweeping past with the impetus gained in two miles of flight with a favoring breeze. Not every one of the sportsman's shots brought down its bird, for now and then there was an unmistakable miss, and sometimes when a chance was taken at long range the pellets could be heard pattering against the thick plumage, yet the stout bird swept on in uninterrupted flight.

The shooter showed neither impatience when he made an ineffectual shot nor exultation when with more frequent occurrence the stricken bird came down in a curved slant and plunged through weeds and water to its last alighting. After a while he gave the gun to Sam, who, profiting by instruction and experience, made some shots good enough to afford consolation for the bad ones, and then they quit their ambuscade and paddled down to the landing under the willows.

The last sunlight was on the eastern mountains and the sportsman made haste to depart on his homeward voyage, he and Sam parting with a mutual desire for further acquaintance and future days of sport together.

" Say, Sam," Antoine whispered eagerly, bursting with news he could scarcely contain till the others were out of hearing, " you 'll ant ast it, did you ? You 'll ant know who he was, ant it ?"

" No," said Sam, " I did n't ask him no questions."

" Wal, seh, bah gosh, he was be de biggest l'yer dey was in Vairgenne.   Dat feller tol' me."

" Git aout Antwine," said Sam, " he hain't no liar.   He's abaout as nice a man as ever I see."

" Oh, Sam, ant you on'stan' Angleesh?   Ah 'll ant say he lie, but he big l'yer.   He goin' be judge, prob'ly gov'ner, mebby."

CHAPTER XIII.

A WILD GOOSE CHASE.

Uncle Lisha and Joseph set forth in the belt of trees that shaded the west bank of Little Otter from the Slab Hole to the South Slang, so intent upon the performance of doughty deeds that they skulked with bent backs till the ache could be endured no longer, and with a loud sigh of relief they straightened up just at the very time and place to disclose themselves to a flock of ducks that were enjoying the seclusion of a marsh-locked pool. Startled by the sound and the sudden apparition of human forms arising within forty paces of their retreat, the ducks sprang into the air with a simultaneous splash and vociferous outcry of alarm. In no less surprise the two gunners stood gaping at the retreating flock, then with one accord they squatted with lowered heads till the whistle of departing wings grew faint in the distance, and then turned their humiliated faces full upon each other.

"Sam Hill!" Joseph ejaculated, "what a chance it seems 's 'ough we 'most hed."

"What a couple o' dumb'd dodunks we be, more like!" Uncle Lisha responded in intense disgust. "Naow le's go 'long an' use aour eyes an' act as if ducks had some tew."

With this determination they proceeded, yet more cautiously, stopping frequently to examine the marsh before them, with heads as gradually uplifted as grass rises after the pressure of the foot. At last they discovered a pool similar to the one at which they had exposed themselves so unwarily, and a careful reconnoissance disclosed a flock of twenty or more dusky ducks taking their ease on the reed-hedged pool, some asleep, their broad bills resting on their round breasts, others leisurely sounding the shallows with elongated necks for choice tidbits, while a few alert old drakes carried their wise heads high, in constant vigilance.

The hunters squatted for a brief, whispered plan of attack, and, having arranged it, moved forward, stooping low, to occupy the spot selected for the onslaught. There was one place in the line of approach where the screen of weeds was so low that it could only be passed without discovery by crawling, and when it was reached the hunters went on all fours, — not on hands and knees, but on hands and feet, — hitching their prone guns along step by step. Now, though their heads were quite out of sight of the ducks and the ducks unseen by them, their posteriors were fully exposed to the view of the vigilant sentinels, who, at the sight of these two strange objects undulating slowly forward above the tops of the rushes, at once sounded the alarm, and the whole flock sprang to wing with an uproar of splashing, fluttering, and quacking.

The unlucky hunters halted without a change of posture, and listened in dismayed silence till the tumult of departure had subsided, before they ventured to drop upon their knees and look in the direction from which the sound of retreat had come. Then they arose and gazed upon the deserted pool, whose nearest semblance to life was in a few scattered feathers drifting across the quiet space.

" Wal " — Uncle Lisha exhaled the word, after holding his breath a long time — " I sh'd like to know what on this livin' airth scairt them 'ere ducks. They never seen nor heard us, that's sartain."

" I swan to man, I do' know," Joseph said, " erless they smelt us, an' it don't sca'cely seem 's 'ough sech tough-nosed critters could smell much anyway. But I d' know. S-s-s-s-h! See that 'ere tormented gre't hen-hawk? Mebby it was him scart 'em. H-s-s-h!" He sank his voice to a whisper as a marsh hawk came cruising low along the rushy level in such intent quest of game that he did not see the two motionless figures, and then with an upward slant alighted on a dead treetop within close range, still scanning the marsh and unconscious of danger, while Joseph cautiously got his gun ready and took deliberate, deadly aim. As his executioner staggered backward from the recoil of the deadly charge, the pirate tumbled from his lookout and fell with a swift, feathery thud on the hard margin of the shore, where Joseph pounced upon him in utter recklessness of beak and talons that still attempted revenge or defense.

"Gosh darn him!" he groaned, as the talons of one foot closed in a dying clutch upon his wrist, and then, as he strove to loosen it with the free hand, that also was caught by the other foot. Then the bird's head drooped, the fire of his eyes went out, but the death grip of his talons was not relaxed, and Joseph, helplessly manacled, turned to Uncle Lisha for relief.

"Wal, you be in a fix. But I could n't help a-laughin' if it was a-killin' ye."

Joseph could see no cause for laughter, as the claws were withdrawn one by one, accompanying each withdrawal by a groan or a suppressed "S-s-s-s-p."

"You 're as bad off as the feller 'at ketched the bear," Uncle Lisha remarked, as he deliberately performed the surgery. "Ye see, he follered a bear track intu a hole, an' the feller 'at was a-huntin' along with him he stayed aoutside. 'I 've ketched a bear,' he hollered from inside.   'All right,' says t' other feller ' fetch him aout an' le' 's see him.'   ' I can't fetch him,' says he.   ' Wal,' says t' other feller, ' come aout yourself.'   ' I can't,' says he, ' he 's got a holt on me an' won't let me,' says he.   There, naow, I 've got ye onhooked."

With an unaccustomed display of temper Joseph seized the hawk by the legs and repeatedly banged the lifeless head against the nearest tree.

" Good airth an' seas!   What ye duin' that for ?   He 's deader 'n a smelt."

" Wal," said Joseph, looking rather foolish as the heat of his wrath abated, " I kinder thought mebby I 'd better let him onderstan' 'at the' 's a herearter for hawks jes' 's much as the' is for other folks.   I 'm a good min' ter give him another polt. Dum him.   Haow he hurt my wris's.   Why, he hain't nothin' but feathers ! " he exclaimed, when he had taken time to try " the heft " of his prize. " You might nigh abaout chuck him right intu a bed jest as he is, seems 's 'ough.   Anyways, he 's wuth a-hevin'."

While reloading his gun he proposed lying in wait by this pool for whatever might chance to come to it, but Uncle Lisha longed for fresh fields of conquest and also thirsted for a draught of drinkable water, which he hoped to find at some spring, and so marched along the bank, leaving his companion to conduct alone his own plan of the campaign.

Joseph seated himself comfortably on a log close to the tallest weeds and did not wait long before a bittern came flapping lazily over the marsh and alighted in the edge of the pool. He had never had so near a view of one and knew not what manner of fowl it might be, but it looked worth killing either for picking or eating. So he trained his gun upon it, and at the discharge it wilted down like a lopped weed. When with some difficulty he drew it within reach by the aid of a pole, he was somewhat disappointed in its weight, but he said to himself : —

"It looks nigh 'nough like one o' them 'ere new fangled Hang-shy rwusters tu be jes' 's good t' eat, which it hain't sayin' no gre't for it, an' then the' 's the feathers, what the' is on 'em, so I guess I hain't done so bad arter all, don't seem 's 'ough I hed."

He had scarcely composed himself to another season of waiting when he was startled by the roar of Uncle Lisha's gun, and after a vain attempt to repress his curiosity shouldered his gun and game and hastened forward to learn the result of a shot so loud that he felt sure it must have achieved something great.

Uncle Lisha had not gone a furlong alone when he came upon another patch of open water, where he saw a flock of large fowl, alarmed at his approach, crowding into a watery path that ran channelward into the depths of the marsh. He managed to get a slow aim upon the entrance just as the last bird was disappearing in it and fired. There was a clamor of consternation, a wild scurry through the rushes, but the nearest bird only beat the sedges convulsively with its broad pinions for a moment and then stretched lifeless head and wings upon the bending weeds. When Uncle Lisha realized how grand a feat he had accomplished he could hardly withhold a shout of exultation, and when Joseph came panting upon the scene he let it out in a great roar.

" Good airth an' seas, Jozeff, I hev act'ally shot a wil' goose, I du b'lieve ! "

" Sam Hill, you hain't, Uncle Lisher," cried Joseph, standing on tiptoe and craning his neck to the utmost. " Not a ra'al wild goose, you don't mean. Wal, I snore, if it don't look like one, seems 's 'ough, jest as true as you live! "

" Why, of course he 's a wil' goose, er was. He 's tame 'nough now, though," said Uncle Lisha, with proud assurance. " An' naow we got tu git him. I s'pose the mud 's more 'n forty foot deep aout there, but I 'll git him if I hafter stay here till the ma'sh freezes. Naow le' 's git some slabs an' things an' lay aout tu him."

Laying aside their guns, they brought slabs and boards with which the spring floods had plentifully strewn the shore, and with no little labor bridged the treacherous marsh, till Joseph, a little the lighter and the least clumsy of the two, gained an unstable footing to the prize, which he lifted, and, cautiously edging his way along the narrow causeway, bore it to the shore.

"There," he said, plumping the gray goose down at the feet of its slayer, who squatted before it, caressing it and feeding his eyes upon it, "I don't b'lieve I wanter kerry it on such a rhud no furder. It don't seem 's 'ough I would, tu hev it, not sca'cely."

"Wal, I would, clean tu Danvis! Good airth an' seas, won't it make Samwil an' Ann Twine's eyes stick aout when they see it, an' them a-shootin' nothin' but leetle insi'nificant ducks. But there ain't no two ways 'baout it, I got tu ha' some water, er choke tu death. Le' 's go over tu that 'ere haouse and git us a drink an' then mog along back to camp. Why, it's the haouse where Samwil left the hosses tu. They 're sorter neighbors, an' I da' say it will please 'em tu see this 'ere faowl, for it hain't ev'ry day 'at folks gits a chance tu look at a wil' goose clus tu. Why, what 's that 'ere you got beside your hen-hawk? Come to think on 't I did hear ye shoot ag'in." In the elation of his own success he had not noticed the addition to Joseph's bunch of game, nor had Joseph, in the midst of excitement and labor, thought to call attention to it.

"That 's more 'n I can tell ye. That is, for

sart'in.   He looks consid'able like one o' these 'ere Hang-shy rhusters, but I don't s'pose he is sca'cely, 'cause I never hearn tell on 'em a-runnin' wil' as I remember on.   Mebby it's one 'at got strayed off f'm hum."

" Wal," said Uncle Lisha, after a critical examination of the bird through his glasses, " I cal'late it 's a mud hen."

"Mebby it's a mud rhuster," Joseph suggested.

' I could n't say of which. sect, but of that spechy.   Wal, le' 's be a-moggin', for I be dryer 'n a graven image, so 't I can't spit 'nough tu enj'y a smoke."

Thereupon they assumed their burdens and trudged across the fields to the farmhouse, which stood foremost in a straggling village of outbuildings.   In response to Uncle Lisha's knock at the open kitchen door, a pleasant-looking woman came out of a cloud of fragrant steam that arose from a brass kettle of cider apple sauce upon the stove. She wore a blue sock on her left arm like an improvised mitten, but the needle caught into the heel and a dangling loop of thread showed that she employed the intervals of watching her cookery in darning the family footwear.

" Good arternoon, marm," said Uncle Lisha. " We stopped in tu see if we could n't git a drink o' water."

She looked the visitors over a moment to assure

herself whether they were of the sort to be served with a tin dipper or a pitcher and glass, and then, removing the sock as she went into the pantry, presently returned with the daintier service, which the old man's honest and respectable face seemed to warrant in spite of his shabby clothes.

" That 'ere 's turrible good water for the time o' — for this part o' the country. We be'n a-huntin'," he continued, as he held the glass to be refilled the third time. " We be'n a-huntin' an' got tormented dry. It 's turrible dry work a-huntin', partic'ly when you 're all the time in sight o' water 't you can't drink. An' I do' know but what it makes a feller drier tu shoot a wil' goose. I do' know as you ever see one." He lifted his trophy from where he had dropped it in careless conspicuity and held it up before her.

" Why, you done well, did n't you," the matron said. " 'T ain't often folks gits 'em. But I 've seen 'em afore. Aour folks ketched one oncte an' we kep' him tew, three year, I guess, an' he mated along with aour tame geese an' we 've got one o' the mixtur' yit. Why ! " with the final exclamation the expression of pleased curiosity in her face hardened to one of unpleasant surprise. " You jes' le' me look o' his neck," and laying hold of it and raising the feathers she disclosed a red string tied around it, at sight of which Uncle Lisha's heart sank with a sickening qualm.

"Yes, sir," she said, "you 've be'n an' killed aour ol' half-bred garnder. Be you some o' the folks that 's a campin' daown here?"

"Yis, marm."

"Well, I guess Mr. Harris 'll be raound there and settle with you for killin' of his garnder. He 'sot consid'able by him."

"Good airth an' seas!" Uncle Lisha whispered in a suppressed roar, as if he feared that he might be heard at camp. "Don't for massy sake let him come raound there talkin' abaout my shootin' of his goose. Where is your man? I c'n settle with him for 't right here. You go an' fetch him."

Mrs. Harris hesitated a moment in fear that they might depart in her absence, then bustled away and presently was heard calling her husband in the back yard. Then their voices were heard approaching in low dialogue till Mr. Harris appeared entering the kitchen from the rear. He was a large, raw-boned man, his shoulders stooped with excessive labor, his fingers hooked like claws ready to pounce upon a hard task or an elusive shilling, while his broad coarse face strove to put on a mask of guileless good humor. He greeted them as if they were all old friends, grinning more effusively, Uncle Lisha thought, than the situation seemed to warrant.

"Du, sir," Uncle Lisha responded, and proceeded at once to business. "My name 's Lisher

Paiggs, an' this 'ere 's my neighbor, Jozeff Hill, an'
we live tu Danvis when we 're tu hum. Jes' naow
we 're a-campin' over here. We don't make a business goin' raound killin' folks' poultry as a gin'al
thing, but it 'pears we hev your 'n, and naow we
want tu settle for 't. What d' ye cal'late the life
o' your goose is wuth? We don't want the car-
kiss."

"Wal, I d' know," Mr. Harris pondered, with
a subsiding grin. "Come in and sed daown.
'T won't cost ye nothin'. Won't ye? Wal, I don'
know czackly. That 'ere was a turrible goose tu
lay an' take care o' goslin's. I never see sech
a " —

"Mr. Harris," his wife said in a severe undertone.

"As I ever see sech a case for layin' an' carin'
for goslin's as she was."

"Mr. Harris," his wife said in a deeper tone of
reproof, and covertly punched him in the back, "it
hain't a goose; it 's a garnder."

"Hey," gasped Mr. Harris, his smile fading out,
but as quickly returning. "Why, yis, land, yis;
so 't is. But I tell ye what, Mis' Harris she sot a
turrible sight by him, I tell ye."

"Wal, wal," and the old man spoke a little impatiently, "it don't make no diffunce haow much
your garnder laid or your womern sot. What
I wanter know is what he was wuth a-livin' an'

haow much he 's wuth dead, an' I 'll pay ye the diffunce pervided I c'n raise the money," and he drew from his pocket the heart case which served him as a purse.

"Wal, naow, I don't know; le' me see," said Mr. Harris, weighing the goose in his hand and feeling its breast. "He hain't turrible meaty, and I carc'late he 'll be tougher 'n tripe, an' it 'll cost abaout as much tu chaw him as he 's wuth. Then ag'in, lookin' at it from a opposite p'int o' view, he was lierble to continer a-livin' a consid'able number o' years, which he was the more val'able in that respeck."

"The' 's the feathers!" Joseph suggested, with a view to bettering his friend's bargain. "The' 's an awful snarl o' feathers on that 'ere goose, which it seems as 'ough they 'd ortu be took accaount on in the trade. Naow if you was a min' tu call it even, I do' know but I 'd be willin' tu throw in this 'ere faowl 'at I got." He held up the bittern before Mr. Harris, who viewed it at first with wonder, then with intense disgust, which his bland smile could not conceal as he exclaimed : —

"Land, what be you a-goin' tu du with that plaguey stake driver? No, I guess I don't want him. I 'll tell ye what, Mr. Peggs, seein' it 's you an' you 're a stranger, you gi' me a half dollar an' we 'll call it square."

Uncle Lisha heaved a sigh of relief, and emptying the heart case into his palm he sorted out the requisite sum from the handful of ninepence and fourpence half-penny bits, cents, and half cents which had been gathered in the mending of many boots and shoes. Mr. Harris counted the much divided half dollar over twice and carefully scrutinized a doubtful penny of Canadian coinage before he reluctantly acknowledged the payment of the debt, and Uncle Lisha felt free to depart without the trophy which he had borne hither in the pride of his heart. Now as he trudged back to camp empty-handed, while Joseph bore his own spoils in humbleness of spirit, he spoke but once and then only with heartfelt emphasis: —

"Damn the goose!"

They found the tent and its environs silent and deserted, and after appeasing their hunger with a cold bite Joseph sat down to pluck his fowls. He had not been long so employed upon the bittern when Antoine and the boatman came strolling up from the landing.

"What you goin' do wid dat t'ing?" Antoine asked, after curiously watching him a few moments.

"Wal," said Joseph, as he carefully plucked out the last feathers, "I kinder thought arter I 'd got the feathers saved, I 'd take an' dress it au' cook it an' see haow it 'ould eat, jes' for the fun on 't."

Antoine wrenched his interior with a groan of

intense disgust, and, snatching the bird from Joseph's hands, tossed it away with all his might. The lank form, with neck and legs asprawl, went clattering through leaves and bushes in a great curve, till it was lost to sight, and was heard to fall with a dull final thud on the sands below the cliff.

" Dar, dat was de bes' way for cook up dat kan' o' vittle. You 'll was cook some bowfins one tam, but you 'll ant goin' for stink de fire wid dat mud hens, bah gosh, no."

Joseph's eyes followed this last featherless flight of the bittern and dwelt a while on the point of its disappearance before he turned upon the Canadian and said reproachfully, but without a trace of anger in his even drawl : —

" Naow, Antwine, seems tu me that 'ere is a 'tarnal mean kind o' caper, an' I do' know but what I 'd ortu take an' fling ye ov' the laidge arter the bird, but it might kinder break frien'ship, an' I guess I won't. But I mus' say it sorter seems tu me 'at for a feller 'at cooks eels an' mud turkles, an' I do' know but frawgs, you be dumb pertic'lar, an', as you might say, nicer 'n you be wise."

" Wal, seh, Zhozeff, Ah dun' know 'f Ah 'll ant prob'ly 'd ought for tol' you 'fore Ah t'row it," Antoine said apologetically, " but, sah, if you 'll heat dat t'ing he was mek you sick lak hol' dev'. You 'll ant goin' heat dat hawk, ant it ? " he asked, as Joseph drew the bird toward him with evident intention of plucking it.

" It hain't sartain but what I will if I seem tu hanker arter sech victuals," Joseph answered ; " but anyways, if you hain't no objections I 'm a-goin' tu save the feathers, which is what I 'm arter in partic'lar."

" Naow, Zhozeff, Ah 'll goin' tol' you de trut'," Antoine said, with impressive seriousness and an accompaniment of emphatic gestures. " If you put de hawk fedder wid de dawk fedder he heat it all up."

" Sho', Antwine ? "

" Dat jes' as true as Frenchmans heat onion," Antoine asserted in the face of Joseph's incredulous stare. " Wait for Ah 'll goin' tol' you. One tam Ah 'll was leetly boy an' leeve in Canada, mah mudder was mek it some bed. fedder of geese's fedder an' she was gat it mos' all stuff up but leetly maght he ant gat nough fedder. Den mah fader was keel two hawk was come raoun' for ketch de chicklin, an' mah mudder was pull de fedder for feenish his bed of it. It was very nice plump beds, an' dey keep it for de bes' one for w'en company come see it, an' nex' year mah gran'pere an' gran'-mere come for visit all naght, an', seh, gran'-mere was gre't big hol' hwomans, an' w'en he come on de room in de morny he was r-r-r-rubby, r-r-r-rubby hesef an' grunt very hard, an' w'en mah mudder ax it what de matter, she say de bed rope cut him all in chonk, 'cause de bed fedder was so t'in, an' mah mudder was supprise mos' for be mad for have it say so 'baout hees bes' bed, but w'en he ex-amine he fin' honly de hawk fedder, de res' it was all heat up. Yas, sah, Zhozeff, dat jes' true you leeve."

" Wal," said Joseph, continuing the employment which he had still pursued while listening to the story, " I c'n keep 'em sep'rit an' put 'em in a piller. Mebby if a feller slep' on it 't 'ould keep him f'm bein' hen-pecked nights."

When Sam returned and the sportsman and his oarsman had departed, a hot supper was prepared and eaten, after which the party sat around the cheerful campfire and recounted the day's adventures, from which were judiciously eliminated the episodes of Joseph's encounter with the hawk and Uncle Lisha's goose shooting.

CHAPTER XIV.

In the morning, when eating breakfast, no plans were laid for spending the day, and after the meal no one made the usual preparation for departure, but all idled about the camp as if without a present object in life but the mere pleasure of existence.

The day was one to invite indolence, the sun bathing the earth in such a mellow warmth that it soon dispelled the morning chill and left no use but pipe-lighting for the fire, which burned with a lazy flicker of transient flame and lazier drifts of smoke jets from snapping embers and brands.

Unruffled by the breath of the sleepy air, nor broken at all save where some waterfowl languidly cleft their surface with a silent wake, lake and creek bore the motionless doubles of painted shore and reedy margin, and the deeper azure of far peaks and cloudless sky ; while from the tranquil scene arose no busier sound of life than the lazy call of a duck or the faint noises of farms so remote that they seemed beyond it. Near at hand, but no more obtrusive, there was a drowsy hum of warmed flies and the slow chirps of crickets and the light scurrying of a chipmunk among the leaves.

" Wal, seh, boys," said Antoine, breaking the silence of the circle as he arose and stretched himself with a yawn, " dis was too pooty day for lose it.   What all you goin' do wid it, hein ? "

" It is a turrible neat day an' that's a fact," Joseph declared with unwonted decision, after a slow and careful contemplation of earth and sky. " An' I be thankful 'at we hain't obleeged tu waste it a-workin'.   It allus did kinder seem tu me as 'ough 's if it was a-sorter heavin' away o' the Lord's blessin's tu spend a ri' daown pleasant day a-workin'.   Some 'at I misused that way years and years ago lays heavy on my conscience yet."

" Naow, Jozeff, don't be no harder on yourself 'an what other folks is," said Uncle Lisha, in mild sarcasm.   " You must have an almighty tender conscience an' an almighty good mem'ry.   I can't remember but precious few such misduin's tu lay up ag'in ye."

" Wal, the' 's more 'n I wish 't the' was," said Joseph, staring retrospectively into the smouldering embers as if they represented the cold ashes of the past.   " It does seem 's 'ough it was wicked, most 'specially 'long in the fall, an' winter comin' on, when the' won't be no rale pleasant days aou' door tu speak on, for a feller tu be a-breakin' of his back diggin' taters, a-humpin' up ag'in the blue sky, with his nose an' eyes tu dead tater tops an' naked sile, when ev'ything looks so putty all around, an' it a'most the last chance o' seein' on 't, or putty nigh, mebby. Then take it in the winter when the' does come one o' them kinder stray days 'at got left over aouten fall, er comes afore its reg'lar time in spring, a feller do' want tu be a-tunkin' at a tree julluk a woodpecker, an' lose all the good on 't, 'ceptin' what sunshine soaks intu his back. Then ag'in come spring you jest wan' tu thaw aout an' git the good on 't yourself, an' not be tapped julluk a maple an' have your sap b'iled daown for other fo'kses benefit. Take it in summer, it 's tew hot most o' the time tu work, anyway, an' when the' is a comf'table day it seems 's 'ough a feller ort tu jest lay in the shade an' see things blow an' grow an' git ripe erless go a-fishin', which I would n't in no boat of nary sect, not for ri' daown enj'yment, don't seem 's 'ough I would, not if they bit faster 'n you e'ld yank 'em."

" Dat was de bes' comfortable Ah 'll can took in dis worl', me," Antoine remarked, while Joseph took breath, " jes' for feesh, an' hab de feesh do hees half."

" I don't s'pose it 's sca'cely right," Joseph continued, " but sometimes it 'most seems 's 'ough I putty nigh wanted tu cuss the man 'at invented work; he sartainly did begin a tormented sight o' trouble."

" Not no gre't for you, Jozeff," Uncle Lisha commented, and went on to say, " I do' know as I hanker arter work, but if I hed me my tools here an' a shoe tu mend, jes' for knittin' work, I cal'late I sh'ld enj'y myself tol'able well."

" Work kinder goes ag'in the grain when it interferes wi' huntin'," Sam said, thrusting a cedar twig into the dying embers and watching its tardy kindling, " but then the work gives a better relish tu the huntin' when you git it."

" One' Lasha spikin' 'baout de shoe mek me t'ink prob'ly Ah 'll bes' was gat mah t'read-needle an' men' mah traowser," bending to inspect his frayed knees, " bah gosh! Ah wish mah clo's was grow up jes' sem lak you' skin w'en you tore it. Ah do' know all what Ursule goin' said w'en he see mah traowser all wore off so. Ah guess Ah goin' tol' him it 'cause Ah 'll been pray for him an' de chil'en so much. It take good many pray' for go raoun' all of it, ant it? Wal, Ah guess Ah em-broider mah knee." Then having got needle and thread and lighted his pipe, he sat down to the uncongenial task.

" Dis mek me rembler one — " he began, and then interrupted himself with a sharp indrawing of breath and an imprecation, " S-s-s-p, Sa-cre ! " as he jabbed the needle point into his knee. " Dat mek me rembler one man Canada."

" Good airth an' seas ! I was a-hopesin' you 'd

forgot him for oncte," Uncle Lisha shouted with such emphasis that it arrested the flow of anecdote. Antoine suddenly became silent and plied his needle with sullen diligence.

"Wal, you might as well trot him aout, Ann Twine," the old man said, moderating his tone, "th' won't be no gettin' red on him naow."

Thus encouraged, Antoine went on with his story, while his audience listened with more interest in the manner of his telling than in the matter.

"Yas, sah, dey was one man Canada, one tam, an' if you 'll ant b'lieved it Ah can tol' you nem de place w'ere he live, honly Ah 'll fregit now. One tam in de fall his waf was mek it new pair clo's all over, new shirt, new coat, new traouser, everyt'ing. De hwomans he feel putty plump 'cause he 'll weave it all heese'f, an' cut it all up an' sew it togedder heese'f, an' he lak for look at hees mans w'en he gat all on, for go on de market.

"One day w'en he go, jes' 'fore he 'll ready for start, he 'll hear hees leetly dog bark very hard in de hwood not more as leetly way from de haouse. He was terribly hunter mans, an' t'ink prob'ly de dog was tree up a coon. So he 'll took hees hol' fusee an' run off for shot it a minute, an' bah gosh, w'at you t'ink?

"It was pant'er, hol' big feller, hugly lak meat-axe. But de mans he 'll ant scare for run. He p'ant hees gaun an' pull it, an' de flint jes' go 'pluck.' An' de pant'er jomp on de man, 'scroonch,' an' tore off all dat new clo's not more as two ninches wide. Oh, bah gosh, Ah 'll tol' you, haow dat hwomans was feel bad w'en she see it all spile up dat clo's she was be so troublesome for mek. Dat was too bad.

" Dar, sah," he said as he regarded his needle-work with proud satisfaction and caressed the grinning stitches, " Ah 'll b'lieved dat was mos' as han'-some as if Ah 'll had quiltin' party work mah knee. All Ah 'll 'fraid for was Ursule t'ink Ah 'll gat some oder hwomans for sew me up."

" Did the man get hurt much, Antwine?" Joseph inquired.

" De man? Oh, he was be keel, Ah b'lieve so. Wal, Ah guess Ah 'll goin' han'some mah oder knee so hees brudder ant be shem of it. Onc' Lasha, if you want it Ah 'll sew you clo's. Ah 'll was be preffic tailor man, me."

When the last stitch was taken he sawed off the thread with his tobacco-clotted knife, put the nee-dle carefully away, and then studied all the land-scape with an undecided air as he said : —

" Wal, Ah do' know if Ah 'll go feeshin', or pick some wa'nut, or borry some happle, or go 'long up de crick for see wat Ah 'll see. Ah guess Ah do dat," he said, coming to a decision as his eyes dwelt on the shaded level shore. " Any of it goin' 'long to me?"

" I guess I 'll jes' laze raound tu-day," Uncle Lisha said after a little consideration, and Joseph after larger deliberation concluded to stay and help him, for " it seemed 's 'ough it was consid'able of a hefty job o' sittin' raound for a man o' Uncle Lisher's years tu ondertake alone."

" If I had Drive here I 'd set some o' these Lakefield foxes tu dancin' tu a Danvis tune," Sam said, studying the lay of the land with a careful eye, " jest tu see haow nigh I 've guessed the runways. As it is, I believe I 'll poke along up tu Mr. Bartlett's, an' take 'em a pair o' ducks."

Failing to induce any of them to accompany him, Antoine shouldered his gun and set forth alone along the shore of the creek, making stealthy approach to every marsh-locked pool that offered harbor to a duck, and searching every nut-tree for squirrels. But the waterfowl were abroad and the squirrels at home, so he continued his quest beyond the imperceptible junction of the shores of creek and Slang.

Now and then he was startled by a bittern springing in awkward haste from the marshy covert, or by a heron launching himself to stately flight from some still pool; but he did not care to chance the uncertainty of a flying shot on such poor game, nor did he discover anything worthy of capture till he came near the log causeway that formed the approach to the Slang bridge.

There he came upon a monstrous turtle scrambling along in a ponderous haste, the eldest patriarch of the marshes, bearing moss of a century's growth upon his venerable back. Antoine rejoiced at the discovery of such noble game and hastened forward to secure it, but the wary old turtle immediately faced him, and pivoting on its hinder legs met every attempt of his assailant to seize him by the tail with quick out-thrusts of the head and vicious snaps of the ugly jaws.

"Bah gosh, you'll ant felt very good-nachel, dis morny, ant it, Onc' Mud Turkey?" cried Antoine, with growing respect for his venerable antagonist. "Wal, Ah'll goin' give you somet'ing for bit ant so soft Ah was," and laying aside his gun he went in search of a suitable stick.

Taking advantage of this cessation of hostilities, the turtle retreated to the bare border of the marsh and began burrowing into the soft muck with such speed that he was more than half his length out of sight in it when Antoine returned after a very brief absence.

Laying hold of the turtle's tail, the stout Canadian tugged with might and main before the creature's obstinate resistance was finally overcome and he was drawn forth and laid sprawling helplessly on his back. One end of a stick was now offered him, which he seized savagely, and was dragged thereby well up on to the grassy bank, where Antoine took counsel with himself concerning the present disposal of his captive.

" 'F Ah 'll took you home jes' you was, you ant han'some for look, an' prob'ly dey ant t'ink you was fit for heat. But meat jes' han'some anybody, so Ah 'll jes' honly took dat for mek you 'quaint of de boy. Ah 'll was very sorry for you, Onc' Mud Turkey, but Ah 'll obleege for cut you necks. You was took you' las' ride on you' hown foots, an' you 'll ant pull some more leetly dauks by hees leg of it an' bit hole on hol' homans geeses prob'ly. Oh, ant you shem for do so gre't weeked ? "

Thus hardening his heart for the execution, he drew out the turtle's neck to its fullest extent by the unreleased grip on the stick and severed it at one stroke, with little apparent effect on the creature's vitality, and proceeded to dress the meat, using the broad shell as a trencher whereon to bestow it.

Having completed this task and washed his hands, he felt need of the refreshment of a smoke and made preparation therefor, but then discovered he had neither matches nor punk, though he was provided with flint and steel for firing the latter. In this extremity, with appetite whetted the keener by disappointment, he looked about for the means of relief, and discovered in a bushy clearing at no great distance a forlorn little cabin.

A wisp of smoke writhing from the low chimney

promised fire enough to light a pipe, and Antoine made toward it, bearing his spoils till he came to a safe place of deposit in a fence corner.

It was a squalid habitation, indicative of shiftless poverty. A path led to it, bordered on one side by some stunted rows of frost-bitten corn, on the other by hills of weed-choked potatoes, and close to the threshold a starved heap of pine roots, the sole miserable representative of a woodpile in the midst of the abundant forest. The place of missing panes in the single sash of the only front window was filled by a weather-beaten straw hat and a faded, tattered remnant of calico in some sort emblematic of the occupants, Antoine thought, when he entered after knocking on the sagged door that could neither be quite opened nor quite shut.

A tall, gaunt, hollow-eyed woman and a tallow-faced boy of similar habit and features sat smoking short pipes by a scant open fire, and turned their listless faces toward him without surprise, scarcely with curiosity, as he accosted them.

"Good morny, ma'm, dat was very nice day dis morny."

"H'm, I s'pose so," the woman assented dubiously in a dolorous, monotonous tone, "for them 'at's well 'nough t' enjoy it. We hain't, me an' Jul'us."

"Ah'll very sorry you ant felt better," said

Antoine, with an expression of deep concern in his voice; "'f Ah could lit mah pipe Ah 'll was felt better, me. Ah 'll ant gat some fire."

He held forward his pipe to indicate his need, and the old woman poked the embers with a stick, hitching her rickety chair aside to make room for him. Antoine scooped up a coal and puffed diligently a moment before he asked: —

"What was be de matter of it, ma'm?"

"Oh, it's the rheumatiz in my limb, an' Jul'us is peakèd. No appetite for nothin' but terbarker. I s'pose it's me a-growin' old an' Jul'us a-growin' so fast — grows lak a weed, he does; la'ge of his age, an' sma't as he is la'ge."

She regarded her son with stolid admiration, while he, sucking his black pipe persistently, as stolidly received her praise of physical and mental growth and the visitor's hearty confirmation of it.

"Yas, ma'm, he 'll was smart boy, lak steel traps, an' he beeg lak hosses. Ah 'll b'lieved he be man 'fore you was, ma'm."

"I do' know haow in this livin' world he grows so, without no more nourishin' victuals," the fond mother continued. "We hain't had nothin' but pertaters an' johnnycake an' green corn t' eat for a fortni't. My limb has pained me so 't I wan't able to arn nothin' duin' for the neighbors, an' he hain't able to work no time — it takes all his stren'th a-growin' — so we hain't hed no meat victuals."

"Dar was plenty dauk an' feesh," Antoine suggested.

"Haow be you goin' to get ducks without no gun ner nobody to shoot it?" she drawled, without changing her monotonous tone. "Er ketch fish when you ain't able? Fish hain't no nourishment neither, if you hain't no fat pork to fry 'em in."

"Dar was a lot of mud turkey," Antoine further suggested.

"Mud turkles!" the old woman exclaimed with an expression of intense disgust in voice and features. "D' you s'pose we 'd eat mud turkles? H'mp! I 'd livser eat snake!"

Antoine felt indignant at the starved crone's contempt of what he considered a choice delicacy, but inquired blandly : —

"Prob'ly you 'll ant lak cheekin pooty good, ant it?"

"Why, yes, me an' Jul'us can eat chicken, the white meat, if the' hain't no skin on 't."

"Wal, naow, Ah 'll tol' you, ma'm, dat was purty good lucky, 'cause you see Ah 'll was gat some cheekin all dressed up dat Ah 'll was carry to mah frien' on de camp, an' Ah 'll be glad for give you some of it 'f you len' me dish for fetch it."

The old woman nodded assent, and pointed over to the table with the air of begrudging a favor. Taking a broken blue-edged ·plate from the table that was scant of everything but untidiness, Antoine went to bring the alms.

"Ah 'll can' help it," he sighed as he knelt before the improvised trencher, and reluctantly selected a generous portion of the lightest colored meat.

"'F Ah 'll goin' taught it for heat mud turkey Ah mus' beegin wid de bes'. Ant he look jes' lak cheekin? Bah gosh, he was cheekin, honly he grow on mud turkey."

He carried his gift to the cabin and presented it to the old woman, who, after a critical inspection, began preparing it for the pot; while her son awoke to such interest in the prospective repast that he sauntered out-doors, and with the dull axe pounded some pine roots into suitable lengths for the fire, which being kindled he sat down again to the restful enjoyment of his pipe and the growing fragrance of the seething stew. Antoine wished he might stay and see with what relish it was eaten, now he was sure his half kindly deception was not suspected, but he could find no excuse for tarrying longer.

"Wal, ma'm," he said, as he dallied long over the fire with the relighting of his pipe, that he might inhale the odor of the pot, "you cheekin smell very good, an Ah hoped he tas'e more better as he smell, prob'ly, an' Ah 'll hoped you 'll gat over your limb. Ah.'ll had one of it one tam in

mah knee, an' he was very bad t'ing for had. An'
Ah 'll hoped you' boy grow long an' wide. Good
morny, bose of it."

"Thank you, an' I 'm obleeged to you," the old
woman said, with some cordiality. "I s'pose you
could n't fetch a drawin' o' tea if you come this
way ag'in ? "

Julius withdrew his rapt gaze from the steaming pot to cast an inquiring glance on the departing visitor, who went his way pretending not to
hear the request.

Antoine took up the precious burden, which had
been somewhat lightened by his generosity, and
bent his careful steps campward, praying that he
might fall in with nothing worth shooting, and
compelled an answer to his prayer by refusing to
see a chance for a shot. He would not look to the
right when a partridge clucked and stirred the
leaves with deliberate footsteps among the under-
growth close beside his path, nor to the left when
an unsuspicious squirrel barked and squalled in the
nearest hickory, nor turn his eyes toward the
marsh to seek the cause of the bickering and splashing that was going on behind the screen of sedges.

So, without interruption, he came to where he
saw the white tent shining like a welcome beacon
among the trees. He presently found Uncle Lisha
and Joseph basking in the sifted sunshine, the one
trying to content himself with idleness, the other
making no effort for the full enjoyment of it.

Antoine set down the shell of meat before them and exclaimed as he pointed proudly toward it : —

"Dar, sah, Ah 'll fetched you somet'ing for heat dat was victuals."

"Good airth an' seas !" cried Uncle Lisha in surprise, "where did ye git some fresh meat? You be'n where they was a-boocherin'? I ain't heard no squealin', an' it ain't no pork nuther. What is 't ?"

"No, sah, Onc' Lisha, Ah 'll be'n butchy mase'f, an' he 'll ant squeel nor beller, an' he was pork an' beefs, an' — wal, dey was fave kan's of it, but Ah 'll fregit toder, 'cep' cheekin ; Ah 'll guess he was all gone prob'ly. Ant you mek aout you min' of it, Zhozeff ?"

"Wal, I don't seem to make aout czackly," said Joseph, deliberating on all fours over the heap of meat and swaying and crouching in various points of observation. "Mebby it 's beef, but I guess it 's pork, an' I do' know but it 's veal, some on 't, an' like 'nough 't hain't nary one. I do' know."

"An' you 'll was gat him 'baout raght, an' it was more better as all. It was mud turkey !"

Joseph recoiled upon his haunches aghast at the revelation, and Uncle Lisha exploded a snort of disgust.

"You 'll ant want for stick you' nose up 'fore you gat it in you' mout'," said Antoine, as he set about his cookery. "You ant w'en you smell heem, an' w'en you heat you be happy."

His companions watched him in silence that was a protest against his operations while he put the meat in the pot and set it on the replenished fire, when after a final approving glance he relegated to them the further care.

"Ah b'lieved Ah 'll goin' keel dauk over on de bay, me, an' if you 'll was goin' loafer raoun' here you can jes' well keep de kittly bile, Zhozeff, an' Onc' Lasha keep you from heat all up of it," and when Joseph after pondering a while did not refuse the duty, Antoine shouldered his gun and strolled out of sight among the trees.

When the sound of his departing footsteps could no longer be heard, Joseph started up with unusual agility and whispered wheezily, "Say, Uncle Lisher, it don't seem 's 'ough we orter eat that dumbed hejus riptyle jes' tu please him, does it naow?" The old shoemaker shook his head in decided negative, and he went on, "Wal, then, I tell ye what, le' 's take an' empty aout the consarned mess an' put in some duck meat in place on 't; he won't never know the diff'ance. Seem 's 'ough it wan't no more 'n sarvin' him right, seein' what a haowdelow he made 'baout me a-cookin' that bowfin an' would n't let me cook my own mud hen, which if it was of the mud specie was 'nough sight better lookin' faowl an' what a mud turkle is."

"I hain't no objections," Uncle Lisha said, "for I don't like the idee o' bein' 'bleeged tu eat what

I don't want tu. But we won't heave it away; we 'll jest hide it till we git aour dinner eat, an' the critter c'n sit up nights an' cook an' eat his 'n if he wants tu."

The conspirators at once set about carrying out their plot, emptying the present contents of the pot into a pan which they hid inside the tent, and substituting therefor the fraud.. Wings, skin, and larger bones were rejected, and no flagrantly incongruous member put in except one gizzard, which Joseph popped into the bottom layer. When all this was accomplished in haste and fear of discovery, and the pot again set to boiling, the two sat down to tend it with more leisurely care, but were hardly settled in their seats when they heard cries of distress arising from below the cliff.

" Oh, One' Lasha! Here, Zhozeff, come fas' you can! Oh, Ah 'll broke off mah leg, bose of it! Ah guess mah arm, prob'ly. Come, quick!' "

Greatly alarmed, they hurried down the steep path with a speed so unwonted that it endangered their own limbs. They searched the foot of the cliff, expecting at every step to come upon the helpless form of their comrade.

" Ann Twine! Ann Twine! where be ye? Grunt if ye can't speak," Uncle Lisha called loudly, but no response came.

" Wha' d' the dumb fool wantu go an' tumble off o' there for? He might ha' knowed it 'ould

pooty nigh kill him.   Mebby he is dead, poor cre'-
tur' ; I wish 't we 'd ha' let his turkle be jes' as he
fixed it."

The most careful search failed to discover Antoine or any trace of him, and after a meditative
silence Uncle Lisha broke out : —

" Consarn his pictur', he be'n a-foolin' on us wi'
his dumb French cadidoes.   'T would n't no more 'n
sarve him right if we hove him over the rocks an'
his mud turkle after him."

" Er make him kerry us up on his back," Joseph suggested as they toiled up the path.   " Seems
's 'ough that 'd suit me tol'able well."

They rested themselves while they watched the
pot, and in the middle of the afternoon Antoine
returned, tired with tramping and sharp set for the
aldermanic feast.

" Darned cunnin' caper, wan't it, a-hollerin'
bloody murder the way you did ? " cried Uncle
Lisha, and wondered at the innocence of the Canadian's face as he answered in surprise : —

" Me?   Ah 'll ant holler, but Ah 'll felt holler
all de tam, an' de more Ah 'll smell dis de more
Ah 'll felt so.   Ah guess it was loon you hear.
Ah 'll see one of it.   Or wal' geeses, prob'ly ; dar
was big drove of it roos' on de lake 'tween de li't-
haouse."

" Ann Twine," Uncle Lisha said sadly, " you be
the lyinest sarpent I ever see."

The others watched Antoine furtively as he eagerly sniffed the steaming pot and peered into it, but they saw no shadow of suspicion on his intent face.

"Dar, sah, Onc' Lasha, an' too you, Zhozeff, ant you 'll cure you foolish all de tam you been smell dat mud turkey git ready for heat?   Oh, Ah tol' you he grea' deal more better as dauk an' he jes' tendry as cheekens," he continued, as he prodded the contents of the pot with a fork and then lifted it from the fire to the centre of the table. "Naow, Zhozeff, brought de plate an' de bread an' de pettetto, an' git ready for beegin.   Come, Onc' Lasha."

"I can't help a spleenin' ag'in it, Ann Twine, but I 'm goin' tu try it a hack, jest tu please you," said Uncle Lisha, taking his place with feigned reluctance, and Joseph followed in like manner, after performing his part in furnishing the table.

Each helped himself sparingly and took tentative morsels, while Antoine fell to with unquestioning faith and good appetite.   The latter was so fully shared with him by his companions that they soon forgot their pretense of aversion and vied with him in the onslaught, and exchanged knowing winks when he extolled the excellence of the dish and smiled upon them in benignant triumph. When hunger was appeased, Joseph began to be uneasy under the burden of his secret and troubled to know how to relieve himself of it, when Antoine gave him the opportunity.

" Dar, sah, Onc' Lasha, Zhozeff, naow you was be heat it, ant you willins for hown he was putty good, hein ? "

" Wal, tol'able, when a feller 's hungry 'nough not to be p'tic'lar," Uncle Lisha admitted, " but I don't call it nothin' stror'nary."

" Tu tell it jest 's 't is, Antwine," said Joseph, after due deliberation, " it r'ally don't seem 's 'ough it was a turrible sight diff'ent f'm duck."

" Oh, he ant, ant he ? " cried Antoine.   " Oh, Zhozeh, what for you ant talk sem you heat ? You was heat more as you was in two day 'fore. Naow, what for you 'll ant hown dat mud turkey was grea' deal more better as dauk, hein ? "

" You won't go tu r'arin' up and gittin' mad 'f I tell ye ? " Joseph asked, swelling with suppressed laughter and hitching a little nearer to Uncle Lisha, who was chuckling audibly.

" No, sah, Ah 'll ant never git mad raght after dinny, 'special w'en he was mud turkey. Dat always mek me good-nachel," Antoine magnanimously declared.

" Wal, you hed n't ortu, 'cause you know you was consid'able uppish abaout me a-cookin' my mud hen an' haow you went on consarnin' a bowfin 'at I fried one time, an' it don't seem 's 'ough ary one looked wus 'n a mud turkle or a eel, so it don't seem 's 'ough you 'd ortu rare up much when I tell ye it hain't nob'dy nor nothin' but duck we be'n a eatin'."

"Oh, he 'll ant, ant he? Wal, he was putty good dauk," Antoine remarked, with imperturbable coolness.

" It wan't nothin' else, an' the way on 't was, you see, me and Uncle Lisher kinder spleened ag'in that 'ere turkle so it did n't seem 's 'ough we could eat it, hungry as we was. So, arter you was gone, we jest emptied it aout 'n the kittle an' filled it up wi' duck, which it is what you be'n a-eatin'. But we did n't heave away your turkle meat. It 's in the tent yender, an' you c'n eat the hull caboodle on 't."

The two conspirators curiously watched their victim, with the expectation of seeing him burn with wrath or wilt with shame, but he calmly continued the careful cleaning of his pipe without speaking until he assured himself of a free draft by vigorously blowing and sucking. Then grinning benignantly on them while he whittled and ground a charge of tobacco, he said : —

" Wal, naow, Ah 'll goin' tol' yo'. Ah was mek four peoples heat mud turkey to-day, an' dey ant know it. Fus', w'en Ah dress him up Ah 'll fan' hol' hwomans an' hees boy; dey ant mos' got not'ing for heat, but dey can' heat mud turkey, oh, no. De good meat walkin' all raound ant quat good 'nough for it; dey mus' had cheekin, an' de hol' hwomans an' hees boy, dey was very satisfy. Den Ah 'll brought de res' an', bah gosh, you was very kin' for cook it an' help me heat it, w'en Ah 'll know you 'll ant lak it for heat mud turkey."

"I tell ye, Ann Twine, it wan't turkle!" Uncle Lisha cried in some heat. "We would n't eat the dumb stuff, an' so we changed it, jest as Jozeff says."

"Dat was so, for Ah 'll see you do it, me. Yes, sah," he continued, complacenfly regarding their astonished faces. "W'en Ah go 'way Ah 'll fregit mah pipe an' Ah 'll come for gat it an' see you an' Zhozeff was fuss wid de pot, an' Ah 'll hid behin' dat bush till you gat it all fix as you want it. W'en you 'll hear me holler you 'll ant fin' me, ant you? Dat tam Ah 'll come back here quick an' Ah 'll swap de meat ag'in, an', bah gosh, sah, you 'll gat lot of dat mud turkey inside of you."

"Ann Twine, you 're a-tellin' one o' your lies," said Uncle Lisha incredulously. For answer Antoine brought forth the pan of duck from the tent and set it before them.

"Dar," he said, pointing to the gizzard conspic- uously displayed on the top, "has mud turkey gat gizzar'? Ant Ah 'll see you put heem on de pot, Zhozeff? Ant Ah 'll see you poke for it when you heat, hein? Oh, you was lak de gizzar' very

much, Zhozeff, but you 'll ant fin' it honly but jes'
de chip Ah 'll put in for improve mah storee for be
true," and after a moment's search at the bottom
of the pot he fished out a cedar chip on the point
of his fork and held it triumphantly before their
faces, whose expression of blank amazement broad-
ened to imbecile grins, while Antoine laughed up-
roariously.

"Oh, Onc' Lasha! Oh, Zhozeff! Ant you
putty smart for foolish me an' gat foolish you'se'f
more as Ah was," and he pranced about in an
ecstasy of triumph, while Uncle Lisha groaned in
disgust.

"The dumb thing makes me feel crawly. I
shall be a snappin' at ye fust ye know."

"Wait, Ah 'll look see if de moss beegin for
grow on you back, Onc' Lasha. Oh, don't you
go crawl on de ma'sh," as the old man stumped
down the path to the landing.

"Say, Antwine," Joseph said confidentially, "it
don't seem 's 'ough the' 'd be any use o' tellin' Samwil. If you won't say nothin' I won't, an' we 'll
come it on him."

But when Sam came he stumbled upon the fresh
turtle shell, and remarked as he kicked it aside:—

"Hello! be'n a-havin' mud turkle, hev ye.
Wal, gi' me some if you got any left. I al'ays
be'n wantin' tu try it."

CHAPTER XV.

A DAY INLAND.

SAM put his gun in the canoe for company or from force of habit, but took no pains to find use for it. His paddle strokes fell so noiselessly that the waterfowl sitting in the edge of the marsh were first notified of his approach by the sight of the canoe's prow nosing its swift way past their hiding-place, or of the paddler's slightly swaying figure and the flash of his dripping blade. Others dozing full-fed were not aroused till the wake of the canoe shook the walls of their rush wigwam, and then with shaken quacks and squeaks of terror sprang to needless flight. A flock of low-flying teal came upon him so suddenly that he instinctively ducked his head as they swerved upward and swept over him, and great fish dashed from beneath his stealthy keel with a startling surge.

Then he saw the two Indians a little way before him, paddling slowly and halting at every muskrat house, in such leisurely conduct of their affairs as if the bright day were endless and the genial season to have no following of storm and bitter cold, less provident than the muskrats, in no more haste than the lazily migrating waterfowl. Their voices, attuned to nature's, sounded no louder than the rustle of their paddles in the sedges as he ran alongside, and they then, first aware of him, showed no more surprise at his sudden appearance than if a weed had drifted past.

"Quiee," Tocksoose gave greeting, and grinned a friendly recognition as he dropped a quarter-grown kit from a trap into the canoe; but his comrade did not so much as turn his sour face toward the newcomer.

"It's tew bad to ketch sech leetle runts," Sam remonstrated. "They hain't wuth fo'pence."

"Me no ketch um, mebby od' man ketch um. Mebby mink ketch um," said Tocksoose. "Me like um git fo' cen', as od' man got twenty cen', nex' year. Lil' moosquas mo' better for eat as ol' one."

"You might as well preach tu the minks an' foxes as tu these critters," Sam thought, driving his canoe forward with vigorous strokes that soon brought him to the mouth of the East Slang, into which he passed and made his way up the narrow, winding channel. Rounding a bend, he came to the foot of a long reach, in which nothing animate could be seen astir but a solitary grebe wrinkling the glassy surface in widening circles at various points of departure and return, in his explorations of the nether watery world. Sam let the canoe drift at the will of the idle current, while he curiously counted the moments of the agile diver's disappearing.

Then his wandering gaze became fixed on a great hawk that came cruising low over the apparently tenantless marsh. With short, restrained beats of his broad pinions the falcon ranged the silent cover till suddenly, with a sharp, downward slant he swooped into its depths, wherefrom, in the same instant, with a clamorous outcry of affrighted squeaks, a hundred wood ducks burst upward with a startling, thunderous roar of wings, threshing water, sedges, and air. As suddenly as they had risen they settled with a resounding splash in the open water of the channel, where they sat motionless, silent, and alert. The baffled marauder mounted heavily from the weeds, and wheeling a moment above the vigilant congregation, each member of which was ready to dive at any sign of attack, he recognized the uselessness of a further attempt and sullenly retired.

The swimming ducks offered a rare opportunity for a deadly shot, but Sam admired so much the adroitness with which they had foiled the onslaught of the hawk that he hesitated to take advantage of it, and while he hesitated they became aware of the presence of a more fearful danger than that which had threatened them from above, now lurking close beside them, and again simultaneously sprang into the air. Then Sam instinctively got his gun in hand, and taking aim at the nearest duck that was laboring upward pulled the trigger; but the cap responded to the stroke of the hammer with only a faint, lifeless click, and before it could be replaced by another one the tardiest laggard was well out of range. When an anathema had been bestowed upon the worthless cap and its maker, Sam tried to make a virtue of the misfire and be glad that it had happened, and thus attempting to fool himself with his own hypocrisy, came to the landing, marked as a place of resort by the ashes and spent brands of fishing fires that had burned in the spring nights when bullpouts were biting.

Measuring the height of the sun, it occurred to him that he might enjoy the excitement of the arrival of the stage-coach by going a little out of his way to Friend Bartlett's, and therefore he held across the fields at a brisk pace toward the tavern, at which the coach halted for a change of horses. As he came to the high rail fence of a stubble field, he surprised a small flock of wild pigeons busily picking up the scattered grain. He had but a glimpse of them on the ground, their backs shining in the slanting sunlight like variously tempered burnished steel, when, with a simultaneous clapping of wings, like a burst of applause, they took flight. He fired into the thick of the flock, and four birds tumbled out of it. He strung them through the under mandibles on two of the long tail feathers tied together at the tips, and hastened on with his burden increased in weight, but more in beauty; for the pigeons were old males, with ruddy breasts and brilliant upper plumage that shone with varied hues in the shifting lights. It soon had another quite as unexpected addition, for as Sam skirted the brink of a hollow, where a brook looped a miniature intervale, in uncertain quest of easiest passage, a partridge, an early wanderer from the woods, burst out of the fringe of trees like a cannon-shot from a palisade and flew straight for the home coverts, now with a blur of rapid, quivering wing-beats, now with set pinions, till Sam, dropping his load and aiming far ahead of the fleeting mark, brought it to the pasture sward in a long incline, as if alighting naturally; but it struck the ground with a rebounding thud, which filled his heart with the pride that always comes to him who brings this noble bird down from its flight.

He made haste to pick it up and go on his way, for he could hear the unmistakable far-sounding cluck of the approaching stage-coach and see the neighborhood gathering at the tavern. When he reached it he was not the latest comer, for two panting boys came running in honest undisguised haste, followed by another, who urged his bare legs to greater speed with sharp commands and vigorous cuts of a switch while he impersonated coach, horses, and driver. After them came a belated grown-up idler trying to stay his steps to a deliberate pace, and from his shop across the road the aproned cooper came bareheaded, with his short-handled adze in his hand and diffusing a wholesome odor of the pine staves and ash hoops of cheese casks.

Now came the stage-coach, the four horses at a brisk trot, the red and yellow body rocking with stately motion under the burden of passengers, baggage, and mails, and greatest of all the driver, known from one end to the other of his route by every one, some of whom had the distinction of being known by him. He pulled up the horses before the low stoop, and throwing the reins to a hostler, descended from his lofty seat to open the door of the coach for such passengers as chose to alight and stretch their legs while the horses were changed. Hospitably welcomed by the smiling landlord, clean-shaven and in shirt-sleeves spotlessly white, all availed themselves of the chance except a woman dressed in deep mourning who held a little boy with long wavy flaxen hair and a brunette complexion, seated upon her lap. He stared out wide-eyed at the juvenile groundlings, envying them their freedom no less than they his distinguished position as a stage-coach passenger, while there was a silent interchange of bashful smiles.

Two of the passengers were spruce city men, wearing their well-fitting garments with the accustomed ease that a sharp-faced old lawyer wore his shabby suit of black, and an air of half contemptuous condescension toward three farmers who like himself were representatives-elect to the Legislature on their way to the State capital. These three were already counting the cost of the honor as they longed for the daily comfort of shirt-sleeves and old clothes, and wondered how they could bear the burden of coats for four long weeks, and what they should do with the strong, hard hands that till now few days but Sundays had found unemployed. Even now one got his knife open and searched the ground for a bit of soft wood to whittle, while another resumed interrupted work upon his finger-nails, which gave promise of employment for some time to come. There was also a bluff Englishman, who at once caught sight of Sam's birds and asked many questions concerning them, as did the city men — he, with a sportsman's interest; they, with a hungry relish of whatever smacked of wild life.

To the untraveled mountaineer the stage-coach, with the mud and dust of other and distant towns upon its wheels and painted sides, and bringing

hither dwellers in great cities and men whose home
was beyond the sea, was as strange an object as a
ship come to quiet port from the turmoil of the
ocean and the busy world beyond it, with the salt
of the sea waves still upon its decks and the breath
of foreign atmospheres not yet quite exhaled. The
sight and touch of it gave him a dreamy vision of
scenes that he could never chance to see, and with
such respect for its strangeness he marveled at
the bold familiarity of the boys, who pranced and
capered as horses at the empty pole, thrust out like
a stripped bowsprit, while one enjoyed a blissful
moment of regal glory on the box.

The little child inside the coach was teasing his
mother for something, and she, after an unavailing
attempt to quiet him, asked Sam — now sitting
alone on the long bench of the stoop — if she
could get a drink of water for the child. He at
once brought a brimming glass from the bar-room,
and with a careful eye upon it as she stretched
forth her hand, he saw a narrow band of unmistakable mulatto skin between the glove and the
sleeve.

He gave a quick start at the unexpected revelation, that spilled a little of the water, and cast a
quick, inquiring glance at the black-veiled face.
The woman, as quickly divining the cause, hastily
drew her sleeve down to her glove. The boy
drank eagerly and she finished the glass under her

veil, returning it with a trembling hand to Sam, who reassured her with a significant shake of his head and a hand upon his lips. The stage-coach had a new interest for him now, but he did not betray it by staring inside it.

The fresh horses were brought out and put on, the travelers took their places, the rural representatives flurried with fear of being left, the lawyer, the Englishman, and others with the easy deliberation of owners, for whom the coach must wait. The driver climbed to the box, cracked his whip, and the heavy conveyance rolled gayly away.

The landlord, the hostlers, and the spectators watched its departure to the first turn of the road.

"By grab! Dan don't drive a livelier team 'an that on his route, I'll bet," said the landlord, withdrawing his admiring gaze from the retreating coach.

"Got quite a load o' rep'sent'tives," another remarked. "Don't know 's they look much better 'n aourn. Wonder if he's goin' by stage."

"M'dah," one answered, evidently not a supporter of the successful candidate. "He's a-goin' tuckernuck, with his own team!"

"By jolly!" the fat cooper ejaculated, "I wish 't I had what it cost tu paint that 'ere Englishman's face. You wouldn't ketch me a-wheltin' hoops."

"That 'ere womern was turrible afeared o' showin' her face," the youngest man of the party said; "but she need n't ha' be'n if she 's as good-lookin' as her boy."

" Some widder womern, proberbly," the landlord said oracularly, and the company dispersed slowly, except the boys' steps were hastened by the imperative rap of the schoolmistress's ruler on the rattling window sash of the schoolhouse. While the corner hamlet lapsed into its ordinary quietude Sam took the road, and presently came to Friend Bartlett's.

The peaceful atmosphere of the place was not disturbed by his approach. The fat dog arose from his basking-place on the sunny side of the horse-block and walked forth to meet him with a slow, non-committal wag of the tail, which was quickened to a friendly greeting when the game was sniffed and Sam's knee had passed olfactory inspection, and then escorted him to the door with dignified cordiality.

Rebecca Bartlett met him with a pleased smile lighting her placid face as she recognized him.

" Why, this is Samuel, is n't it? Well, I 'm real glad to see thee. I 've wanted to talk with thee about poor Pelatiah ever since John saw thee. What, thee has n't brought us more ducks?"

" Wal, yis, marm," said Sam, " ducks was what I started tu fetch ye, but I run ontu a few pigins an' a pa'tridge, an' did n't know but you could work 'em in some way. Pa'tridge is pooty dry-meated, but pigins makes tol'able pigin pies, aour folks thinks."

" Thee has got a partridge? Now I am glad," she declared with great satisfaction and increased interest, as she raised the bird from the bunch and felt the plump breast with a critical hand. " It 's what neighbor Corbin 's craving, and nob'dy 's been able to get him one."

" Onwell, is he, marm? "

" Oh, yes, he 's very low," said Rebecca, modulating her voice to due solemnity. " It 's consumption, and it is n't likely he can continue long, but he thinks a partridge is all he needs to make him well. Thee knows how it is with people in a decline. Now, if thee 's willing, I 'll send it to him."

" Why, sartinly, Mis' Bartlett, it 's yourn to du jest what you 're a min' tu with ; an' I 'll sit ri' daown an' pick it an' dress it."

" No, thank thee, Samuel ; I think it will please him to see it jest as it is. He 's been a great hunter. Perhaps it would be better for him now if he had given his thoughts more to weightier matters ; but it has seemed hard that he could n't have one partridge now, when he used to get so many, and for other people too. Margaret ! "

" Yes, mother," a soft voice answered out of a light stir of housework inside, and in a moment the daughter appeared, without a trace of its recent performance upon her neat attire. A shade of anxiety fell upon her face as she recognized the visitor, to whom she gave friendly greeting.

"Why, how does thee do?" and then turning questioning eyes to her mother, "no bad news of — of the apples, I hope?"

"No news ary way," Sam answered. "I see 'em git a good start tow-ards Canerdy."

"No, it's nothing about them," said Rebecca, "but Samuel has brought us more ducks and some pigeons and this partridge, which seems almost providential. Now thee put on thy bonnet and run right up to neighbor Corbin's with the partridge, will thee? While thee's gone I'll get these pigeons ready and make a pie for dinner. If thee's a mind to help me pick 'em, Samuel, we can talk about Pelatiah, and thee'll stay to dinner with us."

Sam was not loath to accept both invitations, and followed Rebecca to the woodshed. Half of this was floored with plank, neatly swept, but thickly scarred with axe wounds where misdirected blows had fallen along the border nearest the chip-littered ground, on which the tiers of wood arose to the base of the cobwebbed rafters, to which phœbe-birds' nests of past summers clung in various stages of dilapidation. The cheese-press stood at one end of the floor, the lever weighted with worn-out plow-points, making occasional spasmodic, creaking descents, presently followed by an increased trickle of whey into the keeler. A work-bench stood at the other end, with a vise and a few tools upon it, under a dusty window, a rack of augers and a sickle, and a corn-cutter made from a broken scythe. Along the walls between the cheese-press and the work-bench hung various utensils of the dairy and the kitchen, divided by the kitchen and cheese-room doors. Elderly hens made cautious incursions into this debatable ground between indoors and out, where nests were tolerated if once established.

Rebecca sat down on the chopping-block and Sam on the saw-horse, and they stripped the feathers from the birds into the same basket; and so, with hands and tongues employed together, economized time like two gossips at their knitting.

"Poor thing," Rebecca exclaimed, pitying a wound she had uncovered of resplendent feathers, "it does seem cruel to kill such pretty creatures, but they do pick up a great deal of wheat, and they make excellent pies. And now tell me about Pelatiah. Was he greatly cast down?" She sighed deeply and made piteous little sounds with her tongue against her teeth, as she listened to the story of Pelatiah's disappointment and Louisa's death, and when it was ended said in soft, motherly tones : —

" Ah, poor souls, how sad ! Pelatiah was very kindly and faithful, but I used to wish he was more tender. He did n't go to meeting with us very often. I hope he is softened. Louisa was a pleasant young woman, but light. Poor thing! poor thing ! "

" Well, Peltier ain't no gre't hand tu go tu meetin', but I wisht there wan't no worse folks in the world. And he 's as tender-hearted as a gal."

" There, now, I 'll get the broom and sweep thee off," though Sam protested that he was quite clean enough. " My," she exclaimed, as she supplemented the vigorous sweeping of Sam's legs by the application of a moistened forefinger, " how feathers do stick to woolen stuff. Now I guess thee 'll do."

Now Margaret returned glowing with the freshness of the morning, but sobered by recent speech with one who was near the end of life's journey.

" Well, my dear, how did thee find David this morning ? "

" Very feeble ; but he brightened up wonderfully at the sight of the partridge, and says he shall be able to shoot them himself in a little while."

" Ah, poor man," Rebecca sighed, " he 's done with all such things."

" He wanted me to thank thee," Margaret said to Sam.

" Why, it was n't me. It was your mother an' you. But I be sorry for anybody 'at wants to go huntin' an' can't.   That is tough.   It 'ould du him more good tu shoot one pa'tridge 'an to eat a dozen."

" I don't quite see how that could be," said Margaret, with a questioning smile.   Sam answered by asking : —

" Why, would n't you druther pick one wild posy 'at you s'arched for yourself 'an tu hev a hul harnful fetched tu ye ? "

" Oh, yes," and being a woman Margaret shifted ground.   " But I can't understand how people can enjoy killing things, such pretty things as par- tridges."

" They hain't no prettier 'n posies, an' it kills posies tu pick 'em.   But that ain't what you pick 'em for.   It 's to hev 'em."

" But it does n't hurt the posies," she argued.

" That 's more 'n we know, bein' 'at we hain't ' posies, not all on us," and Sam's honest admiring eyes completed the compliment.

" Well, child, we must be doing," said her mother, admonished by the deliberate chime of the kitchen clock.   " Samuel, will thee go and visit John Bartlett or will thee come in and read the ' Liberator ' and the ' Anti-Slavery Standard,' or maybe thee 'd rather read ' Thomas Chalkley's Journal,' or some account of early Friends.   Thee 'll find them very improving."

Sam saw Margaret making a wry face at the

mention of these works, as if at recollection of some unpalatable dose of childhood, and wisely decided to seek recreation in the company of living rather than departed worthies. He found Friend Bartlett in a stony field behind the orchard, persuasively urging a yoke of deliberate oxen who moved with a slow, ponderous progress, in apparent unconsciousness of the plow behind them, though the tense chain creaked under the constant strain, the share groaned and grumbled a subterraneous complaint among the stones, and Michael, bending between the handles, grumbled and cursed in as continuous an undertone, which he took good care should not be loud enough to call a reproof from his employer.

Sam was greeted with quiet cordiality by Friend Bartlett, and, accommodating his long legs to the pace of the procession, enjoyed a peripatetic visit till the mellow conch sounded for dinner. Michael's presence had prevented their speaking of what was uppermost in their thoughts, and now that he went to the barn with the oxen John Bartlett said : —

"Well, I guess our colored friend must be safe over the line by this time."

"They went off a-kitin', anyways," said Sam. "An' I tell you what, Mr. Bartlett, I b'lieve the' 's a couple more on 'em a-p'intin' for Canerdy right in broad daylight," and went on to tell of the two stage-coach passengers.

"Thee don't say ! In the stage this morning !

I had a letter from one of our friends in Middlebury saying that he had a woman and her child in his house and would send 'em along as soon as it seemed safe. But I did n't think he 'd venture to so soon after they were hunting for Robert — and in this way. It was a pretty bold stroke, I say for it."

" Mebby it 's the safest arter all, an' the' won't nob'dy mistrust 'at hain't on the lookout, for the woman keeps her face clust as ever you see, and the young un 's as white as — as any white young un," and Sam instinctively looked toward the east as if he could see through the " Pinnacle " to the Danvis hills, where his own flaxen-haired boy played safe and free in the shelter of the Green Mountains.

" They 'll go right to one of · our friends in Burlington, and he 'll put 'em aboard of the steamboat that 'll take 'em right to St. John's," said the other. " Come, let 's go to dinner."

The neatly served meal and its decorous prelude of silent grace forcibly reminded Sam of the difference between home life and camp life, and just then the latter did not seem quite the best, and it set him to longing for his own fireside. This longing continued to abide with him when the quiet afternoon was half spent and it was time for him to return to camp, for which he felt a kind of disgust, not lessened by the impression of his enter-

tainers' unspoken conviction that his present recreation was a sad waste of time. He could not take
their view of it any more than they could understand his, but he craved their good opinion, and
could not be satisfied with mere toleration.

Till he was out of their sight, half way across
the fields, he felt a shame that he was ashamed of.
Then a westerly waft brought him the heartening
fragrance of the autumnal woods — the odor of pine
and hemlock and ripe leaves. Far behind him
he heard the returning stage-coach clucking like a
hen bringing home her brood, and presently after,
the joyous clamor of the freed school-children, for
the stage-coach was the school-mistress's clock.

Unheeding the incoming waterfowl that swerved
aside or upward from their impetuous flight to pass
him, he paddled steadily down the channel, his
constant wake gilding the silver water far behind
him with pulsing reflections of the sunset that were
reflected again in flickering shafts of duller gold
dropping aslant down the paling of marsh, and so
he came to the end of his peaceful voyage.

CHAPTER XVI.

STORY-TELLING.

The company had been sitting around the fire for some time in meditative silence, Antoine especially in such deep thought that the pipe between his set teeth had gone out for lack of draft. He was racking his brain for the invention of a change in the bill of fare, which had become monotonous with continual repetitions of roast duck, fried duck, and stewed duck till each variation needed a good deal of Spartan sauce to make it palatable. At last he spoke, without removing his pipe from his mouth or his gaze from the fire.

" Cheekin pie was good, an' Ah 'll b'lieved dawk pie was good, but Ah 'll ant tas'e. 'F Ah 'll gat hoven or bake pans an' somet'ing for mek crus', an' board for roll it, an' peg too, an' some pepper we 'll fregit for brought, an' t'ree, four necessity t'ing Ah 'll can't rembler, Ah bet you head Ah 'll was mek you pie to-morry you can' heat 'nough of it, prob'ly. Ah 'll got de dawk."

" It kinder seems," said Joseph, his mouth watering for the prospective feast, " as it looks naow, you 'd hafter make us a pie aouten clear duck, but I d' know fer sartain."

" You might spare him some feathers for crust," Sam suggested.

" Wal, M'ri could n't, though I da' say they 'd make tol'able light top crust."

" Ann Twine's pie is some like the feller's soup 'at I hearn tell on," said Uncle Lisha, fumbling absent-mindedly on the log beside him for a shoe-peg. " He was a-travelin' an' got short o' money, or mebby he was a reg'lar beggar, I do' know, but ary way, he stopped tu a haouse an' ast for somethin' tu eat, an' they would n't give him nothin'. So he ast 'em if they would n't lend him a kittle a spell an' a spwun, so 's 't he c'ld make hisself a kittle o' stun soup, an' so they did just tu see what he 'd du. Wal, he built him a fire side o' the rwud an' sot a kittle o' water a-b'ilin', an' he took an' washed a stun 'baout 's big as his fist an' popped it int' the kittle, an' sot an' watched it b'ile a spell, an' then he dipped up a spoo'f'l an' tasted on 't.

" ' It 's proper good,' says he, ' but it 's kinder fraish, an' I wish 't I hed a leetle grain o' salt tu put into 't,' an' they went and fetched him a han'f'l an' he put that in.

" ' That 's a gre't improvement,' says he, a-tastin' ag'in, ' but it would n't hurt it none if the' was a hunk o' meat in 't; any sort of a scrap 'at you was a-goin' tu heave away. I hain't partic'lar.' An' so they fetched him a good hunk o' meat an' he hove that int' the kittle, an' then says he, 'I s'pose you 'd jes' 's live 's I 'd pull one o' them 'ere turnips over there? This 'ere soup 's goin' tu be putty strong o' stun if it don't ha' some vegetables in 't.'

" So he went an' got him a turnip, an' whilst he was abaout it he got an onion, an' he cut 'em up an' chucked 'em in. An' when he got it b'iled he eat 'nough tu last him tew days, an' says he, a-rubbin' of his stomerk, ' The' hain't nothin' 'at makes better soup 'n a good stun, wi' a few leetle additions, an' I 'm much obleeged tu ye for the use o' your kittle,' says he."

" Dat was mek me rembler of one man Canada," said Antoine, scooping up a coal with the bowl of his pipe and pulling at it with resounding smacks.

" I 'll warrant ye," said Uncle Lisha, " I never knew nothin' 'at did n't."

Antoine gave no heed to the remark, but at once began his story when his pipe was in blast.

" You see, dar was one mans ant very good up, an' he 'll ant gat not'in' for heat on his haouse 'cep' one pea for all his waf an' ten chillens. He tol' hees hwomans for put de pot on de stofe an' full him up wid water an' put dat pea on it. Den bambye w'en he beegin fo' bile he look on de pot an' see dat pea jomp raoun' all 'lone, he say, ' Dat leetly pea was look lonesick, an' Ah 'll goin' see 'f Ah can fin' somet'ings for hees company.'

" So he go in de naght to nudder man's barn, where dey was keel bif critter an' hang it for cold off, an' he was cut good chonk an' take it on his haouse an' t'row it in de pot 'long to de pea w'en his waf he 'll ant see. Bambye w'en de pea was bile plenty an' his waf beegin tas'e for heat, he say:

" ' Bah gosh, Ah 'll ant never see so pea lak dat for mek soup, me.' An de mans tol' him : —

" ' You 'll ant never gat raght kan' o' pea 'fore.' "

" I guess it must be the water in your tew soups 'at makes me think o' the way that 'ere little Wat Palmer got a pint o' rum aouten Hamner here a spell ago," said Sam, as he broke a dry branch across his knee and slowly fed the fire with the pieces.

" It wan't good rum, I 'll bate ye," said Uncle Lisha.

" Wal, sech as it was, he got it aouten Hamner for nothin', which is more 'n most c'n du, an' he got drunk as a bee on 't an' then tol' haow he done it."

" Wal, haow 'd he come it on him ? "

" Wal, Wat he was dre'f'lly dry an' not a red cent in his pocket nor nob'dy tu treat him. So he gits him tew pint bottles jest czactly alike an' fills one on 'em wi' water an' sticks that intu one cut-tail pocket an' the empty one int' t' other an' marches up to Hamner's bar 's promp' 's a major

an' calls for a pint o' the best rum. Bein' so
promp' Hamner cal'lated 'at of course he was goin'
tu pay ri' daown, an' so he drawed the sperits an'
handed it over to Wat, an' he tucked it in his
pocket, and says he, ' Mr. Hamner, you jest chalk
this daown ag'in me an' I 'll pay for 't the nex' job
o' fiddlin' I git,' and Hamner said, not by a jugful,
he would n't, an' if Wat wan't goin' tu pay for 't
then tu jest hand it right back.   Wat, he begged
hard, but it wan't no use, the money or the liquor
Hamner would hev, an' so Wat gin him the bottle o' water, a-partin' with 't as 'ough 't was his
heart's blood, an' off he went wi' the rum, an' in an
haour was drunker 'n a hatter, an' Hamner poured
the water intu his barrel, never mistrustin', but
a-ticklin' himself 'at he 'd saved ninepunce, an' so
he hed, r'al'y.   But it bothered him haow Wat hed
got so all-fired drunk."

" Wal, seh, boy, if de folks dat was went to
Hamny ant gat more as pant water in de barrel
rawm, it won't hurt dem."

" Wal," said Joseph, " it kinder seems as 'ough
another pint o'' water was a leetle mite more 'n
Hamner's rum 'ould stan', accordin' tu my rec'lec-
tions o' the taste on 't, but I d' know, mebby it
will."

The company became silent again, each busy
with his own thoughts, till Antoine began to sing
as if to himself what may have been an improvisa-

tion, but was more likely a free translation of an
old song : —

> " All tam w'en de leaf turn yeller
>   It mek it kan o' lonesick, me,
>   For t'ink w'en Ah 'll was leetly feller
>   An' go sleep on mah mudder's knee,
> ' Dor, dor, dor, petit !   Dor, dor, dor, petit ! '
>   Same hol' song she sing to me.
>
> " Den de folkses an' de medder,
>   An' de ribber an' de tree,
>   Beegin swimmin' raoun' togedder
>   W'en mah mudder sing to me,
> ' Dor, dor, dor, petit !   Dor, dor, dor, petit ! '
>   So he sing his song to me.
>
> "Sometam Ah 'll wish for be dat bebby,
>   Jus' de sem Ah 'll use for be.
>   Ah 'll ant care 'f he scol' it, mebby,
>   'F Ah 'll hear mah mudder sing to me,
> ' Dor, dor, dor, petit !   Dor, dor, dor, petit ! '
>   Jus' sem he use for sing to me.
>   Sem mah mudder sing to me."

Antoine pocketed his pipe and yawned sleepily,
" Wal, dis ant mek any dawk pie.   Ah 'll b'lieved
Ah can mek it jus' as fas' 'f Ah go sleep," and he
made his way into the tent, whither the others
presently followed, Sam lingering last to scan the
patches of starlit sky between the branches, and
forecast the morrow's weather.

Then, while the dying fire snapped itself out and
the dancing shadows sank into the universal gloom,
the tired hunters were lulled to sleep by the slow
wash of waves and the low song of the cedars.

CHAPTER XVII.

UNCLE LISHA woke early from a troubled dream of slaughtered geese that when picked up changed to a leering, disagreeable man clad in a garment of feathers and a red woolen comforter tied about his neck. As the unpleasant vision dissolved in the vanishing mists of dreamland, his awakening senses realized the dim, chilling dawn of the autumn day, its silver promise of golden hours, its absence of bird songs, the near stillness stirred but not broken by far-away sounds, the raucous call of dusky ducks, the chiming whistle of a flock of golden-eyes already on the wing, and the crazy laughter of a distant loon calling the sleeping winds.

These sounds became more separate and distinct when he crept forth into the open air without disturbing his companions and stood shivering by the cold fireplace. He heard what more attracted his attention, the rustle of quick nervous footsteps in dry leaves near by and a sharp " K-r-r-r, quit, quit, quit, quit " that at once told their origin. He cautiously drew his gun from the tent and went in stealthy pursuit of the partridge, which led him down to the brink of the cliff before it burst into flight and went clattering far out of sight among the trees.

Uncle Lisha stared a moment into the brief disturbance of branches along the bird's aerial path, and then through a narrow aperture in the green wall of cedars he turned his eyes upon the lake, always an object of admiration to him, a dweller among the mountains.

He saw Split Rock and the farther shore of the bay becoming distinct in the growing light, and looming above the low-spread veil of mist, whose nearer frayed edge dissolved in the silvery sheen of the water, smooth as glass, yet gently undulating with long swells that were not perceptible except as they swept downward the lengthening reflections of Garden Island trees, or washed the sands with recurrent, slumberous murmurs.

As he peered out upon the tranquil scene through the narrow casement of boughs, he heard a sonorous gabble of voices mingled with the soft wash of the swells, evidently close at hand, yet coming from an unseen source, for there was no living object in sight but a small flock of ducks crinkling the glassy surface with their wake just in the edge of the mist. Raising himself on tiptoe and looking nearer, his heart almost choked him at the sight of five noble geese standing midleg deep in the sandy shallows almost beneath him. One tall old gander stood on guard, stretched to his utmost height, while his companions delved in the submerged gravel.

With breathless caution the old man trained his gun upon them. Remembering all he had ever heard of the danger of overshooting in downhill shots, and aiming low at two that stood in range, the trigger was pulled, the mimic thunder rolled across the bay, and as the multiplied echoes came tumbling back from distant hills and shores the lifting smoke unveiled two sprawling forms floundering in the shallows and a brief vision of the survivors climbing skyward with flurried wing-beats.

He knew not how, but with a speed and safety that seemed in him miraculous, Uncle Lisha descended the cliff and secured his victims.

"There you be, anyway!" he panted as he stood exultantly regarding them, "an' if you 're tame wil' geese you 're almighty smart ones, an' if any dumb man claims ye he 'll be an almighty smart one if he gits ye away f'm your Uncle Lisher!"

Casting a furtive glance around, he gathered them by the legs, carefully examined their necks for any hidden mark of ownership, and made all haste along the beach. Though he had not far to go to reach camp, his breath was well-nigh spent, his short old legs were weak, and his arm ached with a pain that he was proud of when he had climbed the steep path, and bracing himself for a final effort, held up his game before his gaping comrades.

"There, boys," he cried, "haow 'll that du for a 'fore breakfus' job? I tell ye it 's the airly bird 'at gits the worm. These 'ere geese is the birds an' I 'm the worm."

Then in response to a shower of questions he related all the incidents of his exploit, while each of his companions " hefted " the geese separately and together and burned with envy or glowed with admiration.

" An' naow le 's ha' some breakfus'," he cried when the recital was concluded, " for it 's hungry work a-huntin' geese an' strainin' work a-luggin' on 'em, as you may not know, but I du."

" I s'pose you won't hev no 'bjections tu my hevin' the feathers if I 'll pick 'em? " Joseph asked as they sat around the stone table, and between bites he turned his eyes upon the geese, and with slow rumination calculated their yield of down.

" Not a ident'cal feather comes off 'm them geese till they gits tu Danvis, an' Jerushy an' the hull consarn on 'em sees 'em jest as they be, feathers an' all. No, sir," the old man continued with increasing emphasis, as he waved the half-picked thigh of a duck in the direction of the subject of his remarks, " the' ain't a-goin' tu be nothin' duberous abaout them 'ere geese, ner nob'dy a-twit-tin' on me 'at they 're someb'dy 'nother 's tame geese 'at I shot."

" Prob'ly you 'll goin' prove it by de smell of it too, Onc' Lasha! Dey was git purty hol' 'nough for smell w'en you gat it home."

" I 'll resk but what they 'll keep three, four days, an' you 'll be a-goin' hum by that time, won't ye, Samwil ? "

" Yes, I guess we 'll git 'nough on 't by that time," Sam answered. " An' I would kerry 'em jest as they be if I was you, for they 're better worth showin' 'an anything we 've got erless it 's aourselves. What be you an' Jozeff goin' tu du t'day? Me an' Antwine 's a-goin' up the Saouth Slang tu hunt some an' see the Injins make the' canew. Want tu go 'long up in the scaow ? "

" No, I don't sca'cely b'lieve we du, du we, Jozeff? I be'n a-cal'latin' tu gwup the crik a piece some day an' see an ol' feller 'at I useter know time o' the war 'at I hain't seen for fifteen year, an' I guess if Jozeff 's a min' ter go an' hunt along up that way in the scaow, we 'll go. I 'd ruther see an ol' friend 'an all the dumb b'ilin' o' Injins in the 'Nited States, an' I don't care no gre't 'baout seein' 'em make a canew. If 't was mockersins, it might be interestin'. What say, Jozeff ? "

Joseph pondered long before he answered, casting doubtful glances out upon the creek while he slowly mopped his plate with a bit of bread.

" Wal, I do' know, sca'cely, Uncle Lisher.   Du you understan' haow tu oar a boat an' gee an' haw it ?   'Cause ye see I don't, an' the plaguey dumb things goes a-shoolin' raoun' jest where they 're a minter, a dumb sight contrayer 'n a hawg, seem 's 'ough.   I cal'late they got it 'baout right when they called 'em she.   I do' know but what it can be l'arnt, but I kinder reckon a feller 's got tu hev the gift o' managin' on 'em, same as o' women folks, which some hain't ner can't git.   Naow if 't was M'ri er Ruby, I should know jest haow tu go tu work, but darn a boat, anyways."

" Good airth an' seas, Jozeff, 't ain't nothin' to manage ary one.   You jest got tu humor 'em, that 's all.   I can run that scaow boat anywheres on this 'ere crik, I bate ye."

" Wal, if you c'n du it, it 's all right, an' I 'll go, but if you hafter depend any on me, we shan't git anywheres ner nowheres else."

Joseph's doubts being overcome, they set forth on their voyage, Uncle Lisha at the oars, shaping his course by frequent glances over his shoulder.

The weather was in the genial mood that autumnal days often assume as if to make amends for later sullenness and turbulence.   The sun shone warm and bright, and the genial air was stirred by so light a breeze that it only wrinkled the outer channel with ripples that flashed back the sunlight and repeated the azure of the sky in quavering

lines of blue, cut athwart by gold and russet reflections of farther woods and nearer rushy margins.
The marshes were webbed so thick with a veil of
spiders' weaving that they looked as if a hoar frost
lay upon them, while the sun threw a glade of burnished gold across the broad silvery level, broken
by the curving seam of the channel and the brown
domes of the muskrat houses.

Uncle Lisha pulled an even, steady stroke, but
a noisy one, with a creak and splash that awoke
echoes and aroused flocks of wildfowl, while the
boat snored placidly on its course, its broad bow
seeming to exhale long respirations as it met the
ripples with a decadent surge. A party of crows
came out of the woods, cruising overhead in a brief
tour of observation, whereof they made discordant
report as they flapped back to cover. A kingfisher
sallied from his perch to meet the voyagers with a
rattling volley of clatter that did not cease till he
slanted in upward flight to a steadfast poise above
a shoal of minnows, into which he presently plunged
like a plummet, and then retired in silence to his
Lenten breakfast.

So they pursued the voyage, Uncle Lisha too
busily employed and Joseph in too great trepidation
for much conversation, till the mouth of the South
Slang was passed, when the latter cleared his
throat and remarked : —

"I tell ye what 't is, Uncle Lisher, it kinder

seems 's 'ough a feller 'd feel consid'able stiddier an' safer on one o' them 'ere mushrat haousen 'an what he does a-bolancin' hisself in this 'ere plaguey ol' wobblin' boat, seems 's 'ough he would."

"He wouldn't git fur on one on 'em, I don't cal'late," the old man answered.

"Mebbe he might git fur in 'em," said Joseph, feeling guilty for venturing to pun in such a perilous situation; but Uncle Lisha did not deign to notice it and he continued in serious vein. "But ye see I hain't wantin' tu go nowher', on'y tu git aout ont' the land ag'in, which the' hain't no chance o' duin' here, 'ceptin' I land on one o' them mushrat haousen."

Uncle Lisha vouchsafed no answer, but half turned in his seat to study his course, thereby slightly tipping the scow.

"Sam Hill! Look aout!" cried Joseph, pulling hard on the gunwale. "You'll hev the dumb tottlish consarn t' other side up fust ye know!"

"Go 'long wi' your nonsense," Uncle Lisha answered. "You couldn't tip it over." In proof whereof he wagged his head and shoulders from side to side and raised a wash that shook the boat, yet not so much as it did Joseph.

"For the Lord's sake stop it, Uncle Lisher," he pleaded, "I can't swim no more 'n a grin'stun."

"Nob'dy wants ye tu. You jes' sit still an' I'll navigate ye." Uncle Lisha smiled benignly as he resumed his stroke.

"Set still?   It don't seem 's 'ough I could, no more 'n on a hetchel, an' the tarnal boat won't let me.   Say, Uncle Lisher, I wanter git aout an' set on a mushrat haouse till you come along back. Like 'nough I c'ld shoot a mushrat er suthin'."

"Sho, the' would n't none come anigh ye."

"Wal, I don't care if they would n't.   I've rid fur 'nough, an' don't want to go nowheres!   You back up tu that big one an' le' me git aout.   My back aches an' my laigs cramps, an' I'm dizzy-headed an' sick tu my stomerk an' I don't feel very well myself.   You le' me git aout."

"Why, Jozeff, be you in ri' daown airnest?" Uncle Lisha asked, resting his oars.   Joseph's scared face gave sufficient answer without supplement of speech.

"Yes, I be.   It seems 's 'ough I would n't ask for nothin' in this world 'an tu be sot on suthin' 'at would n't tottle every time I drawed my breath or rolled my eye.   You jest lemme git aout."

"Sho, now don't be sech a 'fraid-cat.   It hain't more 'n a miled furder tu where we 're a-goin', an' then you can huff it back tu camp, 'crost the bridge an' so raound."

"I tell ye I 've rid fur 'nough.   You back up an' lemme git aout.   Come now, du, Uncle Lisher. Whoa!   Back!   S-h-s-h!   Dumb the plaguey ol' contr'y thing!   Whoa!   Hush!"

"Wal, if you will, you will, I s'pose," Uncle

Lisha said, stopping the scow's headway with a great surge of the oars and backing her in the direction of the largest muskrat house. "But you 'll git turrible lunsome, an' you can't move raound none."

"I 've moved raound 'nough tu last me a month. An' I 'll be contented as a clam a-waitin' fer ye. Seems 's 'ough I would till — till the ma'sh froze, so I c'ld walk ashore."

The slanting stern of the scow slid up the sloped side of the house, and Joseph, hitching his gun along beside him, crawled out on all fours to the top, where he seated himself with a sigh of intense relief.

"There, naow, if 't wan't fer thinkin' o' gittin' away f'm here, I sh'ld be as independent as a man on the taown. You need n't hurry none 'baout comin' back. Seems 's 'ough I wanted consid'able time tu git settled an' rested up an' look raound."

"Guess you 'll git settled an' sick on 't 'fore I git aout o' sight. If ye du, you holler, an' I 'll come back an' git ye. Good-by."

Uncle Lisha bent to his oars and with a strong pull, assisted by a push of Joseph's foot, resumed his course, continuing it with moderate speed till quite out of sight, in momentary expectation of a recall. He passed the mouth of the East Slang and the long curve of the reach above it, when he came where shore and channel became neighborly at a sandy landing, the cleanliest of all the old homestead ports that the inland voyager finds between the lake and the first falls of Little Otter. He pulled in at the foot of a great elm and stepped out on the flint-strewn shore, stretching his legs and straightening his back before he beached his boat and climbed the breast-high bank, which was cut to a steep incline by the wash of the spring floods, and overhung with a fringe of naked roots of shrubs and grass.

A level meadow lay before him, the rank aftermath dappled with purple heads of the second blossoms of clover and starred with late daisies. Beyond it a farmhouse and barns nestled among locust, cherry, and apple trees, and a footpath led to it from the landing. This Uncle Lisha followed till the old house assumed a familiar appearance as he approached it from the unaccustomed direction. The smoke of an outdoor fire drifted up from behind a row of cherry-trees that bordered the garden, and with it broken clouds of steam that diffused a savory odor of mixed cookery, the old-time hog's hotch-potch of pumpkins, potatoes, and apples.

When his feet brushed the plantain and scuffed the chips of the back yard, Uncle Lisha came close upon the source of the smoke and steam, a great potash kettle slung to a thick pole by a log chain over a brisk fire of stubborn odds and ends of the wood-pile. A wiry little man of about his own

age was sidling around the windward side of the
fire, punching it here with a wooden poker, kicking
it there with a quick thrust of his cowhide boot,
and then, pulling a hat apparently as old as himself
well over his brows and sinking his chin deep into
the grizzled ruff of beard that surrounded his
throat, stooped and peered into the bubbling kettle,
getting brief glimpses of wallowing chunks of
pumpkins, bursting potatoes, and dropsical apples.
He was in this position as Uncle Lisha approached
in the rear, and touched him lightly on the most
prominent part of his person with his gun. The
guardian of the kettle was not at all startled, but
only called out without turning his head : —

"Hy, ye leetle sarpint, tryin' tu skeer yer gran'-
dad, be ye ?"

Uncle Lisha touched him again, when, making
a sudden clutch with his free hand, he caught the
stock of a gun. Then he quickly faced about, the
look of surprise growing on his face when it met
the complacent grin on another face as old as his
own and on a level with it. The expression of
blank amazement softened to one of pleased recognition when the visitor roared : —

"Good airth an' seas ! Abil, don't ye know
me ?" and the host responded in a higher pitched
but as hearty a voice : —

"Why, Lisher Peggs, you goo' for nothin' ol'
sinner, is it you ? Where 'n time 'd you come

from, an' haow be ye, anyway?" and the hands of
the old friends clasped each other in a vise-like
grip. " I never thought o' it a-bein' nobody ner
nothin' but some o' the young uns a-foolin'.
They're keen ones, I tell ye. But, by hokey, I'm
glad tu see ye. Where'd ye come from, anyway,
an' haow be ye?" Abel Benham ran on in an uninterrupted flow while he lugged a block of wood
in front of the fire. " There, set ri' daown an'
make yourself tu hum. Got yer pipe? Wal,
here's some terbarker. Light up an' le's have a
smoke." While he filled his own pipe he stood off
and made a critical examination of his friend,
beaming upon him a slow smile of approval.
" Wal, ye look jest as nat'ral as an ol' shoe.
Leetle older an' a leetle fatter, but jest as humbly
as ever. Where'd ye come from, anyway?"

Uncle Lisha accounted for his presence, and the
two fell into a discourse concerning past experiences
till Abel bethought him of another hospitable offering.

"Say, there's a berril o' cider 'at's worked
some. 'T hain't very sartain, but it's better'n
water. Won't ye ha' some?"

He brought a brimming quart dipper of it, from
which they drank in turn, and Uncle Lisha gave
it the usual compliment of " being good for the
time o' year," while he thought of poor Joseph in
thirsty isolation. They ate the mellowest apples

in the variegated fragrant pile that was flanked by a yellow mound of pumpkins on one side and on the other by a great heap of potatoes, blushing a dusky red through the clinging soil. When conversation lagged Uncle Lisha was taken to see the hogs, which were duly admired and their weight guessed, while a treat of back-scratching and corn nubbins made the visit a mutual pleasure. Then the dinner - horn sounded, and the visitor was forced, not much against his will, to partake of a bountiful meal, served in civilized fashion, which he realized was the better and more comfortable way, for he was beginning to tire of eating with his fingers and sleeping in his clothes, and of the untidiness of womanless housekeeping, and he was glad to eat food nicely cooked, unseasoned with smoke and ashes, off a clean plate, in the companionship of women and children, and finish the meal with a dessert of pumpkin pie, so dear to the Yankee.

Now and then he had brief mental visions of Joseph munching his dry, unsocial repast on the roof of the marsh dweller's hut, and felt some qualms of pity for his friend's solitary plight; but both were as fleeting as they are apt to be when one in the midst of plenty considers the condition of the wretched.

Not till he noticed how his shadow had lengthened while he smoked and chatted beside the wan-

ing fire did he realize how long poor Joseph had
been left in solitary exile. Then he bade his
friend farewell and set forth on his return.

With a long and strong pull Uncle Lisha sent
the scow surging down the channel, and though he
grew scant of breath with the unwonted exertion,
he abated not the length nor strength of his stroke
till he drew near the place where his comrade had
been left, frightening scores of ducks to unnoticed
flight a furlong in advance of his noisy progress.

Then he began to look forward, the lifted oar
blades dripping a dotted wake while he turned his
head, or trailed, bumping the gunwales and creat-
ing a succession of miniature whirlpools while he
twisted his short body for a long look ahead. Discovering no one, he became anxious, but tried to
quiet his feelings with the idea that he had mis-
taken his reckoning, and again plied the oars
vigorously, casting frequent glances on either side.
Presently he passed a muskrat house that he was
sure must be the one upon which he had left his
companion, for it was the largest in the neighborhood, and the weeds in front were pressed flat
where the boat's stern crushed them down, and in
further proof of its identity a piece of paper that
had held Joseph's luncheon lay on the shelving
verge, one sodden half, anchoring the other that
fluttered in the light wind.

Uncle Lisha checked the boat's headway with a

backward stroke and headed toward the house, calling out as he approached it, with his face over his
shoulder, in a deprecatory tone : —

" There, naow, Jozeff, you need n't try tu hide
ye. You can't skeer me wi' your foolin'. Git
right up an' git right in here."

There was no response, and as the bow grounded
with a soft, semi-elastic bump he called again,
rather impatiently, at the same time getting upon
his feet and facing about : —

" Come, naow, quit your foolin' an' git in here."

His face became blank with amazement as he
peered over the top of the muskrat house and saw
only the naked slope of its farther wall.

" Good airth an' seas, has the critter got asleep
an' rolled off an' draownded hisself ? " he cried in
real alarm, then took an oar and gently prodded
the shallow water on all sides, but met only the
soft resistance of the oozy bottom.

" 'Shaw, he could n't never," he assured himself.
" 'T ain't deep enough, an' he 'd ha' left his gun.
But what on airth can ha' become on him ? If
he 'd ha' waded ashore he 'd ha' left a track in the
ma'sh like a tew-year-ol' steer, an' he could n't git
through the mud, anyways. The' hain't be'n no
boat come along 'at he da'st go in. Where in tunket has the critter gone ? Jozeff ! Jozeff ! Jozeff ! "
he lifted up his voice and called, first accenting
and prolonging the first syllable, then the second,

and then both, but there came no answer save the mocking echoes repeating his call from the woods.

" Con-dumb the tarnal fool ! Wha' 'd he wanter go tu roost on a mushrat haouse for anyhaow, julluk a cussed mudhen ? " the old man growled in a tremulous voice when he had taken breath after futile listening. " And wha' 'd I ever let him for? I 'd give all my ol' boots an' shoes tu see him a settin' in this 'ere boat ag'in. Yis, sir, I would."

He looked long and carefully all around far and near, and then shoved off into the channel and resuming the oars pulled lustily toward the camp.

CHAPTER XVIII.

JOSEPH HILL stretched his cramped limbs with a sense of great relief to both body and mind while he watched the scow pass out of sight around the next bend, and caught the last glimpse of Uncle Lisha's hat rising and falling with slow regularity behind the tops of the marsh growth. The clank and splash of the oars faded out of hearing, and as far as he could see or hear he was the sole human occupant of the marshes.

Now and then a duck could be heard quacking a lazy call to comrades or uttering a startled note of alarm, and occasionally the quick, pulsing whistle of passing wings, and far away on the lake the wild cry of a loon, and high overhead the petulant scream of a hawk. Close at hand there was an infrequent rustle and splash of some invisible inhabitant of the marshes, but Joseph listened intently before he could catch the faintest sound of human life, such as the rumble of a distant wagon or ox-cart, or the mellowed shout of the teamster coming to him as if from a different world from that which held his indolent environment.　He was quite contented with the isolation and the quietude as he sat at ease on the soft but stable roof smoking his pipe and patiently waiting for something to come and be killed.

Presently a huge pickerel appeared like an apparition in the dooryard of the muskrat, his cruel eyes and mottled sides shining with a magnified gleam through the clear, still water that barely covered his dorsal fin.　Joseph had a mountaineer's admiration for this species, and deemed such a specimen a worthy trophy.　His heart almost stood still as he realized the opportunity for securing such a noble prize.　He made a cautious movement to bring his gun to bear upon it, but the wary fish detected it and dashed away with a sudden surge that tore the smooth surface into boiling eddies.　Joseph dodged as if a blow had been struck him and gasped his disappointment.

"Gosh darn the luck!　Wan't he a wolloper, though!　Wal, the' hain't no feathers on him, anyway!"

Comforting himself with this qualified consolation, he set to patient waiting again, with some hope that his recent visitor might return.　The last ripple subsided and the schools of minnows, recovered from their fright, began to dart back into the restored quiet of the pool, when its surface was moved by the sluggish undulation of an under wake, then silently broken as a muskrat's head appeared, regarding the strange occupant of its abode with a grim curiosity that would have been alarming if exhibited by a larger animal. The creature remained quite motionless, while Joseph with the utmost caution raised his gun to a deadly aim, and at such short range that it occurred to him, as his finger tightened on the trigger, that the furry skin would be riddled into worthlessness, and he had no desire for wanton destruction.

"I shall blow ye all tu flinders, I know I shall," he whispered to himself as his finger relaxed. His left foot was drawn well under him, his arm resting across his bent knee and supporting the long gun barrel. "If he 'd swim off jes' a leetle mite furder," he soliloquized as he looked straight into the fierce deep-set little eyes, " it seems jes' 's 'ough I might."

Suddenly his heel slipped down the sloping wall, the gun barrel as suddenly descended, and the muskrat dived with a splash like the plunge of a ten-pound shot. It is said that the scream of a panther and the plunge of a muskrat will startle the steadiest and most accustomed nerves as often as heard or seen, and Joseph jumped as if he had suffered the double shock.

"Gosh all Connecticut! " he ejaculated, gasping as if he himself had been plunged in the cold water. "Why don't ye scare a feller aouten his boots! I snum, I most wish I 'd ha' let ye hev, an' spottered ye all over the ma'sh, seems 's 'ough I did, a'most."

Gradually he recovered his equanimity and now gave his attention to feathered game ; but though he lay close on the back side of the house, hoping that some passing flock or single bird might chance to alight in the channel within gunshot, all such espied him and veered off with swifter flight or climbed higher above him, giving his poor ambuscade a wide berth. Only once a flock of teal, following the channel in low flight as if it was a path, flashed past him, slanting lower with set wings to alight, but dropped out of sight beyond the next bend before he heard the fluttering splash that told of their descent. After a while they reappeared, swimming down stream in a devious way, circling, ducking, diving, and nibbling the water, till at last they started with a sudden impulse directly toward him. His gun was leveled upon them, the muzzle gradually lowering, and shaking with the tumultuous beating of his heart as they drew nearer. Now they were almost within certain range, and his finger began to press the hard trigger and his teeth were set in expectation of the inevitable recoil, when all at once they became suspicious of the singular appearance of an old felt hat showing above the top of a muskrat house, and with one accord sprang to flight and vanished like wind-blown smoke.

"Wal, it does beat Sam Hill what tarnal luck I du hev right stret along this hul endurin' day! But them wan't nothin' but leetle pindlin' teal. I b'lieve the' wan't; not much meat on 'em, an' the feathers mere nothin'! But I swan, I wish I 'd ha' got 'em!"

Half an hour passed, and he was drowsy with lying in the warm sunshine, when he was aroused by a stir of the rushes close by the nearest musk-rat house, and then saw a large dusky gray duck swim out of the weeds and climb boldly and deliberately to its top. The slow upward movement of Joseph's gun was arrested by the thought that this could not be a wild duck, and he congratulated himself that he had not obeyed his first impulse.

"It 's a dumb putty idee, folks a-lettin' the' poultry run loose, hither an' yon, an' then make folks pay for 'em when they git shot accidental." Then Joseph addressed the duck aloud: "Do ye know 'at you come almighty nigh a-gittin' shot, you ol' fool?"

The bird stood bolt upright and stretched its neck to the utmost, and Joseph, clambering to the top of the house, swung his hat and shouted lustily:—

"G' 'long home, you ol' fool, 'fore someb'dy shoots ye! Shew!"

The duck squatted and sprang into the air with rapid wing-beats, uttering discordant quacks of terror, and shrank to a wavering speck in the distance, while Joseph gaped at the vanishing form in blank and speechless amazement.

"The very ol' scratch is in everything!" he said at last, and sat down, laying his gun aside as if he had no further use for it. "Dumbed if I try tu shoot anything, an' I wish 't Uncle Lisher 'd come along back."

He took his luncheon from his pocket and ate it slowly, more to pass away the time than to appease hunger. The droughtiness of the repast was aggravated by the abundance of unpalatable water that surrounded him, clear and bright to the eye, but saturated with rank-flavored weeds and nauseous to a mountaineer's palate accustomed to draughts from ice-cold springs. The channel was ruffled by the light northerly breeze, and as he watched the swift ripples continually flickering past it seemed as if he on the artificial islet was being carried as rapidly in the opposite direction by the current. At times slight tremors were imparted to the house by some violent movement of its inmates, and this added to the impression of its instability till Joseph's head swam, and he could not convince himself that he was not afloat, though his relative position to surrounding objects remained unchanged.

"I don't see why in Sam Hill Uncle Lisher don't come along! Wonder 'f he's hired his board up there? I know this 'ere haouse hain't floatin' off, but it seems jes' 's 'ough it was, an' I do' know but what them tormented mushrats is undermindin' on 't, an' 'll let me daown kerswash fust I know! Shew! Ye plaguey leetle torments, scat!" he shouted as he pounded the side of the house with fists and heels.

So passed an hour of discomfort and apprehension, relieved at last by the welcome sound of an approaching boat, which he doubted not was the long expected craft of Uncle Lisha. But when with provoking slowness it appeared around the bend, he saw an unfamiliar figure stooping and rising to the deliberate strokes of the oars, that, though wielded with the skill of an experienced oarsman, shrieked and clanked in doleful discord in their unlubricated swivels. Two short fish-poles protruded from either side, and the fisherman, who wore a black felt hat and a red-backed waistcoat, now and then ceased rowing to overhaul his lines, and once to boat a big pickerel that Joseph could hear thrashing the boat's bottom to the accompaniment of the shrieking swivels when their music was resumed.

Joseph had an impression that he had seen the ancient hat and red-backed waistcoat before, and when the boat passed him and its occupant's profile was revealed, he recognized the stolid features of Uncle Tyler, with whom he had had a brief acquaintance during a previous voyage on these waters. Remembering the old man's deafness he hailed him lustily, but the unconscious face gave no sign and the regular rise and fall of the oars was uninterrupted. Joseph drew in his lungsful of air and let it out in a hail that would have done credit to Uncle Lisha himself; but if the old fisherman heard it, he mistook the direction from which it came, for he turned his head the other way.

"Hello there!" Joseph repeated; "come he-ere! Help! murder! fi-er."

But Uncle Tyler did not become aware of him till he had rowed quite past, and saw him prancing about on the narrow footing of the muskrat house and frantically swinging his hat.

"Was you a-speakin' tu me?" he bawled in an unmodulated tone as he ceased rowing. "What ye want? What ye duin' on top o' that 'ere mushrat haouse? Where's your bwut?"

"Hain't got no boat! Come back here an' git me!"

"No, I hain't got no terbarker. Sent up tu the store by a feller tu git me some last night, but he forgot it. Smoked my last pipeful a-comin' long daown."

"Gol dumb it, come back here an' take me int' your boat!" Joseph howled till his voice cracked. "I'll give ye all the terbarker I've got," and he beckoned with his hat, reinforcing the signal by

waving a blue paper of Lorillard's long cut. This
had the desired effect upon the old man's compre-
hension, and after carefully winding in his trolling
lines, he put about and ran in to Joseph, who
crept eagerly but cautiously on board the scow.

" Git int' the starn there ! " Uncle Tyler commanded.

" Int' the what ? " Joseph asked at the top of
his voice.

" Int' the starn ! the starn ! " Uncle Tyler repeated as loudly, indicating the direction with all
the fingers of one hand.

" Starn ? " Joseph repeated, still unenlightened,
as he crouched on hands and knees beside the ancient mariner and shouted in his ear, while he
scanned the after part of the scow with a puzzled
face. " I don't seem tu see nothin'. Guess you
forgot tu fetch it, did n't ye ? "

" Good land o' massy ! You do' know no more
'baout a bwut 'an a hen ! " Uncle Tyler declared
in disgust. " Go an' set daown in that 'ere seat.
That 'ere 's the starn an' t' other eend 's the
bow, an' this 'ere 's 'midships. There, sed daown
an' gin me that terbarker."

Joseph obeyed the last command first and crept
to his designated place, steadying himself with a
hand on either gunwale as he picked careful footsteps among seven or eight large pickerel that lay
dead or at the last gasp on the slippery floor.

These he had time to admire while Uncle Tyler leisurely filled and lighted his pipe, remarking as he did so : —

"I sent up tu the store for some terbarker las' night by a feller, but he forgot it."

"You are some nigher gittin' on 't 'an you was four, five year ago," said Joseph. "If I don't disremember you forgot tu send for it then. I should n't wonder but what like 'nough you 'd git ye some in four, five year more." But the old man chose not to hear him till he asked in no louder voice, "Why did n't ye stop the boat when I hollered fust ? "

"Did ye holler afore ? Wal, naow, I hear'd suthin', but I reckoned 't was n't nothin' but Harris's bull a-bellerin'. I wan't a-lookin' for nobody rwustin' on a mushrat haouse. Haow come ye here anyway ? "

"I got left here," Joseph shouted.

"Deaf in yer left ear ? Can't ye hear me ? Turrible disagreeable tu be deaf, I s'pose, most ev'rybody speaks so low naow-er-days. I ast ye haow ye come here — on this mushrat haouse ? Onderstand ? "

"Come in a boat ! Got on here tu shoot ducks ! "

"Ooh, tu shoot ducks," said Uncle Tyler, backing his scow into the channel. "Yes, yes, 'spected tu find ducks in a mushrat haouse ! Wal, wal, that's a cur'us idee." The old man gave way to an expression of mirth which was like the laughter of a ghost, being without sound. Having got his boat and his pipe well a-going, Uncle Tyler was enabled to observe his passenger more closely, when a gleam of recognition lighted up his stolid face.

" Good land o' massy ! " he mumbled, trying to speak with the pipe wabbling between his gums and then letting the oars trail that he might remove it for freer speech. " I b'lieve I 've seen you afore ! Wan't you daown here afore, last year or year afore, or some 'er's along there, you an' another feller 'at did n't know no more 'n you du 'baout a bwut; gin me a polt top o' the head wi' an oar — hain't you one on 'em ? " He took off his hat and searched for the exact spot on his bald pate as if to establish evidence or refresh his memory.

" Yes, I b'lieve I was one o' the ones," said Joseph, and proceeded to give a loud and brief account of himself and friends, to which the old man, as he plied the oars, listened as well as he could with his pipe preventing the opening of his mouth, which he apparently depended upon as much as his ears as an organ of hearing. When Joseph concluded with the relation of his latest adventure his auditor fell into another silently boisterous laughter, which brought on a violent fit of coughing, and after that he recovered speech.

"Oh, good land' o' massy! You must be sick for tu think ducks 'ould come tu ye settin' right in plain sight. Wal, wal, you must be sick! I 'll tell ye haow tu shoot ducks if ye won't tell nobody. You jest take an' shove a slab way aout int' the aidge o' the ma'sh an' sprinkle a mess o' oats onto 't, an' you fix ye up a bough haouse so 't you can rake it eendways, an' bimeby when the ducks dis-kiver the bait and git wonted they 'll come there reg'lar to feed, an' then you lay low fer 'em airly in the mornin'. Mebby you 'll ketch a hull slabful on 'em a feedin' tu oncte, an' then, sir, you c'n rip up the hull magazine. That's the way tu shoot ducks! You c'n git 'em that way! Any lunk-head can! Naow you take an' let aout one o' them trollin' lines an' ketch a pickerel. You do' know 's you can? Wal, any dumb fool can heng a-holt of a pole, an' yarn in a fish arter he 's ketched hisself. I guess you can, an' you 'd orter git a good one a-goin' by the Saouth Slang."

Joseph was diffident, but otherwise not loath to accept a chance of redeeming his ill luck, and awk-wardly paid out one of the clumsy lines while his skilled companion handily got the other to its work, though his attention was also given to keeping the boat moving in its proper course, his pipe in blast, and a critical oversight of Joseph's management of the tackle.

"I do' know ezackly," the latter shouted, bringing his mouth to bear on the other, after some intent moments of watching his line, " but it most seems 's 'ough I druther ketch a whoppin' big pickerel 'an tu shoot a duck, seems 's 'ough I druther, tu-day."

" Wal, like 'nough you 'll git you 're druther," Uncle Tyler responded, and sure enough when his lure was trailing past the mouth of the South Slang it was arrested by a sullen, vicious pull that made the stout pole bend like a drawn bow and brought Joseph's heart into his throat at one leap. Remembering the lesson of a former year, he drew the tip of the pole forward till he could lay hold of the line and then hauled it in hand over hand. Then amid a conflict of hopes and fears he saw a monster pickerel coming toward the boat with jaws as wide open as if he had an intention of swallowing it and the crew. Good fortune and a stout line and hook combined to favor Joseph in getting the fish on board in spite of flustered awkwardness, and he was fairly faint with pride and thankfulness when he saw his prize at his feet threshing the bottom of the boat and snapping the wide jaws, toothed as cruelly as a wolf trap. In the midst of his excitement he did not notice that Uncle Tyler had quit rowing and was calmly hauling in his own strained line till, with an easy motion, the old man lifted a fish as big as his own into the boat, remarking as he did so : —

" That 's the way tu ketch a pickerel ! "

Thence to the landing at the willows the voyage was occasionally enlivened by the capture of a fish, and arriving there, Joseph offered the hospitalities of the camp to his rescuer, unlimited tobacco and such victuals as the place afforded in the absence of the cook.

In consideration of their mutual obligations, they became very friendly and conversed so constantly and loudly that the arrival of Uncle Lisha's boat was unheard, as was his no less noisy ascent of the path, slipping, stumbling, and puffing asthmatically.

" Good airth an' seas ! Be you here, Jozeff ? I snum, I never was tickleder tu see a man in this livin' airth. Why in time did n't ye stay where you was till I come ? What d' ye wanter git on there for anyway ? "

With alternate expressions of mirth, vexation, and rejoicing over his safe return, he listened to Joseph's relation of the adventures of his exile, which Joseph ended with a solemn declaration that he would never again under any circumstances embark in any craft smaller than a canal boat, no matter how he might be tempted by fish or fowl.

CHAPTER XIX.

THE two uncles of all their acquaintances got on exceedingly well together, for it transpired that Uncle Tyler had been a Plattsburg volunteer, which was a close bond of friendship, and in their exchange of reminiscences he had no difficulty in understanding the other, who, he said, " talked jest as folks used tu."

" Some on 'em says 'at I 'm a-gittin' deaf, but I tell 'em it 's 'cause they don't speak plain. The' don't nobody, sca'cely, naow-er-days. But I can hear you a-talkin' jest as plain as I could hear the cannon tu Plattsburg. An' the' wan't no trouble o' hearin' them, was the'? "

" No, ner the hollerin' nuther," said Uncle Lisha.

" Du you reckerleck haow that minister hollered?" continued the other. " He come from over your way somewher's, cap'n of a comperny he was, all the menfolks of his congregation his comperny was, an' he got 'em all squatted daown behin' a stun wall, an' when the British come a-marchin' up, some on 'em kep' a-stickin' of the' heads up an' a-peekin' at 'em, an' the minister he kep' a-tellin' on 'em tu lay low, but they would n't, for all naow an' ag'in one on 'em would git a chunk o' lead in his head which it spilte him fer fightin', till bimeby the minister he got mad an' damned 'em up hill an' daown an' grabbed a mus- kit an' swore he 'd shoot the fust one 'at peeked over the wall. Yes, he did ; damned 'em right tu the' heads. An' so arter he got hum they hed a church meetin' an' hauled the minister over the coals for cussin', an' by gol, sir, they voted tu 'scuse him, 'cause they 'lowed his swearin' was a military needcessity."

Uncle Tyler indulged in such immoderate silent laughter over his story that he brought on a violent fit of coughing, from which he recovered after so protracted a struggle for breath that his enter- tainers were relieved to see him depart homeward before he should die on their hands.

" He 's a crabbed ol' creetur, but he 's got his good p'ints," Uncle Lisha remarked, as they watched him rounding the great bend, his pipe in full blast and puffing with the regularity, if not quite the volume, of a high-pressure steamboat. " Deaf folks an' blin' folks lives in worlds by theirselves, still worlds an' dark worlds, an' I cal'late it makes a man sort o' crabbed tu live by hisself. But the ol' creetur hes got his good p'ints."

"Yes," Joseph assented, "so he hes, an' it kinder seems 's 'ough his best ones was oarin' a boat an' ketchin' fish, an' I do' know but borryin' ter-barker in a way 'at you can't deny him, 'cause he allers meant tu ha' hed some o' his own. But he is a turrible man tu oar a boat an' a turrible man tu ketch pickerels. I do' know 's I ever see a more one. An' naow I s'pose these 'ere 'at he helped me ketch has got tu be dressed."

He heaved a sigh of resignation as he slowly drew his jackknife from his pocket and as slowly opened the rickety blade, while his eyes made deliberate selection of a worthy subject for his skill. This he laid upon a convenient slab, and began the task with increased courage when he saw Uncle Lisha opening his knife with an evident intention of lending a helping hand. As they scraped gray-green backs, spotted sides and silvery bellies to an even whiteness, and beguiled the most irksome of the angler's labors with friendly discourse, they heard Sam's return heralded by occasional shots faintly echoed far up the Slang, then saw the infrequent puffs of powder smoke whisked away by the wind before the tardy report burst on their ears, with briefer intervals, till the light birch canoe came swimming, swift and silent, around the last bend like a great duck, and glided into port close beside them.

Antoine rejoiced over the prospective change in

the bill of fare from fowl to fish, and promised such skill in cookery as should no less gladden the others.

"Oh, bah gosh! Ah 'll tol' you, Zhozeff," he cried, as he sidled around with his arms akimbo when they were not engaged in gesture, and his head tilted to one side and the other, in inspection of the progress of the work, " w'en you 'll gat dat peekrils scrope so he white lak snowballs, Ah 'll goin' cook him so you 'll wish you was kingfish'n' bird an' heat feesh every day, all de tam, sem lak one man Canada."

Uncle Lisha scraped his fish softly while he listened in expectation of a story, but Antoine seemed to have forgotten that he had one to tell, though the old man prompted him with an interrogative " Wal ?"

" Wal," he repeated after a while, " I 've allers be'n wantin' tu hear suthin' abaout a man in Canerdy, an' if you 've got anythin' tu tell le' 's hev it.   But whilst you 're a-talkin', Ann Twine, you might be a rippin' one o' these 'ere fish."

" No, seh, Onc' Lasha, Ah 'll can't oversaw de work an' tol' de storee an' work mahse'f all de once."

" Wal, tell yer story then, if you 've got it thought up.   You would n't half clean the fish if you sot aout tu."

" Wal, seh, Onc' Lasha," Antoine began, as he

deliberately filled his pipe, " great many while 'go, w'en de tam was hol', dar was one man Canada was lak for feesh so much he ant do mos' not'ing but dat. W'en his corn ought for be plant his waf was plant it, if he gat plant 't all, an' he go feeshin'. W'en his corn was ought for be hoe, he go feeshin'. W'en it was tam for cut off, his waf cut it off, an' de mans go feeshin' an' de sem for husk it, an' jes' de sem for rip his wheat, an' t'rash it, his waf he do it, all of it. An' w'en his hwood was ought for be cut he go feeshin' in de ice. An' w'en de Govny want it for go faght de Hinjin an' de Angleesh, he 'll run 'way an' go feeshin', so bamby de pries' he 'll gat mad at it an' he tol' it 'f he ant 'have hese'f for be so shiflin', he goin' turn it into kingfishin' an' den see 'f he 'll gat 'nough feeshin'.

" De mans he some scare an' promise for be better, 'fore soon he fregit an' go feeshin' all de tam jes de sem. Den de pries', Oh, haow he 'll was mad an' turn dat man into kingfishin' raght off. De man he was supprise prob'ly, for feel hese'f such leetly feller all cover wid fedder, but pooty soon he feel glad for t'ink he 'll ant gat for wear clo's dat was trouble for git, an' cau go feeshin' all de tam.

" He go up de river, ' K-r-r-r-r,' an' he go daown de river, ' K-r-r-r-r,' an' wen he see leetly feesh, 'baout so big he can swaller, ' splosh', he jomp on it an' flew on a tree for heat it an' say, ' T'ank you, Père Jerome, it was funs for be kingfishin'.'

When he was flew pas' hees hown haouse on de river an' see hees waf homp hees back hoein' an' rippin' in de sun an' hees chillren cry for hongry he 'll holler 'K-r-r-r,' jes' lak he was laught at it, he such gre't wicked.

" Wal, sch, he 'll had good tam all summer an' long in de fall 'fore it come col'.　Den he ant hear de sing bird yaller any more 'cause dey all gone 'cep' de jay an' de hwoodpeckit; den de river froze on top, but he 'll ant know 'nough for go to de warm wedder.　He guess he was be hable for stay jes' long anybody.　One morny de river was be froze on top, but he 'll ant know when he go for his breakfis' an' he go 'K-r-r-r,' lookin' for see some feesh, an' bamby he 'll see leetly feesh swim under de ice an' he holler 'K-r-r-r-r' an' go firs' head raght on top of it, 'Floop,' an' bus' his head on de ice an' broke his brain all off an' dat was de en' of it."

" Sho, Ann Twine, you 'd a gre't sight better be'n a-dressin' fish 'an a-wastin' your time a-tellin' sech a dumb lie ! " Uncle Lisha commented. " Naow you rence 'em off an' kerry 'em up tu camp, fer Jozeff an' me hes done aour sheer."

While Uncle Lisha made his way to the water side with hands and knife held abroad till he stooped to cleanse them, Antoine began washing the fish, protesting meanwhile : —

" Oh, Onc' Lasha, you was want me tol' it.　You

was jes' lak man feeshin' an' git leetly bite, an' he keep feeshin' for ketch it, an' w'en he ketch it, it was punkin seed, an' he mad 'cause it ant bull pawt. It bes' was for be satisfy. Naow, hurrah for de suppy!"

With that they bore their fish to camp, where Sam had preceded them and got the fire in full blast. Presently Antoine pranced around it in a culinary ecstasy, while the others watched him in rapt regard and grew hungrier with every whiff borne to their nostrils from the screeching pan. When at last they sat down to their rock table Uncle Lisha heaved a sigh of satisfaction as he adjusted his spectacles for detection of bones.

"Ah-h-h! This 'ere 's suthin' like. The fact on 't is, I 've eat duck till I 'm a-gittin' web-footed."

"An' bah gosh! Ah 'll pull up some fedder on mah back dis morny. Ah 'll was put it on Zhozeff's bag if you ant believed it."

"I swan, Antwine," said Joseph, "if you 'll let 'em grow all over ye, I 'll pick ye at the halves."

"Say what you 're a mintur," said Sam, "a good fat duck hain't tu be sneezed at. I cal'late them leetle teal ducks is the ch'icest eatin', and wood duck next, an' black duck next, but any on 'em 's good enough for poor folks. Arter all, the' 's more fun in gettin' on 'em 'an the' is a-hevin' on 'em, same as it is in most all huntin' an' fishin' in the true sperit. I guess it 's a feller's soul 'at enj'ys it. But then ag'in the' 's dawgs 'at enj'ys it, and folks says they hain't got no souls, but I don't b'lieve it."

" Ner I nuther," said Uncle Lisha. " I 've seen some dawgs an' some hosses 'at thinks more 'n some men du an' reasons aout things tew."

" Yes," Sam continued, " an' jest think o' humern fools an' tew-legged hawgs a-goin' tu heaven, an' good dawgs 'at thinks an' dreams an' sticks tu ye through thick an' thin a-goin' aout intu nothin'. It hain't no fair shake ! I cal'late dreamin' is a sign of a soul. The body 's all asleep, but the' 's suthin' keeps a-goin' on a-thinkin' arter a fashion, an' what is 't if 't hain't a soul? You never heard a hawg du nothin' on'y snore when he sleeps, but you 'll hear a leetle bird in the dead o' night an' darkness a-singin' aout on his rwust suthin' he hed left over from daytime, so faint an' fur off, you know he 's asleep. An' a dawg 'll show 'at the' 's a part on him a-huntin' in his sleep jest as much as folks feels tu be when they 're asleep. A dawg 's got some advantage over us in not hevin' no gun tu git off. It 's cur'us 'at a dream gun never will go off. You pull till you shet your teeth an' eyes, an' when the hommer falls it goes daown abaout 's quick as a wiltin' weed an' abaout as heavy, an' your dumb gun won't go off. But what I was a-goin' tu say, a haoun' dawg 'll foller a fox all day an' all

night a-singin' glory halleluiah all the time, an'
when you shoot the fox afore him he 'll on'y jest
chaw his backbone a minute an' give him a shake
an' then curl up an' lay daown as comf'table as
a kitten an' jest as contented. His stomerk 's as
empty as a contribution box, but his soul is satisfied jest as much as a man's is.   But I 'm a-losin'
my chance o' gittin' my supper, a-gabbin'! Shove
the fryin' pan this way, Antwine."

When they had their fill of fish they enjoyed
their loaf by the fire and recounted the day's do-
ings.   Sam and Antoine told of the Indians' progress in canoe-building, Joseph his brief experience
of Crusoe life, and Uncle Lisha of his visit to his
old friend and his alarm at Joseph's disappearance.

" I did n't know but them 'ere nigger hunters
hed kerried the creatur' off," he said, " but I
know'd they 'd bring him back arter they 'd tried
workin' on him an' boardin' on him a spell.   But
I tell ye I was glad tu find the creatur' a-hollerin'
to that ol' Tyler, 'cause I feel kinder 'caountable
for his safe-keepin'."

" I druther hev a deaf man tu talk tu 'an not tu
hev nob'dy, if it is strainin' work," said Joseph,
caressing his throat with a tender touch. " Gol,
my throat 's all furred up."

" Dat was feeshbone, prob'ly. You 'll ant wan'
heat more hurry as you spoke, Zhozeff."

After planning how to spend the morrow, which

was to be their last day in camp, they turned into their blankets and drowsed into restful sleep to the sound of the crickets' faint, monotonous complaint and the fleeting whistle of passing wings.

CHAPTER XX.

SAM'S comrades were in delicious, semi-torpid enjoyment of a morning nap when he quietly left his place among them and, after making a breakfast of stealthily gathered fragments, set forth in fulfillment of a promise made to himself of a day alone in Sungahneetook, the fish-weir river of the old Waubanakees. He was not unsocial, but yet at times was fonder of solitude than of company. Like a true lover of nature, he desired not to go with a crowd to woo his mistress.

Creek and lake were thickly shrouded in a tattered web of mist whose gray shreds slowly undulated in the motionless air, disclosing near glints of unruffled silver water and farther away brief glimpses of russet and green marsh, beyond which the unveiled forest glowed in the faint dawn with all the divers hues of autumnal flame. Every single-pointed willow and many-pointed maple leaf was giving its contribution to the slow shower of crystal drops that pattered on rushes and fallen leaves, or tinkled on the quiet waters. The soft continuous sound was punctuated at intervals by the louder voices of awakening life, the sharp whistle of passing wings, the raucous diminuendo of a duck's call.   Then came from afar inland the challenge of a cock, the mellow lowing of kine and quavering bleat of sheep, or from the lake the clatter of an anchored sloop's capstan, the echoed voices of her crew, mingled with the crazy laughter of a loon.

To these drowsy sounds of awakening day Sam added the dip and drip of his paddle, as with head above the mist that wreathed the canoe he shaped his easy course across the shallow head of the bay. Then he entered the stream's gateway, gorgeous with the autumnal colors of the water maples. Looking around and backward, he could imagine himself in the solitude of the primeval wilderness, for there was no visible sign of man's intrusion on the wooded banks at either side, nor on the silent lake, nor on the rugged crags of Split Rock Mountain, and these were the bounds of vision.

A few rods up stream the illusion was dispelled where the cleared bank opened to an old pasture. The turf was cut with wheel tracks of wagons that had brought apples to the Canadian boat, signs of her recent presence that set Sam wondering how it fared with her contraband freight.

Passing the next bend, he was between wooded shores, where ferns and other moisture-loving plants crowded each other in rampant growth. Ducks frequently arose before him, singly and in flocks, taking wing from the water or jutting logs, out of range before he discovered them or could bring his unready gun to bear on them. He saw that shots were only to be got by prowling along on foot, and ran in behind a little island that hugged the left bank. It was crowded with great trees ; most conspicuous among them was a towering elm and an immense buttonwood, whose trunk shone unearthly white amid the forest shadows, like the ghost of a giant, and all were embowered in a tangle of wild grapevines.

As Sam stepped on shore he caught a glimpse through the treetops of a flock of ducks whistling with lowering flight toward some spot below him and back from the stream. Thither he cautiously made his way and presently saw an open space among the trees, toward which he made a stealthy approach under cover of a clump of alders. When he reached this he discovered a narrow lagoon lying close before him. It was some twenty rods in length, bordered by a growth of wild rice and covered with duck weed. A great branchless tree lay lengthwise of it at the nearer end, an inviting roosting-place for wood ducks, a score of which were occupying it with heads uplifted and alert, or comfortably resting on their mottled breasts or tucked beneath their wings, the males resplendent with bright color, the females shining with gilded bronze, yet all strangely inconspicuous in nature's nice adjustment to their environment, never failing to blend them with the hues of her changing seasons. As many more swam idly to and fro, meshing the green scum of duckweed with a network of watery paths.

If Sam was aware of a qualm of conscience it came too late to withhold him from the unfair chance, and he raked the log with such deadly aim that more than half its happy crew tumbled overboard, killed outright or, in the last extremity, splashed aimlessly, sorely wounded, struggling instinctively toward the cover of the weeds, while the affrighted survivors jostled each other in flurried flight, knowing not what to make of the catastrophe which had befallen their comrades, but wheeled and pivoted in confused wonderment till Sam came forth to secure his victims, when they took flight, yet returned to circle and hover overhead, reluctant to leave a haunt where man so seldom intruded. Another shot fired to secure a cripple served to convince them of its present unsafety, and when Sam bore away his abundant trophies he left the pool as silent and deserted as it is to-day, when it is known to every gunner of this region, and even the poor heron and bittern avoid its precincts.

After depositing the ducks in the canoe and following the bank a little farther, Sam came opposite a landing where a scow was moored and a dugout lay with its nose in the bank. On the level sward a seine was spread and a man was kneeling upon it, busily engaged in mending it. A little boy with hair like sun-burned tow stood watching the net-mender and making frequent proffers of help that were ungraciously refused. The man's inquisitive eyes soon made him aware of Sam's presence, but he made no sign of his discovery except to bawl out without raising his head : —

" Haow d' du, Capt'in Tawmus," and he did not change his position till he had finished the rent he was tying. Then he threw down his netting needle and rising to his feet came to the bank with a peculiar awkward swaggering gait and a swing of the arms that continued after he stood still, like the slowly ceasing vibrations of a pendulum, motions by which Sam recognized an old acquaintance, one of the money diggers of Garden Island.

The child followed the man to the bank, dividing his gaping attention to the stranger with inspection of a cedar fish-pole that was set with its sharpened butt in the bank and supported by a crotched stick at the water's edge. He skipped from one occupation to the other with an awkward agility that seemed to have been acquired in dodging gratuitous cuffs. He drew out his hook, spat upon it, and cast it with such faith and skill of a true angler that Sam's heart warmed to him, the more for his forlornness.

"Why, goodness gracious-Peter-ah!" the man cried in dull surprise, "I took ye tu be Tawmus Baker, an' consequently I called you Captain Tawmus. Haow's your folks-ah? Crops tol'able good? I do' know's I c'n call your name. What is 't when you 're tu hum, anyway-ah?"

Sam gave him the desired information and he continued : —

"You don't say! A-huntin' ducks, be ye? Wal, you won't git none. The' ha' none-ah up the crick ner nowheres. I be'n daown the crick myself an' all I got was this 'ere-ah." He took a coot out from the log canoe and held it aloft for Sam's inspection. "I do' know what sort o' critter he is, but I 'm a-goin' tu see haow he 'll eat. I fooled that 'ere duck, sir. He sot right aout in plain sight, but I went a-sploshin' along in the ma'sh an' a-lookin' t' other way, an' made him think I was arter su'thin' else, an' I got right up tu him. Fooled him, I did, by gracious-Peter! The' hain't no use in your a-goin' up the crick ner daown the crick nuther," the man declared, giving meantime no more attention to the presence of his child than he would have done to that of a dog.

"I 'm 'bleeged tu you for tellin' me, but I guess I 'll go 'long up a piece. I kinder want tu see what the crick looks like, an' I don't care no gre't abaout ducks anyway."

"Wal, go and be darned," the other snarled, "but you might jest as well leave your gun-ah. An' you'll come tu a gut o' the ma'sh 'at you can't git acrost-ah."

In spite of such discouraging advice Sam went on with his ready gun in the hollow of his arm, and his thumb and forefinger on hammer and trigger, and a watchful eye on the stream as each bend unfolded a new reach. He crossed the formidable gut at one stride, and at the next turn came to a long westward reach down which the rising sun shone full in his face, dazzling him with level beams that sheeted the rippling water with a sun glade of wrinkled gold, and glorified the mist with more and brighter colors than the rainbow bears, all minutely mirrored in the innumerable drops that beaded every twig and bejeweled every leaf.

Shading his eyes with his hand, he searched the resplendent reach to its farther end, and there discovered a figure skulking swiftly along the bank. The form and motion, though revealed but in glimpses, were unmistakably those of his late interlocutor, whose purpose of forestalling Sam was easily guessed.

"Wal, go and be darned," said Sam, quoting the man's ungracious godspeed with a chuckle. "I guess I'll lay low right here a spell."

A group of lusty basswoods, sprung from the mouldering parent tree, overhung the bank with a drooping spread of branches, and Sam crept beneath the leafy tent, stretching himself on the green sward to wait at ease for what might come to him. The monotonous babble of a shallow rapid not far above him, and the softer irregular swirl of deeper water around a half-sunken log near at hand, were the loudest sounds that reached his ears for a while, and then the quiet of the morning was broken by an echoing roar, and before the echoes ceased there was a rush of wings, recurring again and again as flock after flock of frightened ducks came hurrying past, unseen but in fleeting glimpses through openings in the branches. At last there was a clattering splash of an alighting flock, and in a few moments he discovered them swimming down stream toward him. When they came near enough he fired into the thick of them, with a result that would have sickened with envy the heart of his rival had he beheld it. Six ducks lay feebly beating the water with their wings, or clawing the air with upturned paddles, and a seventh dived and fluttered down stream in a futile attempt to escape, till Sam reloaded his gun and ended its struggles.

Then with the aid of a pole he gathered in the game and again retired to his ambuscade. Laying his loaded gun within easy reach, he sat down to the enjoyment of a comfortable smoke, idly watch-

ing the patch of water gliding past him, tangling
in its eddies the quivering reflections of the other
shore with floating frost-painted leaves, some waterlogged with far voyaging, others newly launched
and buoyant, sailing across the current in wafts of
the breeze till stranded on the bank or swept on-
ward in the stronger current.

Then as silently, but more swiftly and suddenly,
and scarcely less gayly colored than the drifting
leaves, a flock of wood ducks swam into the narrow
arena. After tacking up stream a moment to inspect an evidently favorite resort, they crept in on
to a willowy sand spit that jutted down stream and
formed a tiny cove almost beneath Sam's hiding-
place. Instinctively he stretched his hand toward
his gun, but withheld it as he became more interested in watching the unsuspicious birds crowding
and jostling each other for the best places, then
one after another standing upright and shaking
out their wings, then settling down and preening
their plumage. They were so near him that he
could see the flash of their bright eyes, the red and
olive markings on the drakes' bills, the colors of
their crests, and almost count the arrow-shaped
spots on their breasts.

"By the gre't horn spoon!" he whispered to
himself, "they 're tew harnsome tu spile, an'
they 're so clust tu, I sh'll knock 'em all tu flinders.
I 've got 'nough anyway, seven here an' 'leven in

the canew, so what 's the good o' murderin'?　But
they be turrible temptin'."

Just then he caught sight of the money digger
at the bend above.　It was evident that he saw the
ducks, for he stopped a moment, then cautiously
backed away and began a wide détour to reach a
point opposite them.　Sam drew a stout piece of a
fallen limb to him, carefully balanced it in his
hand, and then watched intently the crest of the
other bank.　After a considerable time the crown
of an unkempt head slowly arose from behind a
log of driftwood stranded among the trees in the
spring freshet, and then a pair of eyes slowly scanning the shore till they fixed on the object of their
search, then sank out of sight, then reappeared
behind the rusty barrel of a slowly leveled musket.

As Sam saw a brawny hand reaching out to
cock the clumsy hammer after assured aim, and
wondered that the audible double click did not
alarm the ducks, he threw the club at them.　Before the hurtling missile splashed in the margin of
the sand spit the ducks sprang into the air, uttering
quavering *wee-uks, wee-uks* of alarm.

For a moment the musket held to its blank aim,
then was uplifted as the disappointed gunner
slowly arose to his feet and came out upon the
bank, craning his neck up stream and down stream
to discover the cause of the mischance, till at last
he drawled : —

"What in all smutteration scairt them 'ere ducks-ah?" and then after vainly waiting for an answer, "Gol dum the tarnal luck."

Shaking with smothered laughter, Sam watched the man vent his disappointment in stamping and fuming, till at last he saw him depart, bearing a couple of ducks, the sole trophies of his stolen march.

Sam resumed his exploration of the stream, and after coming to a great raft of driftwood that bridged it he discovered another little lagoon in the edge of the narrow intervale, so close to the level upland that it was shaded by its hemlocks, and ducks and partridges were near neighbors, each in their favorite haunts.

Then he came to banks clad with willows, and they in turn with wild grapevines, purple underneath with clusters of frost-ripened fruit. Out of one of these wild bowers a partridge and a wood duck took sudden flight from their interrupted feast, one making for the woods, the other for the water. Sam tumbled the duck back among the willows by a snap shot that he was prouder of than of those which had given much greater scores.

The next bend of the stream disclosed the majestic peak of Camel's Hump through the vista of a willowy bank and a pine-crowned knoll, and when the hunter had warmed his heart with a long look at the grandest of his beloved mountains he turned back, for the landscape was beginning to show more farmsteads than woods.

The way back over a path once traveled seemed so long that Sam had been expecting to come upon the bowery island for some time before he caught sight of its ghostly guardian buttonwood shining afar off through the shadows of the water maples. He was about to shorten the way by a cut across the bend when he heard the agonized scream of a child. It apparently came from the landing, and he bent his steps that way with a premonition that help was needed.

He was running at top speed when he came to the place and at a glance saw the dugout adrift slowly rocking on the agitated water with a cedar fish-pole floating near it. With eyes intent on the water he dropped his burdens and threw off hat and coat and waistcoat.

In the same instant a scared little face and a pair of clutching hands broke the surface. Making a long leap, Sam plunged and found himself not beyond his depth, but so near it that he could swim faster than he could wade, and a few strokes brought him within reach of the child. He caught him by the hair and bore him to the shore.

The little fellow had life enough in him to impede his rescuer with wild clutches and to cling desperately at the grassy margin when he was brought within reach of it, so that when Sam had dragged his own waterlogged self up the steep, slippery bank he had less trouble in pulling the boy up it than in bringing him to it.

The poor little fellow had not much breath to spare, but plenty of water, to rid him of which Sam laid him across a log and gently rolled him from side to side, his patient moaning and crying feebly between fits of strangling.

When he had recovered speech and natural breathing and a disposition to cry continually, Sam took him up tenderly in his arms and carried him toward the house, which stood a quarter of a mile away behind a straggling orchard, whose unpruned lichened trees were as old, forlorn, and neglected as the weather-beaten house and ruinous barn.

" Haow old be ye ? " Sam began, catechizing his charge.

" Seben, goin' on eight."

" Haow come ye in the crik ? "

" Fishin'," was the laconic response, and then with sudden interest the child added, " Say-ah, 'd ye git my fish-pole ? "

" No, I had all I wanted tu git you."

" Wal, you 'd ortu git it.   The' 's an ol' roncher on it-ah.   Pulled me right in.   They 'll lick me for losin' on 't, ah," the boy whimpered.

" No, they won't, nuther.   Don't you worry, they 'll be glad 'nough tu git you.   Naow, you look a-here.   You 're tew leetle a feller tu go fishin' alone.   Your father 'd ortu known better 'n tu left ye.   The' won't allers be somebody raoun' tu pull you out.   Don't ye go again.   Naow, don't fergit."   Sam gave him a gentle shake to emphasize his injunction, and the boy nodded assent. Then discovering they were drawing near the house he struggled to get down.

"You lemme go," he whimpered, "I wanter go an' dry me.   Marm 'll lick me for gittin' wet."

"By the gre't horn spoon! if she does I 'll draowned the hull fam'ly.   Haow many on 'em is the'?   Wal, nev' mind, you keep quiet," Sam added, guessing the computation was beyond so young a head, when he saw a full half-dozen tow-thatched heads swarming out of the door to stare at him a moment and then vanish as suddenly as a litter of frightened woodchucks.

A gaunt, unkempt woman appeared, shading her inquiring eyes and blank, wondering face with both hands till she recognized the visitor's dripping burden.   Then her face grew white with terror and she wailed out with her hands piteously outstretched : —

"Oh, Joby 's draounded!   Oh, dear! oh, dear!"

"No, he hain't draounded, marm," Sam declared in a cheery voice, "but he 's almightedly soaked an' you 'd better dry him off an' put him tu bed."

Her face became a little less woeful, yet she would not be assured, but cried out : —

“ Oh, Joby, hain’t you draownded ? ”

“ No, marm, I hain’t,” the boy answered feebly.

“ Yis, you be tew draounded,” she protested.

The children gathered behind her in an awed semicircle that broke to let Sam and their mother pass in, and closed in again in their rear, while he kicked a rocking-chair to a place by the stove, motioned her by a nod to be seated in it, and put the child in her lap.

“ You take off his wet clo’s an’ put him tu bed,” he commanded, “ an’ I ’ll roust up the fire,” and while she began to obey him he fed the cracked old rotary stove with an armful of wood.

“ Sis, you run aout an’ git a han’ful o’ catnip an’ steep it up in a tin o’ b’ilin’ water,” he said to a girl of twelve who stood staring at him in abashed amazement, then addressing the mother, who was struggling with the clinging ragged garments : “ You give him a good lot on ’t, hot as he c’n take it.”

After seeing the catnip tea a-brewing, Sam went to the barn and took off and wrung out his clothes, affording an interesting spectacle to three of the boys who followed and watched him through the half-open door till he dispersed them by throwing one of his boots at them.

When he returned to the house, shivering, but no longer dribbling a trail by which he could be traced, he found his late audience of the barn giggling in safe retreat behind the stove, the patient in bed, and his mother administering doses of hot catnip tea, with the comforting assurance that " he 'd ketch it when his pa got hum."

" I don't care," poor Joby whimpered under the blankets; " I wan't a mite tu blame. I got holt of a ol' roncher an' he yanked me in, so naow. I wish I 'd got him. He was a ol' roncher." And he began to cry piteously over the loss of the fish and the impending chastisement.

" There, there, bub, don't ye take on," said Sam, shivering over the stove. " If your fish hain't le' go when I git back there, I 'll haul him aout and lay him on the bank for ye, an' your pa won't tech ye, I know. It 's bad 'nough tu git draounded 'thaout bein' licked for it. Boo! it 's consid'able cool bathin' this time o' year ! "

" Why, you be cold, hain't ye ? " the woman said. " I was so took up wi' Joby I never thought. Won't ye hev ye some sperits ? We hain't a drop in the haouse, but won't ye hev some ? The' 's some camfire ; that 'ould kinder warm ye. It 's warmin'."

Sam declined the spirits that were not and the camphor that was.

" You need n't think I hain't obleeged if I hain't said so," the woman said, looking more gratitude than her words expressed, as she followed him to the door. " If his brother was here I 'd tell your fortin' an' not charge ye nothin'. His brother gives me the influence. I hev secont sight."

" You 'd ort tu hev looked fur enough ahead tu kep' your boy from tumblin' int' the crik," Sam said as he left her, and she called after him : —

" Wal, I foreseen he was a-goin' tu git draounded, an' I 've said so all summer."

Sam warmed himself with a run to the landing, where he had the luck to find the dugout stranded on that side. He picked up the boy's pole with a big pickerel fast to the line, and leaving it conspicuously displayed on the bank, crossed the stream. When he had rescued the child he noticed the scow and seine were gone, and concluded that the owner was seeking for better luck in fishing than in duck hunting. He picked up his things, and was soon afloat in his own canoe.

As silently as the outsped current the canoe glided down stream, and Sam with eyes constantly alert scanned banks and water without discovering anything worthy of note till, upon rounding a bend, he found himself close beside a man kneeling by a hollow log on the verge of the bank. It was the negro Jim, who, as the bow of the canoe slid noiselessly into his field of vision, turned a startled face toward Sam.

" Good Lord, Mr. Lovel, haow you did scare me!" he exclaimed with emphatic jerks of his head. " You 'pear tu be allus a-scarin' of me!

My Lord, haow you did scare me that night."
He laughed as if at the recollection of an excellent
joke, then became suddenly serious. "But 't wan't
nothin' to what come arter! No, sir!" He
dropped his voice to a lower but no less emphatic
tone and came nearer Sam, who held the canoe by
an overhanging bough. "'Baout half an haour
arter I come back four fellers come a-r'arin int' the
ol' shanty, lookin' arter Bob. Yes, sir! 'Where's
that nigger you be'n hidin'? Where's that nigger?'
'No niggers here but what belongs here," says I;
'me an' Nancy an' the young un, an' them's as
many as I can 'tend tu.' But no, I was all sorts
of a lyin' nigger, an' they knowed I'd got him hid,
an' through the haouse they went, up stairs an'
daown, an' under the bed an' int' the butt'ry; but
nary Bob nowheres, an' mighty good for some o'
their healths 'at the' wan't naow, I tell you. One
spell they'd cuss an' 'nuther spell they'd coax, but
ary way they could n't make me know nothin', an'
bimeby they cleared aout, an' you'd better b'lieve
I wan't sorry; no, sir, not one mite. An' I tell
you what, Mr. Lovel, I don't want no more o' my
Southern relations tu come a-visitin' on me; no sir!
They're tew interestin' tu white folks! Nancy an'
the young un is all the darkies I want tu bother
my brains with."

"You hain't heared nothin' but what he got
away all right?" Sam asked.

"Mr. Bartlett thinks he did, sure, an' he says that nigger hunter 's gin it up an' cleared aout. I guess Bob 's shakin' his heels in Canerdy by this time, don't you, Mr. Lovel?"

"I hope so," said Sam, and then with professional interest in the other's evident employment, "Hain't it middlin' airly for trappin' mink?"

"I reckon they 'll du me more good naow 'n they will if somebody else gits 'em by 'm by," Jim said, with repeated and decided jerks of the head.

"Wal, they hain't my mink," said Sam, loosing his hold of the branch and letting the canoe drift away. "Ta' care of your relations when they happen along."

"Yes, sir, Mr. Lovel, I will, sartain, but I don't want tu see none of 'em, no, sir," and chuckling and wagging his head he resumed the setting of the trap as Sam drove the canoe on its course.

A smart breeze ruffled the green water of the bay with waves that flashed like fire in the broad glade of the low sun and flecked the far blue of the lake with leaping whitecaps as the canoe slid over the long undulations of the shallows toward her port.

A flock of golden eyes took flight before her, their wing-beats ringing like the quick clangor of tiny bells, and flocks of teal and dusky ducks whistled past, coming in early on the favoring breeze from their day's outing on the lake. One by one a company of herons forsook the shallows beneath the cliffs and sagged on slow vans toward the woods of Little Otter, and high above all an eagle made stately progress through his aerial realm. The wash of waves was left behind when the canoe entered the creek, and presently it slipped in at the landing, where Sam found his friends already returned and awaiting his coming.

CHAPTER XXI.

AN INLAND EXPLORATION.

Of the remaining inmates of the tent Uncle Lisha was the first to arise, for after threescore years of partial disproof he was still a believer in the maxim that inculcates the benefits of early rising. He lighted the fire and made a trip to the waterside, returning therefrom in the glow of recent ablution and the exertion of lugging a pail of water up the steep path before his companions came stumbling forth, yawning and blinking in the secondary stage of reviving consciousness.

"Bah gosh! Onc' Lasha, Ah guess you 'll was try for ketch nudder waum dis morny, ant it, hein?" Antoine asked, rubbing his eyes with one hand and searching his pockets for his pipe with the other.

"If you an' the worm ever meets, he 'll haftu du the s'archin'. Come, Ann Twine, le' 's git us suthin' t' eat time 'nough tu call it breakfus stid o' dinner. You an' Jozeff go an' wash ye whilst I git the taters on. What is 't this mornin', duck or fish?"

" Feesh was de quickes', 'cause he all ready for jomp on de pan."

" An' best, seem 's 'ough, arter duck so contin'al? " said Joseph. " I 'm kinder thinkin' ducks would n't be much 'caount if 't wan't for the feathers, that is, for a stiddy thing. But I du lufter shoot 'em, though."

" I should like tu know haow you know you du," said Uncle Lisha, counting out the potatoes from the sack. " Three for Ann Twine — come, hyper, an' when you git back I 'll tell ye what we 'll du tu-day — tew for Jozeff, an' one for me."

In due time the fish was fried, the potatoes boiled, the tea brewed, and the little company gathered around the stone table.

" What I was a-cal'latin' was," Uncle Lisha began, and then deferred speech while he cooled the tea in his tin cup with a gusty blast accompanied by a vigorous shake, " 'at we 'd take a rantomscoot over west tu where we was stationed time o' the war. I kinder want tu see the place ag'in, an' it 'ould be interestin' tu you an' Ann Twine, an' we c'n take aour guns along an' mebby shoot suthin' 'nother, an' a bag, an' pick up some wa'nuts, which they 'd be a proper good treat tu the folks up hum. What d' ye say to it — 'mongst ye? "

" Ah 'll ant want for go feeshin's, an' Ah 'll ant want for go hunt on de crik, an' Ah 'll willin' for go loafer 'long to you, Onc' Lasha."

" Most anything 'll suit me," said Joseph, " if it hain't goin' in a boat, which it don't seem as 'ough I would du under no circumstances exceptin' in the case of a reg'lar ol' Noer flood, an' then I b'lieve I 'd climb the last tree 'fore I 'd trust myself tu any tarnal boat, he or she, smaller 'n the ark or a steamboat, which I do' know nothin' 'baout, or leastways a canawl boat, 'at I hev ventured ontu."

So, being of one mind, when breakfast was eaten and the act by courtesy called dishwashing had been performed, they set forth westward across the fields and by the woodside, where ferns and asters invaded the grass land, and the timothy and clover crept into the shadow of the woods. As, advancing abreast, they climbed a knoll and their heads arose above its crest, Antoine's quick eye caught sight of a gray squirrel running from the woods to an outlying hickory.

" S-s-h !" Antoine whispered, " go softle till he gat on de tree, den we supprise him an' kill it."

These tactics were successfully carried out as far as the surprise, but the beleaguered squirrel hid so closely among the topmost leaves that the besiegers were unable to discover it. A random shot was fired into the thickest bunch of leaves, and the frightened squirrel sprang to the ground. Recovering in an instant from the shock of the desperate leap, it scudded away to the cover of the woods at a rate that defied the pottering aim of two guns, and their futile charges raked the turf far in its rear. Of course the event reminded Antoine of one man in Canada whose adventure he proceeded to relate, while the others, crawling on their hands and knees, gathered the fallen nuts.

"You see, seh, boy, he 'll was huntin' jus' sem lak we was, honly he was hunt for bear an' he was 'lone, jus' one poor leetly Frenchmans 'stid of two fat hol' Yankee an' one big hugly Frenchmans. Wal, seh, he foller bear tracks where it go in hole, an' he 'll was si' do'n for wait of it come off de hole so he can shot it. W'en he 'll set t'ree, prob'ly two naour, he beegin for gat dry, an' he stan' up hees gaun gin tree an' go on de brook for drink, an', seh, de bear happen for gat dry too, an' it come off de hole an' gat raght 'tween de mans an' de gaun, bah gosh! An' dat mans he 'll had for run home an' lef' hees gaun. What you t'ink for dat, hein? But dat ant so funny lak 'nudder man Canada. He was gat bag jus' sem we was, honly grea' deal more bigger, an' "—

"Oh, shet your head, Ann Twine. You 'd a dumb sight better be a-pickin' up wa'nuts 'an tu stan' there a-makin' up lies."

"Dat jus' what Ah 'll was goin' for do, but you an' Zhozeff gat it all pick up. Dat was too bad! Hoorah, le 's go scare some more squirly."

Going forward, they soon came to the head of the bay, which was memorable as the scene of

Uncle Lisha's and Joseph's first duck shooting. To-day its only visible occupant was a solitary heron so slowly wading the glassy shallows that he scarcely broke the perfect contour of his mirrored semblance. He was in long range of a clump of cedars, under cover of which Antoine made a stealthy approach, and was just on the point of firing when he was discovered by the wary heron, who launched himself upon the air in a long upward slant of labored flight. Antoine followed him with uncertain aim, and only pulled trigger when the bird was hopelessly out of range and a hundred feet above the lake. But to the wonder of the three beholders, as the shot whistled past the heron he turned a half somersault, and with beak back drawn for a stroke came tumbling and sprawling downward in apparent helplessness. Antoine raised a shout of triumph, Joseph began to congratulate himself on a handsome addition to his stock of feathers, and Uncle Lisha had already upon his lips a rebuke for the wanton destruction of a harmless and worthless bird, when to his delight, the others' disgust, and the amazement of all, the heron was seen to recover himself after a tumble of twenty feet and resume his even flight. The sudden terror that seized him, when to his ears the whistle of the hurtling shot was the rush of an eagle's pinions, was relieved when he saw no foe above him to repel, and with regular wing-beats he climbed the long incline of retreat, till indrawn neck, broad vans, and trailing legs were blurred in a wavering speck of gray that vanished behind a cedar-crowned headland.

"Bah gosh," Antoine ejaculated, recovering speech and suspended respiration, "what yo' s'pose mek dat feller git over be keel so quick, hein?"

"I 'm dumb glad on 't, Ann Twine. What d' ye w'ntu pester that poor ol' lunsome crane for? He ain't wuth the paowder you burnt, an' don't trouble nob'dy."

"Seem 's 'ough he kerried off a mess o' feathers 'at I 'd ortu had," Joseph sighed.

"Ah 'll bet you head he 's gone off for die."

"Of ol' age, I hope," said Uncle Lisha.

Going a little farther, they came to a small rock-walled cove, where a rude fireplace and an inverted washtub gave evidence of a family washing place. Here they sat down to enjoy a restful smoke. They were aroused from their reverie by shrill outcries of distress arising from a little distance, and hastening forward through the fringe of woods to learn the cause, they discovered a girl of ten or eleven years with a younger child on a great pine stump in the middle of the field, where they were besieged by a gaunt old ram, who, uttering hoarse bleats, made frequent circuits of the tower of refuge, which now and then he butted with blows that sounded like the strokes of a beetle.

Uncle Lisha and his party advanced to the rescue with loud shouts, which at once attracted the attention of the ram, but did not daunt him in the least, for no sooner did he find himself threatened by an attack in the rear than he charged upon his assailants so fiercely that Joseph and Antoine fled with all speed to the shelter of the woods, whither the ram followed in hot pursuit. Antoine climbed nimbly up a low-branched tree, while Joseph sought refuge in a thicket of cedars, wherein he was assisted, as he scrambled on all fours, by a blow that drove him into the evergreen curtain quite out of sight of his pursuer.

Having routed the main body, the doughty champion turned and charged upon Uncle Lisha, who, as unable as he was indisposed to run from an enemy, still held forward to the rescue of the children. He had almost reached them when the elder child cried out in great alarm, —

"Oh, look out. Look out, mister, he 'll hit ye. Oh, dear."

As Uncle Lisha faced about, his antagonist was close upon him, coming at full speed with lowered head and assured aim, but the old man stepped aside and dexterously caught the ram by one horn as he passed. The sheep made vicious sidewise thrusts and struggled desperately for liberty, and though his captor was made to take some unusually lively steps his hold could not be loosened.

"Say, sissy," Uncle Lisha called in broken words and sentences, "you git daown — consarn yer ol' picter — an' fetch me a club er a — Oh, you won't git away erless your horn comes off — stun an' I'll give him all the hommerin' he wants. You dasn't? Wal, then, you an' bubby git daown an' clipper fer the fence. I won' let the ol' torment git away. Clipper, naow. Ann Twine! Jozeff! Come 'ere an' fetch me a club er a stun. Oh, you plaguey fraid-cats. I wish 't I c'ld sick him ontu ye. I'd let him drive ye int' the lake, I swan I would."

"Seems 's 'ough you might kinder tie his laigs, Uncle Lisher," Joseph suggested, venturing to peep from his hiding-place.

"Tie yer granny! I don't kerry ropes raound wi' me."

"Put it on de bag, Onc' Lisha, an' tie de bag," Antoine shouted.

"Fetch me the bag and I swan I will," Uncle Lisha responded.

"It bes' was you hol' him hees hin' leg of it an' Ah 'll shot it, bah gosh!" Antoine now proposed.

"Honh! You want tu pay for him? Well, I hain't a buyin' mutton. Oh, you dumb slinks! You hain't spunk 'nough tu break up a settin' hen! Come along here, you tarnal ol' sarpent," and despairing of receiving aid, Uncle Lisha led his captive about the field while he searched for a suitable weapon. This he found at last in the form of a good-sized stone, wherewith he belabored the ram's nose till the fight was quite taken out of him and his only desire was to escape. When this became evident to Uncle Lisha he released his prisoner, who made a speedy retreat for a short distance and then partly turned about as if with some intention of renewing hostilities. The old man hurled the stone with such true aim that it struck him full on the ribs, knocking the breath out of him with the last vestige of valor, and he retreated on the ends of his toes, with his back humped and his head violently shaken, and his stumpy tail wiggling till it imparted a tremor to his whole body.

"There, dumb yer ol' Meriner picter, hev ye got 'nough on 't?" Uncle Lisha shouted, while his victory was cheered with cries of delight by the children, who had watched the progress of the battle through the rails of the fence, and by Joseph and Antoine with more discreet celebration, less likely to attract the attention of the ram.

"I guess you might ventur' aout here naow," Uncle Lisha called as the two men edged along the border of the woods, and he picked up the gun which he had dropped at the beginning of the encounter. "Oh, I 'm 'shamed on ye," he continued when with frequent backward glances they rejoined him and led the way toward the fence. "Tew

gre't growed-up men afeared of a poor, insi'nificant sheep."

" Wal, seh, Onc' Lasha, Ah 'll goin' tol' you,
Ah 'll ant was be 'fraid of it, but Ah 'll know 'f
Ah 'll was gat mad, Ah 'll keel it, me, an' Ah 'll
ant want it for pay it.   Ah 'll glad Ah 'll ant gat
mad. But Ah 'll mos' was w'en, Ah 'll up dat tree."

" Wal, I never had no knack o' gittin' along wi'
sheep, never seemed 's 'ough I hed," said Joseph.
" I could n't never drive 'em ner call 'em. Don't
you cal'late they be turrible contr'y critters, Uncle
Lisher ? "

The victorious champion vouchsafed no answer
but a contemptuous snort, and now that the fence
was crossed took the lead in the direction of a ram-
bling old gray farmhouse whither the children had
gone.

"That 'ere 's the haouse where aour officers got
the' put-up-punce," he said, presently recovering
his usual tranquillity of temper. " We common
folks slep' in the buildin's when we wan't aout on
the P'int. We 'll g' aout there w'en I git me a
drink, for it 's turrible sightly. The' use' tu be a
good well o' water here twenty-five year ago, an' if
it 's here yit I want some on 't, for I got consid'-
able he't up tusslin' wi' that ol' rip."

As they approached the house a comely young
matron came to the open kitchen door, welcoming
them with a pleasant smile and a cheery voice,

while her keen eyes made a quick but comprehensive survey of the group.

"Good-mornin', gentlemen. You're the ones
'at drove that cross ol' buck away from the children?"

"Yes, ma'am," said Antoine, coming to the
front with his politest manners; "we was be de
zhontemans."

But Joseph had not the effrontery to claim
much of the glory for himself and Antoine, and
said, jerking his thumb toward Uncle Lisha, "He
done most on 't, ma'am. Ye see, he kind o' seemed
tu hev the fust chance, an' so he took it."

"Yes, I know," the young woman said, growing red in the face with suppressed laughter;
"Janey here told me all about it," and the little
girl retired from view behind her mother, who continued addressing Uncle Lisha. "I'm dreffly
obleeged tu you, sir. But set your guns in the
shed an' come right in, all of you, an' have a fried
cake an' some cider."

"Thank you, marm, I guess we won't go in,"
said Uncle Lisha; "but I wouldn't go ag'in a nut
cake, for I hain't seen one for a week, and I be
turrible dry, which fetched me here; but you
needn't put yourself aout tu git cider, water's
good 'nough for us."

"'T ain't no trouble," and the woman bustled in,
closely followed by the children, and returned with

a heaped pan of doughnuts, fresh and hot from the kettle. "Naow jest help yourselves whilst I go an' draw some cider."

"Don't ye," Uncle Lisha expostulated, "water's plenty good enough for us."

But the hospitality of their hostess was not to be restrained, and she presently brought a brimming pitcher of cider, to the great satisfaction of two of the party.

"I 'm afeared these fried cakes hes soaked fat," she said, breaking one and examining it critically when her guests were served. "They be fat-soaked," she declared in a grieved tone, "but mebby they 'll go better 'n none, if you hain't had none lately."

"Queen Victory couldn't make no better," Uncle Lisha declared, "nor yit the President's wife, an' I da' say nary one on 'em gits so good, for I s'pose likely they depends on hired gals tu make 'em." And his companions heartily seconded the praise.

"It looks consid'able nat'ral raound here," he said, as his eyes roved over the old house and its surroundings, "on'y jest a leetle older 'n it was twenty-five, mebby thirty year ago — time o' the war, anyway — when I was here 'long wi' the m'lishy."

"You don't say!" his hostess cried. "Why, I can jest remember a-seein' the soldiers here all raound, an' haow scairt I was! My!"

" It hain't posscrble! You don't look as if you could ha' be'n borned then," Uncle Lisha gallantly declared.

" Wal, I was then," she answered with a pleased little laugh, " an' I remember seein' the soldiers here an' the British boats 'way acrost the lake an' hearin' the cannons firin' over tu the P'int." And so the two fell to telling of scenes that had been impressed distinctly on the memory of one in the prime of manhood, and no less so on the infantile mind of the other.

" Wal, we shall haftu be a-goin'," Uncle Lisha said, turning away reluctantly, " I want tu take these men aout ont' the P'int here where they can see the broad lake."

" An' you want to go to the landin'. It 's got tu be quite a place, with a hoss boat a-runnin' on the ferry to Grog Harbor."

" A hoss boat? You don't say! Wal, that 's suthin' I never did see, ner these men nuther, I 'll warrant. We 're a thaousand times obleeged tu ye for the nutcakes an' cider, marm."

" An' so be I tu you," said she heartily. " I tell aour folks they 'd ortu kill that ol' torment. He 's treed me oncte, an' naow I take a club when I go where he is ; but aour folks say he ain't cross, on'y jest notional."

" Darn sech notions," said Joseph, caressing his recent bruises ; " I wish 't he 'd got 'em aouten his head 'fore I met him."

" Why, Jozeff, you did n't exactly meet him, he kind o' overtook ye," said the old man, with a merry twinkle in his eye. " Wal, good-day, marm; " and they strolled away to the woods and the end of the point where the sheer wall bears its green crown of cedar high above the lake.

The broad bay lay before them, and beyond the bold promontories of Thompson's Point and Split Rock the broader lake stretched far north to reach the sky. The lake was ruffled by a northerly breeze, and the white sails of the sloops and schooners running before it, or beating against it, gleamed against blue waves and sky, but among them all not one such imposing tower of canvas as Uncle Lisha had seen when the British brigs were swooping down on their expected prey.

" Why, they looked julluk meetin' haousen, a-comin' over the water, an' the gunboats swarmin' raound 'em looked sassy, I tell ye. I s'pose aour folks was afeared they might land a mess o' sojers here an' go over cross lots tu where aour ships lay in t' other crik an' destr'y 'em, an' that 's why we was posted here. But they never come a-nigh us an' kep' right on to where the' was a good lickin' a-waitin' for 'em, an' they got it, tew."

When Joseph had crept to the verge of the cliff and ventured one brief glance downward where the waves chuckled wickedly in the low-roofed caves, he was ready to go, and they wended their way to the ferry just in time to see the horse boat come splashing into port, the four horses plodding their unprogressive journey on the revolving wheel, whose foothold always slid away beneath and behind them, and continually returned in a perpetual round of monotony.

A drove of cattle in the first day of their long journey on the hoof to Boston markets crowded the deck with their drivers and a few other passengers, while the captain steered his craft in austere silence till he shouted " Whoa " to his crew, who was the driver of the horses and passed the command to them, whereat they stood still and the boat surged up to the wharf with a bump that jostled all her animate freight and shook some profanity from the lips of her commander.

When the boat was made fast there was a stir of preparation in the group of prospective passengers on the wharf, while the cattle swarmed ashore, urged by their drivers and followed by their other fellow voyagers edging after them, step by step, in slow impatience, and all regarded with impartial interest by the little company of spectators.

These presently turned their attention to a tin-peddler, who was driving his red cart aboard bound on a trading expedition among the foreigners of the other shore. A bunch of brooms stuck upright in the hinder end of it, like the banner of the Dutch admiral, yet emblematic only of a peaceable conquest of housewives' hoarded rags and dried apples, some spoils of which were already gathered in sacks and bales on the roof of the cart. The peddler was a much less important figure in the world than either the sharp-faced wool-buyer or the oily old cheese speculator who now led their horse and buggy aboard, but he and his red cart with its visible proof of traffic were greater objects of interest to the spectators, as was the grizzled old hunter who had outlived the deer of Vermont, and with his gaunt hounds, so long-eared and sad-faced that Uncle Lisha regretted Sam's absence, was on his way to put his long rifle to its old use in the still happy hunting-grounds beyond the lake.

After the ferryboat had waited a while for a possible additional fare, which indeed came at top speed from the door of the stone tavern, the captain gave the order to the crew, the crew cracked his whip and shouted to the horses, who began their stumbling tramp, and the boat paddled off on her course.

As the loungers dribbled away, some to the socialities of the barroom, others to their homes, and the lowing of the cattle and the shouts of the drovers were blended in the distance, Uncle Lisha and his comrades strolled in the direction of the farmhouse.

"I do' know but it's ridin' a free hoss tew fur, but I'm a-goin' tu ask 'em for a pocketful o' them apples 'at 's a-layin' on the ground," the old man said. "Looks 's if the' was more 'n they knowed what tu du with."

" All raght, Onc' Lasha, Ah 'll go on de lake an' wait for you an' Zhozeff, an' mebby Ah 'll shot some dawk." So saying, Antoine skirted the orchard on his way toward the shore while the others went to the house. There they lingered a while to talk with their hostess, and then, their request being cheerfully granted, they filled their pockets with mellow apples and went on to join Antoine.

Their steps were hastened by the roar of his gun, and they found him rejoicing over three plump teal which were the result of the shot. After giving the particulars of the exploit, Antoine shouldered the bag, which had grown plethoric since he left them, and picking up his gun and game, set forth to camp.

" Why, Ann Twine," Uncle Lisha remarked as the Canadian trudged on before him, " you hev be'n spry tu git three ducks an' sech a snag o' wa'nuts sen you left us. You hain't shucked 'em, I know by the bulge on 'em, but it don't seem 's 'ough you 'd ortu took quite so many 'thaout askin'."

" Was Ah 'll ask it de squirly ? He was all de one gat it," was the laconic answer.

Arriving at camp without further incident,

Antoine flung down his burden with a sigh of relief, exclaiming as he straightened his shoulders : —

"Bah gosh, dat happle pooty heavy for carry ! "

"Apples ? " Uncle Lisha repeated in surprise. "Is them apples ? Where on airth did you git 'em ? "

"Wal, seh, Onc' Lasha," said Antoine, with an air of supreme satisfaction, "Ah 'll was peck it up while you was ask for it. Ah 'll t'ink dat was save tam prob'ly, an' if dey 'll ant give it, dat was save de happle. Hein, Onc' Lisha ? "

"So you went an' stole them folkses apples," cried the old man indignantly. "You tarnal mean, mis'able creetur, I 'm a good min' tu make ye kerry 'em right stret back. I be, I swan ! "

"Ah 'll can' do it, Onc' Lasha ; Ah 'll too tire, me. But if you 'll want for carry it, Ah 'll was help you load it on you back."

"Ann Twine," Uncle Lisha roared with kindling wrath, "you pick up them apples an' kerry 'em stret back where you got 'em, or I 'll shake ye aouten yer boots ! " and the flash of fire in the gray eyes implied certain execution of the threat.

Antoine at once swung the bag up on his shoulder and started off with it in sullen silence. It is probable that he went no further than fairly out of sight, and then emptying its ill-gotten contents spent the hour of his supposed journey in a comfortable nap; but Uncle Lisha's conscience was relieved.

The remainder of the day was spent in idling about camp, till at sundown the party repaired to the landing to watch for Sam's return.

CHAPTER XXII.

"Wal, here you be, boy," said Uncle Lisha, "an' I 'm glad tu see ye, for it 's a-gittin' consid'able ca'julluky aout yender for your milkweed pod. Good airth an' seas! What a snag o' ducks you got! Sixteen, sebenteen, eighteen, nineteen! Yes, sir; nineteen! Jullook o' there, Ann Twine; he 's skunked the hull caboodle on us! Le' me see, you got three, an' me an' Jozeff — wal, we hain't caounted aourn yit."

"Pooh, dat ant notings!" said Antoine, contemptuously poking the pile of ducks with his toe. "Ant he 'll gat honly nanteen dawk in dat crik all to hese'f? Dat ant much for do, an' what lectly feller dey was! One tam w'en Ah 'll leeve in Canada Ah 'll keel forty wid club; yes, seh, an' dey was gre't beeg feller. Yes, seh, dey was geeses."

"Sho, Ann Twine, I guess they was in the aig."

"No, seh, dey was in Canada, sem Ah 'll tol' you, an' if you 'll ant b'lieved me Ah 'll goin' tol' you de trute. You see de way of it, he come on

stubbly graoun' for pick de hoat was jus' sow, an'
he steek hees foot on de mud so he can' pull it, an'
den he froze heem fas' 'cause it mos' winter; so
den Ah 'll ant not'ing for do honly knock hees
head of it."

"What be you a-tellin'?" Uncle Lisha groaned.
"Oats jes' sowed on stubble in the fall! Du, fer
massy's sake, lie reason'ble if you must lie."

"Oh, Onc' Lasha!" Antoine said, in an injured
tone. "If Ah prove mah storce you 'll ant b'lieved
it. Haow you s'pose mans was goin' for rembler
everyt'ing was happen in hees laftam w'en he
happen so many, hein? It was two tam Ah 'll
keel forty wid stick, one tam in de sprim an' one
tam in de fall! Come, le' 's go on de camp. De
patack was mos' all bile, prob'ly, an' de dawk ready
for cook. Sam, you wan' save dis leetly feller?"
touching the ducks again with a scornful toe.

"Sam Hill," said Joseph, just finding words to
express his admiration. "If that 'ere hain't a
harnsome mess o' feathers. Samwil, if you 'll let
me pick them tu the halves, M'ri 'll be more 'n
willin' 'at I come, or leastways she 'd ort tu be,
seems 's 'ough."

"You c'n hev the hull on 'em tu feather your
nest, for all me," Sam replied, cringing from a
fresh contact with his wet trousers in a way that
attracted Uncle Lisha's attention.

"Why, Samwil," he cried, as he laid a tentative

hand on one of the legs. " You 've be'n in the water. Hes that 'ere mis'able aigshell be'n a spillin' on ye? I allers said it 'ould. I wish 't the dumbed Injin contraption was smashed finer 'n a barn fore it draounds ye."

" It never tipped over wi' me yit," Sam protested. " I went int' the water a purpose."

" A-wadin' arter ducks? You tarnal fool, this time o' year? "

" No, I did n't," Sam answered doggedly.

" Wal, then, what did ye for ? "

" Wal, if you 've got tu know, the' was a leetle chap tumbled int' the crik a-fishin' all alone, an' I hed tu fish him aout, tu keep him from draoundin', an' it nat'rally was sort of a wet job."

" I wan't cal'latin' tu scold ye for no sech a thing, Samwil," Uncle Lisha said in a low voice as he laid his hand on Sam's shoulder, " but you 'd better go an' dry ye off by the fire." And so they all set forth toward the camp, these two leading the way.

As they drew near it they were astonished to hear the unmistakable sound of female voices, and singularly familiar ones. Sam coming first in sight of the place signaled silence and a halt to his companions, who gathered close at his back, and all stood and stared in wonder not unmingled with dismay upon the unexpected invasion of the camp.

Two women were nosing about, turning their

sun-bonnets like telescopes this way and that in diligent inspection of every object, now focusing a common centre of interest, now separately, in search of new diversions and discoveries. These movements were accompanied by remarks which were not very flattering. The faces were indistinct in the depths of the sun-bonnets, but there was no mistaking the forms, motions, and voices of Aunt Jerusha and Huldah.

"I don't b'lieve they've swep' up sence they be'n here," said the first, making a slow inspection of the fireplace and its littered surroundings.

"Swep'?" the other returned sarcastically. "Why, they hain't got so much as a hemlock broom, I warrant ye, which they might easy enough, for jullook at the cedar a-growin' all araound."

"I know it," Aunt Jerusha acquiesced, "jest as good if not full better, not scatterin' itself so bad."

"An' will you look at that 'ere fryin'-pan?" cried Huldah, holding off the utensil with gingerly hands at a distance, yet bringing the muzzle of her bonnet to closer inspection. "I can caount the leavin's o' three cookin's in 't, plain."

"Sam Hill, hain't I glad M'ri hain't here tu see that 'ere," Joseph whispered, "an acre o' feathers would n't caount ag'in leavin' on 't so; wal, mebbe that's settin' on 't high, say half an acre."

"An' see them pertaters. I 'll be baound they 're all b'ilin' tu pieces," cried Aunt Jerusha, fluttering over to the pot and peering into it while she blew away the steam. "Yes, they be, true 's you live. Can't you take 'em off, Huldy?"

" 'T ain't likely there 's no sech a thing as a holder. I da' say they use a bunch o' leaves or a dirty stockin'," said Huldah, rushing to the rescue of the potatoes; "but thank goodness I 've got my apron," and she whisked the kettle off, keeled it and set it by the fire in a trice.

" Or mebby the' hats," Aunt Jerusha suggested, still dwelling on holders. " Jest think on 't, Lisher might ha' fetched his luther apron." And Uncle Lisha gave Sam an appreciative dig in the side with his elbow.

Then the two women backed off a little to take a comprehensive view of the scene, making inquiries and responses of, "Did you ever?" and "No, I never," till they fell into a fit of laughter which they were obliged to sit down to finish, while the spectators made a silent exchange of imbecile grins. When the camp inspectors had exhausted their mirth, they discovered the tent and flew to it. Now their heads were thrust far inside in minute inspection, now withdrawn and the muzzles turned to each other with divers nods and shakes of assent and dissent, accompanied by spasmodic movements of their bodies, all of which gave evidence of invidious remarks and indulgence in unseemly mirth. All this was endured in silence by the spectators of the inquest till the older woman began poking at the contents of the tent with a long stick, when Uncle Lisha could restrain himself no longer, but rushed forward and shouted at the top of his voice:

" Hello, you women; what you duin' in there! "

Thereupon the intruders backed out of the tent, and facing about showed the rightful occupants a far bolder front than they could muster, caught as they were in all unseemly ways of housekeeping.

" Why, Lisher Paiggs, haow du ye du?" cried Aunt Jerusha, beaming upon her husband, and Huldah called out heartily: —

" Haow be ye, Sam, an' all of ye? "

" Good airth an' seas, is that you?" Uncle Lisha shouted. " Why, I thought you was couple o' schoolgals a-snoopin' raound. Wal, seein' you ast, I do' know 's I'm none the better for seein' you, considerin' haow you talk abaout aour haousekeepin'."

" Wal, naow, Lisher, you can't deny but it's a leetle mite thick under the nail," said his wife.

" By gosh, Aunt Jerrushy," cried Antoine, coming to the front, " you was come de wrong day. Dis ant aour day for wash de dish. We jes' daown to de lake for see if dere was waters 'nough for wash to-morry, an' we make off aour min' we got for wait till he rise."

"Haow come ye tu come, anyway?" Uncle Lisha demanded. "Sed daown an' make yourselves tu hum, an' tell us 'baout it," and he waved them hospitably to one of the fireside logs. "Aour gal 'll git tea ready tu rights. Come, Miss Ann Twine, you want tu be gittin' aout your sweetcake an' plum sass an' jell, for we got comp'ny."

"Ah 'll gat all of it in de pettetto keetly, an' de res' of it Ah 'll gat pooty soon," Antoine answered promptly, and began bustling about the fire, heating the frying-pan and scouring it with a stone — as he would never have thought of doing but for the presence of the guests. They eyed his movements, but politely refrained from audible comment. Then seeing the ducks, they fell into a poultry-wives' admiration of them.

"My, I never see sech harnsome ducks," cried Huldah, "an' you got all them sence you come here?"

"Why, I got these tu-day, jes' myself, an' I do' know what the rest on 'em has got," Sam answered, and then Huldah detected the condition of his nether garments, and she took him to task forthwith.

"Why, Sam Lovel, what in this livin' world you be'n a-duin' to your trowses? You be'n wadin' int' the river with 'em? An' the water jest as cold as ice. An' you've be'n a-duin' on 't every day sence you come here an' got the rheumatiz tucked outu ye an' the phthisic an' nob'dy knows what all, jest tu shoot a duck. You 'll ketch your death jest as sure as you live, for a few leetle mis'able ducks. You shan't never come here again, not if I c'n help it. Hain't it a caution. Naow you go intu that tent an' take right off them trowses an' hand 'em aout tu me an' le' me dry 'em an' you cover up in the blankets till they be. I should think you 'd know better an' should n't ha' s'posed Uncle Lisher 'd ha' let ye."

Before Sam could say a word in his own defense he was judged and sentenced, but when Huldah stopped to breathe Uncle Lisha put in a plea for him.

"Naow, Huldy, you quit a-scoldin' on him, for he hain't be'n in the water afore sen' we be'n here, an' he went into 't tu save a leetle boy from draoundin'. I guess that 'ere leetle shaver's mother would n't wanter hev Samwil scolded."

Huldah's voice shook a little, and the look she gave her husband was anything but reproachful as she said : —

"Why, Sam, haow 'd I know? You set ri' daown here by the fire an' dry ye an' tell me all about it. Folks hain't half so apt tu ketch cold if they let the' clo's dry on 'em. Le' me fill your pipe for ye. Did you run a turrible resk? Did he come all right? Haow old was he?"

These and many more questions he was called

upon to answer as he toasted his legs between whiles of keeping them out of Antoine's way, who as nearly as could be was on all sides of the fire at once.

At the same time Aunt Jerusha hovered about him, intent on motherly offices from which she could not be diverted until Uncle Lisha had shouted at her three times with increasing volume of voice.

"Haow come ye tu come? Good airth an' seas! that 's what I want tu know," while Joseph could not find a chance to inquire after the welfare of his father or to ask what message M'ri had sent.

"What was 't you was sayin', father?" Aunt Jerusha asked at last, yet still giving her attention to Sam. "Haow 'd we come? Why, we tackled right up the waggin an' come along. But we never tol' nob'dy 'at we was a-comin' here. The' 'd ha' be'n objections, no eend on 'em, if we 'd ha' tol'. Hed n't you better pull ye' boots off, Samwil, an' stick ye' feet up on that chunk? An' so you see, Huldy she hed some dried apple 'at she wanted tu trade off, an' we jest fixed it up betwixt us 'at we 'd fetch it daown tu Vergennes an' stay over night tu Cousin Chase's an' then come here! An' so we did, an' here we be. Hain't you glad tu see us? You don't act as if you was, not turrible."

"Why, yes, we be tew," Uncle Lisha protested; "but you see, you took us kinder onawares."

"We did n't hev time tu put on aour tother clo's," said Sam.

"Wal, tu tell the truth an' not no jokin' abaout it," said Aunt Jerusha, "we fetched daown all on ye's tother clo's as fur as Cousin Chase's, an' there they be."

"You did n't never, Jerushy Paiggs," said her husband incredulously; but she nodded repeated affirmatives and smiled serenely.

"Wal, then, what did ye for? Be you goin' tu sell 'em or be you goin' tu take us to meetin' or a-visitin', or what is 't?"

"No, not nary one," said she after a moment's enjoyment of her auditors' mystification; "but tu the caravan 'at 's comin' nex' day arter tu-morrer. We cal'lated you 'd plan tu go to 't, an' we 'd go tew, on Bub's 'caount. His gran'pa an' gran'ma 's goin' tu fetch him, an' we wan't a-going tu hev you raound in your ol' ev'yday clo's."

"Good airth an' seas, if I had n't clean forgot it!" Uncle Lisha declared in genuine surprise at his forgetfulness of so important an event.

"Seems 's 'ough I did kinder think on 't when you was a-carummuxin' wi' that ol' ram," said Joseph; "but I hain't thought on 't sence an' I do' know when afore."

"Forgot it!" Aunt Jerusha exclaimed with

mild scorn; "that's a likely story, an' it all pic-
tered aout in red an' yaller ev'ywheres.   Anyways, it is naow up tu Danvis even on tu folkses
barns, an' ev'ybody's a-goin'."

"On Bub's 'caount, I s'pose," her husband remarked, bestowing a wink upon the company.   "I
do' know what we'd all du if it wan't for that
boy."

"I don't nuther," Aunt Jerusha assented heartily. "But it don't signify. "We're all a-goin'
an' a-goin' lookin' somehaow.   Oh, you need n't
think me an' Huldy did n't fetch aour tother bun-
nits," as she detected a quizzical glance at the
gingham sun-bonnets. "An' you need n't worry
none; we made cal'lations on your not bein' prepared for comp'ny an' laid in wi' the folks where
we left aour hoss and waggin tu keep us over night
in case you did n't hev spare beds."

"We got feathers 'nough, seems 's 'ough," Joseph said, "but I don't know 'baout the tick, not
sca'cely."

"An' we fetched along a loaf o' bread an' some
butter, an' some b'iled aigs an' some quick pickles," .
Aunt Jerusha continued, casting a doubtful eye
upon Antoine's panful of fried duck, "'cause we
did n't know but what you might be gittin' short;
but I will say it smells better 'n it looks. Be ye
gittin' dried off, Samwil? They be rael socierable
folks where we left the hoss. Harris is the name

—I b'le' so, an' they 'peared tu be consid'able 'quainted wi' some on ye." She cast a quizzical glance around, ending at Huldah, who shook her head. "Why, good land! what hurt 'll it du? Don' they all know what they done?"

"What in time be you a-drivin' at?" Sam asked. Huldah still shook her head and gave at the same time a deprecatory "S-h-h," but Aunt Jerusha persisted in telling her tale.

"Why, nothin', only them folks was a-tellin' haow 't an ol' man an' a fat man come there one day with a wil' goose 'at they 'd shot, praouder 'n tew rhusters, an' come tu it was a tame wil' goose 'at them folkses hed. Oh, my sakes!" She ended with a fit of laughter in which Sam and Antoine joined as they comprehended the gist of the story, while the heroes of it looked foolish, though Uncle Lisha tried to make light of it by saying: —

"Sho, women folks 'll b'lieve anything you tel' 'em. That 'ere Harris 'll lie faster 'n a hoss c'n trot. What was that 'ere yarn he tol' you, Samwil?" But he failed to divert inquiry and was obliged to admit the truth of the charge. Yet he was consoled for this humiliation by the admiration that his real wild geese drew forth when he exhibited them, and Joseph's store of feathers were given unqualified praise.

Then Antoine announced supper and the embarrassed hosts led their guests to the repast, which they attacked with no great zest, having seen the cook wipe on his trousers the fork with which he turned the contents of the pan, and use his hat for a holder. Yet they praised what was set before them, while making a meal mostly from the provisions they had brought with them. Then they helped to clear the table and made the dishes cleaner than they had been since their first use here.

After this all the company gathered around the fire, the men smoking, Aunt Jerusha regaling herself with snuff, Hulda unwontedly idle for lack of knitting, while all the latest Danvis news was told and with judicious omissions all the adventures of the camp, and so well did the visitors enjoy their first taste of this life that they decided to lodge in the tent, where a luxurious bed was prepared for them with a double allowance of cedar twigs.

At sundown the north wind died, but the pulse of waves still beat upon the beach in regular recurrence above the slumberous murmur of distant shores. A company of bitterns were performing a farewell rite on the eve of migration, uttering uncouth squawks as they wheeled high above the marshes in awkward gyrations, and frequent flights of ducks were whistling past and splashing into channel and marsh.

The busy air was filled with sounds that were strange to Huldah's ear; the shuddering cry of a screech owl and the sad monotony of the crickets

were the only familiar ones among them all.
These with the slow wash of waves were the voices
that her dreams shaped themselves to, when with
a lingering sense of strange environment she fell
asleep.

CHAPTER XXIII.

THE full light of morning had chased the shadows from the camp and even possessed the recesses of the tent when the drowsy inmates awoke and crept forth yawning and shivering in the unsunned air until the rekindled fire warmed them.

Then the women folks got the tidiest breakfast the camp had ever known, and when all save Antoine, who sulked on his faded laurels, had eaten it with great relish, Huldah went out and feasted her eyes full of the wonder and beauty of the lake, where it doubled painted shores in the glassy mirror of near waters, its far expanse melting into ethereal hills and further sky, where distant islands hung in the blended azure.

Then while Joseph and Antoine, forlorn bachelors by brevet, kept camp, the reunited couples embarked in the scow for a cruise along the shore of the bay.

The experience gained while voyaging on the canal and the Western lakes put Aunt Jerusha quite at ease on these quiet waters, and with such an example before her Huldah was too proud to show any trepidation and too sensible to affect it.

"Wal, Huldy," said Uncle Lisha, watching her as he steered while Sam wielded the oars, "you be a nat'ral born sailor, an' you never in a boat before, I'll warrant. Why don't you jump raound and squawk ev' time the boat jiggles?"

"Why, I hain't no time tu, the''s so much tu look at," said she, her eyes roving far and near over the unfamiliar landscape. "Hain't them pine-trees? We don't hev no sech tu home. An' if there hain't the Hump, for there can't be no other like it — an' hain't that Tater Hill? My, what a ways off they be, so blue they don't look much nigher 'n the sky. I should hate tu live so far from 'em all the time. Oh, look at that boat, an' hain't that a black man in it? It sartainly is," and she pointed across and up stream to where Jim was paddling out of his marshy harbor.

"Why, yes," said Uncle Lisha, "that's one o' your husband's friends, Huldy. You'd admire tu see what comp'ny he keeps when he's daown here, — Injins an' niggers an' I do' know what all."

"Quakers an' lawyers an' shoemakers," Sam supplemented.

"An' you hain't no idee what cadidoes he cuts up," the old man continued, regarding his audience with a solemn countenance, "a-fishin' leetle boys aouten the crik, an' wuss 'n all, what you don't never want tu tell nobody, a-helpin' Quakers steal runaway niggers away f'm the' owners. Yes, sir, he done it an' he da's n't deny it," and Uncle Lisha frowned benignly on the culprit.

"Why, Samwil," Huldah said, in a low voice, beaming affection and admiration upon her husband, while Aunt Jerusha laid a gentle hand upon his shoulder.

"Wal, no wonder both on ye's mad an' he 'shamed, but we won't tell on 't if he don't du it ag'in," said Uncle Lisha.

"Sho, Uncle Lisher, what nonsense hev you be'n a-s'misin' up," Sam demanded, with a bold assumption of innocence.

"Good airth an' seas, boy! don't ye s'pose I know brand when the bag 's ontied? Wha' d ye go over tu that Canuck's boat for? Sellin' apples proberbly. Wha' 'd ye kerry them ducks up tu Bartlett's for? Thought they was starvin' proberbly. What made ye so tickled when ye seen the Canuck boat p'intin' for Canerdy? Turrible glad tu git red on him, wan't ye? Oh, you be almighty cunnin', hain't ye?"

Sam's downcast eyes discovered something on the boat's bottom which promised a change of the subject of conversation.

"Why, if there hain't a trollin' line an' hook wi' a piece o' pork rin' an' red rag on 't all rigged for fishin'. It must be Antwine had it, but I don't know when. You put it aout, Huldy, an' mebby you c'n ketch a pickerel."

" Me? My goodness, I could n't never. I 've ketched traouts, but I can't never ketch a pickerel, I know. Would n't I feel big tu, though?"

The line was let out, the boat was slowed down to the proper rate of speed as it skirted the channel, and Huldah held the hand line with a grip that showed a determination to be hauled overboard rather than relinquish it. When the boat reached the mouth of the creek her resolution seemed about to be tested, for the line tightened suddenly with a jerk that drew her arms out to their utmost stretch.

" Whoa! whoa! Back up your waggin, Sam," she cried. " I 've got ketched on a lawg or the hull bottom of the river."

" You hain't nuther!" shouted Uncle Lisha, at once recognizing the cause of the intermittent strain. " It 's a fish, an' an ol' solaker. Pull stiddy, Huldy, stiddy. Oh, good airth an' seas! If you c'n on'y git him! Keep a tight line on him!"

" I sh'ld think he was a-doin' that," said Huldah, her voice shaken by the beating of her heart, though she presented an outside appearance of coolness. Foot by foot the big pickerel was drawn toward the boat till the cold gleam of his wicked eyes could be seen, and then by Uncle Lisha's direction he was given line, then hauled in again till the old man could get a grip on his gills and toss him into the boat. Huldah gave a great gasp of relief and was ready to cry for pride when Sam swung his hat and gave a lusty cheer that was echoed by Jim, who had been watching the struggle and now came paddling over, jerking his head and laughing and offering congratulations while yet twenty rods away.

"I tell ye what, Mr. Lovel, he is a good one!" Jim cried, as he ran his canoe alongside the scow and looked at the fish with a sort of proprietary pride and with almost as much satisfaction as if he had caught it. "Yes, sir, he is a good one, Mr. Lovel. Is it Mis' Lovel 'at ketched him? Well, ma'am, you handled him just as well as ever I ever see anybody. Yes, sir, you did. Could n't no man done better — could n't myself. Naow, if you want tu try it, you might troll aout raound the island. Mighty good place that is for ol' big fellers," and Jim emphasized every item of praise and advice by a jerk of the head, continuing both till the crew of the scow passed out of hearing, and Huldah remarked, still gloating over her captive : —

"Wal, Uncle Lisher, Samwil might find wus comp'ny, for he 'pears tu be a real sensible, candid sort of a man."

When they entered the lake Aunt Jerusha was

induced by much persuasion to take the line and a
chance of distinguishing herself. She held it anxiously and under continual protest of inability to
do so at all.

"I can't hold it so 't any fish 'll ever bite, I
know I can't. If anything gits a holt of it, I shall
lose it, I know I shall. You 'd better take it,
Huldy; you 've got used to 't! There! There!
There 's suthin' a nibblin'! No, the' hain't nuther.
I knowed the' would n't nothin', never! My land!
The' is tew! Lisher, Samwil, Huldy! I 've got
him. He 'll git away! He 'll pull me in!'"

With frequent abortive snatches at it, she frantically hauled in the line, that yielded. to her spasmodic efforts with a heavy, sluggish resistance.
Uncle Lisha unconsciously lifted the paddle from
the water, Sam quit rowing, and Huldah withdrew
her admiring gaze from the fish at her feet, and
the three spectators watched the struggle with
intense interest.

"Lisher Paiggs," cried Aunt Jerusha with unusual sharpness, "why don't you take a holt an'
help me stid o' settin' there like a scairt fool?"

In ready obedience to this demand, Uncle Lisha
underrun the line with the paddle and brought it
to hand, and then slowly and carefully hauled it in
till, reaching down to the surface, he lifted the bur-
dened hook and swung inboard a big clam.

"Wal, ol' woman," said he, collapsing from

high expectation to deep disgust, " you hev done it, hain't ye ? "　With his knife he loosened the vise-like grip of the mussel and was about to toss it overboard.

" Here, don't ye never, Lisher Paiggs," cried Aunt Jerusha, suddenly recovering speech ; " you gi' me that.　It 's jest what I wanted."

" Good airth an' seas, Jerushy, wha'd' ye want on 't ?　You can't eat one on 'em no more you could a chunk o' soaked so' luther."

" No more I don't want tu.　You jest clean the meat aout on 't an' heave it away an' gi' me the shells.　There," she continued when possessed of them, and holding them up she regarded them with unaffected admiration, " them 's jest what I be'n a-wantin' ever sen I be'n a-haousekeepin', for they be the completest thing tu scrape aout a kittle an' tu skim milk an' tu scoop sugar 'at ever was. Mother hed some 'at she fetched f'm Rhode Islan', an' I 've allus be'n a-wantin' tu git a holt o' some. Naow I 've got 'em, an' I 'd a great sight druther hev 'em 'an a fish 'at 'll be eat right up.　Naow, Lisher, you heave that 'ere fishin' thingumbob int' the water ag'in an' I 'll ketch Huldy some clam-shells."

Aunt Jerusha did not succeed in fulfilling this benevolent intention, for they were now in deep water, but as they coasted along the gray northern wall of Garden Island she was thrown into a second fever of excitement by a livelier tug at the line. This time it was a pickerel, which, by dint of stout tackle and good fortune, was brought to boat, and in spite of her protested indifference to such a capture, she rejoiced over it exceedingly.

They landed on the island, and with Sam acting as guide explored its interior. The garden-like bloom of its shrubbery no longer verified the island's name, but there were evidences of it in the abundant black clusters of viburnum berries and scarlet haws of wild roses, and there were yet enough blue and white blossoms of asters to make the place pleasant to flower-loving women.

The money diggers' pit in the centre of the island was a place of interest to the men, for whom a hole in the ground always has a fascination. Then all went over to the east end, where Aunt Jerusha found some stranded clam-shells for Huldah, cleaner and brighter than her own, and all found arrow points of flint on the narrow strip of gravelly beach.

"It does beat all natur' haow the critters made 'em!" said Uncle Lisha, pondering over a handsome hornstone arrow-head. "We could n't, wi' all the tools we got, an' I hearn an ol' feller tell aout West 'at the Injins done it wi' a sort o' bone thingumajig, jest by pushin' on 't with the hand, an' he claimed he 'd seen 'em at it, but I d' know 'baout it. That 'ere 'd make a toll'able good gun-flint, an' I guess I 'll keep it.   An' naow," he continued, after trying the flint with his knife and pocketing both, "if you 've looked at posies an' cur'osities long enough le' 's go over int' the bay yunder an' g' up tu the haouse where I was yist'-day an' git some apples for the women folks. They 're dre'df'l clever folks up there."

This plan being approved, the party voyaged across the tranquil bay, and then making a détour to avoid the realm of the warlike old Spaniard, went across the fields to the house.

As they drew near they sniffed a familiarly pleasant and pungent odor of smoke and lye which led them to an outdoor fire where Uncle Lisha's yesterday's acquaintance was boiling soap. Uncle Lisha introduced his companions, who were cordially welcomed by the mistress, without an apology for the man's hat and coat she wore, except to say : —

" If you ever made soap you know folks don't want tu dress up much for it, an' you c'n see I hain't."

" I guess you don't want tu," said Aunt Jerusha sympathetically.   " It is turrible messin', clarifyin' the grease, an' the lye 'll take the color aout 'n eve'ything it teches."

" An' so onsartain," Huldah added.   " You never know whether it 's a-goin' tu be soap."

" I know it," cried the housewife.   " It is the

provokin'est! Your lye 'll bear an aig like a cork, an' your grease 'll be all right, an' yit they won't be soap. I wonder what 's come of my man. If you men folks could find him mebby it 'ould be more interestin' 'an aour gabbin'. He went tu git some chunks. Soap-b'ilin' 's a good time tu burn up chunks. Gid — Gid-eon! where be ye? I guess he 'll come," she said, after listening a moment; and then returning to the subject of soap-making, "Some says it 's 'cause the wind 's north, but I do' know. Anyways, it does act onaccountable."

"I believe the witches or the Ol' Cat hisself gits into 't," Aunt Jerusha declared.

"Same as intu cream sometimes," said Huldah. "Solon Briggs says 'at a piece o' silver money 'll drive the witches aout o' that, an' mebby it 'ould aout of soap."

"Wal, I 'm goin' tu see whether it 's soap or not," the soapmaker said, tucking her dress between her knees, pulling her hat over her eyes, and blowing the steam away while she dipped a few spoonfuls of the contents of the kettle into an old saucer. This she stirred and cooled with her breath, watching it anxiously, while her feminine guests looked on with almost as much interest, as the liquid dribbled in a thin stream from the spoon.

"Mebby they was beech ashes," Uncle Lisha suggested, regarding it and the disappointed and vexed face of the matron.

"No, they was most all ellum," she answered. "Plague on 't, it don't look like nothin'."

"Wal, the' hain't no better ashes than ellum, so it ain't that," said the old man.

"Try a leetle dash o' water in 't," Aunt Jerusha suggested, and when this was done the liquid at once thickened in the saucer and the face of the fair soapmaker relaxed to an expression of supreme satisfaction, which was sympathetically repeated in the countenances of her visitors.

Gideon now appeared with an armful of refractory outcasts from the woodpile and the little girls at his heels. He was introduced in the same breath that the good tidings were communicated to him, and he rejoiced also, while the little girls silently welcomed their doughty old champion with bashful smiles, and, nibbling finger tips and apron corners, shyly made the acquaintance of his companions.

When the guests were comforted with apples and stayed with flagons, they went over to the ferry harbor and beheld with intense admiration that maritime wonder, the horse boat, arrive and depart. Uncle Lisha recounted once more to Aunt Jerusha's willing ears the events of his life as a soldier, and she was proud to be on the very ground where he began his military career, and declared with great satisfaction: "This was 'nough tu pay her for comin'," while Sam and Huldah were so much interested the old man felt himself quite a hero.

Then they strolled back to their own humble craft and coasted along shore toward camp. Long before they saw his figure idly pacing the beach, they heard Antoine's sonorous voice doing its best with some words of the " Exile of Erin " which he had picked up somewhere : —

> " Dar come on de beach a poor eggshell of heron,
>   De dew on hees chin rub it heavy an' chill.
> For he caount on he side his two rib a pair in,
>   An' one dar alone in de wind by de hill."

He was at the landing to receive them and was profuse in his compliments to the anglers when their trophies were shown him.

" Bah gosh, Aunt Jerrushy! Bah t'under, Ma'am Hudly! You bose of it beat Onc' Lasha an' Zhozeff an' Sam for feesh, an' 'mos' me, w'en Ah ant try. Prob'ly if Ah 'll was go wid you, you ketch lot of it. But you do pooty good, Ah tol' you."

" Yes, they did, sartain," said Uncle Lisha. " An' you 'd ort tu seen her haul in a clam. He fit like a good feller, but 't wan't no use, the ol' woman was tew many for him an' she muckled him. An' both women 's a heap better sailors 'an Jozeff is."

" Zhozeff," said Antoine, with supreme contempt, " Ah 'll was jes' soon try for mek feesh walk on de graoun' as for mek Zhozeff be sailor mans. An' all de tam we keep haouse to-day he worry, worry for 'fraid you be draown' on de lake."

The next morning the preparative bustle of departure began, and though no one openly confessed it, each felt a shade of sadness as the place grew bare and desolate where such pleasant hours had been spent.

"It beats all natur' haow a feller gits wonted tu a place where he's hed a good time, an' hates tu leave it," Sam said, as he turned away, "but it's hopesin' we'll come ag'in."

"What's sass for gander's sass for goose, an' when you come ag'in I'm a-comin' tew," said Huldah decidedly.

"If de hwomans was comin', Ah'll ant, me," Antoine declared; "it was spile up all de funs for try for live too pooty."

"Wal," Uncle Lisha sighed, "it hain't noways likely 'at I'll ever come ag'in."

"But if ye du, Lisher, I'm a-comin' tew," Aunt Jerusha said, as they departed.

The last ember snapped out in dull explosion and the last thin wisp of smoke dissolved in the colorless air, and amid the silence of desertion the falling leaves began the slow obliteration of man's transitory sojourn.

CHAPTER XXIV.

THE CARAVAN.

TOWARD the middle of the afternoon Uncle Lisha and his friends entered the outskirts of the little city, where the unusual appearance of a camping outfit attracted considerable attention and was generally believed to be one of the side shows belonging to the coming caravan.

It presently gathered a following of boys, and when Sam drew rein in front of Cousin Chase's tidy house these were joined by several grown-up and no less curious idlers, and all surrounded the wagon in an interested group.

"It's a nigger show, I bet ye," one boy confidently asserted.

"Yah. What you talkin' 'bout?" cried another contemptuously. "It's the Injin show! Don't you see the canew? An' that black feller up there's one of 'em; the ol' chief, he is."

"My, don't he look ugly, though?" loudly whispered another, staring in fascinated horror at Antoine, who, overhearing these remarks, at once fell into humoring them.

"Yas, sah, Ah'll was big Injin, me! Ant you see haow Ah'll was sca'p dis hol' mans?" He lifted Uncle Lisha's hat, displaying the shining bald pate, and then after a moment's impressive silence continued, "Wal, seh, boy, Ah was tore off you hairs jes' lak dat 'f you'll ant ta' careful. You want for hear me spik Injin more better as Angleesh?

"Cangra musquash nawah alamose woisoose chunkamug peskegan. Ooop!"

His audience listened with deep admiration to the first specimen of aboriginal eloquence which they had ever heard.

"You want to go on and turn to the left to get to the show ground," said a florid gentleman of leisure, dressed in a drab fur hat, blue coat, and tightly strapped trousers, and he pointed up street with his cane, which he then tucked under his arm, while he took a pinch of snuff and meditatively surveyed the occupants of the wagon. "I hope you folks don't have any tight-rope dancing and the like," he continued with a deprecatory air. "That's contrary to the laws of the State, you know."

"Wal, naow, that's tew bad," said Uncle Lisha in a grieved voice, and indicating Joseph with a jerk of the thumb, "for this 'ere young man is turrible hefty on the wires."

The florid gentleman thought he recognized the

blush of modest merit in Joseph's abashed face, and with a sly wink at Uncle Lisha said in a husky undertone : —

" We might fix up a leetle private entertainment — in a barn — you know, to-night. Select and quiet, you know."

" No, sir ! We 're law-abidin' folks," said Uncle Lisha with virtuous decision. " Say, can any on ye tell me whether no Ab'm Chase lives in this 'ere haouse. Good airth an' seas ! If he don't come an' tell us where tu go pooty soon we sh'll hefter hev a show tu git red o' the folks."

" Say, mister," an eager boy whispered, clutching Sam's knee, " if I 'd fetch water for your hosses, won't ye let me go in for nothin', me an' my little brother ; he hain't bigger 'n nothin' ! We hain't got no money. Will ye, mister ? "

" Why, bub," said Sam, " we hain't no show. We jest come tu see the show, that 's all."

The boy stared incredulously into the honest face till assured there was no guile in it, and then retired in disappointment, leading his little brother.

Now the front door of the house opened and Abram Chase came hurrying out in a state of excitement quite incongruous with his smooth-shaven face and plain, neat attire, when he found his Cousin Jerusha's husband and his friends standing unwelcomed at his threshold and surrounded by a crowd of curious idlers.

" God zounds ! Lisher, what be you settin' there for ? Why did n't ye come right in ? Back up a leetle an' haw right in here an' drive tu the barn. Clear aout, boys. What be you a-hengin' raound here for ? "

As he opened the great gate and the wagon was driven into the barn the crowd realized its mistake and dispersed, the blue-coated gentleman saunter- ing up the street in dignified indifference, while the boys made a joke of their disappointment and tried to out-jeer one another.

" Ya-ay, Kelly, how much 's the tickets to your Injin show? Ya-ay ! " and Kelly retorted : —

" Ya-ay, Smithy, 'baout as much as it 'll be to git int' your nigger show. Ya-ay ! " and both factions shouted " Ya-ay ! " with a clamor like that of a congregation of crows, and Uncle Lisha was im- pressed by the depravity of town boys in calling each other by their last names.

" Well, Lisher, haow be you, anyway ? " Abram Chase inquired, when, after a bustle of general hospitality, he found time to give attention to in- dividuals. " An' haow be you, Samwil? An' hain't this Joseph Hill ? "

" Wal, I don't sca'cely seem tu know whether no it 's me 'r a Injin 'r a balance master 'r some other sort o' show feller," said Joseph, feeling his head and looking at his short, stumpy legs to assure himself of his identity. " I was beginnin' tu 'xpect Uncle Lisher 'd hev me a-stannin' on my head 'r a-turnin' summersets 'fore I knowed it."

" Bah gosh, Ah 'll give more for see dat as all de show dey had to-morry," cried Antoine. With that he departed to his numerous compatriots in the " French village " at the other end of the town, and the others went into the house, where Cousin Chase's good wife was entertaining Jerusha and Huldah.

Henceforth till bedtime these town mice and country mice compared experiences, now to the envy of one, now the other.

When morning came no one thought of anything but the great event of the day already heralded in the gray dawn by the rumble of the heavy baggage vans. Habitual early risers were out betimes full clad, to admire the teams of large, handsome horses and gayly painted wagons, and sluggards came forth half dressed with garments in hand and unshod feet, rubbing sleepy eyes and fumbling at buttons with alternate hands as they blinked at the lumbering procession with a fellow feeling for the drowsy drivers and the weary showmen asleep on the jolting piles of canvas.

The vans rumbled past, transferring the present interest to the show grounds, and the brief excitement of the street subsided temporarily while the citizens breakfasted.

Then the first influx of sightseers came hurrying

in, fearful of being late, though they reported the caravan two miles behind, delayed at the last stream by the elephants refusing to cross the bridge. Gradually the incoming tide of sightseers increased, some on foot, whole families in heavy farm wagons, and young fellows with their sweethearts in the cumbersome single pleasure wagons of those days, some of which had boxes shaped like bread trays, others square ones substantially framed and paneled, with high-backed seats cushioned with russet-colored leather and perched at such a lofty height that ascent and descent were not to be lightly undertaken.

At last the grand triumphal chariot appeared, blazing and glittering with scarlet and gold, and drawn by four white horses driven by a liveried driver, behind whom the band was enthroned, blowing lustily on brazen bugles, French horns, trombones, and ophicleides, all in time to the thunderous beating of a bigger drum than had ever been heard at a general muster. Then came two elephants, one of whom bore a howdah in which the lion tamer sat dressed like a Roman gladiator and quietly smoking an incongruous pipe. These were followed by four camels ridden by Arabs, whose genuineness became doubtful when one was heard to address his beast with "Git on wid yez, ye spalpeen." Then came the train of closed mysterious cages, some silent, others giving forth growls and screams of strange beasts and birds.

Close upon these came a crowd, hurrying for fear of being late, though it was two hours before the advertised opening of the show. Uncle Lisha and his party, reinforced by Mr. and Mrs. Purington, Sis and her nephew Bub, were early upon the ground, eagerly enjoying all the novel sights and sounds of the busy scene.

Here was an excited group of Canadians, interspersed with a sprinkling of cool-headed Yankee jockeys, gathered around three or four sorry nags that looked as if the impending changes of ownership could make little difference to them or any one else.

"Wal, Joe," drawled a solemn-visaged man, after an examination of one of these animals from all points of view, " it kinder looks tu me 's if your hoss hed got the heaves tucked ontu him consid'-able bad."

"Yas, Harrum, 'e got some o' dem," the owner, a jolly little pock-marked Frenchman, frankly admitted in a husky voice, "mais, dey ant hurt him mite. You 'oss 'e hol', hol' every tam 'e hol', Harrum, and 'e gat splavin lak geese egg."

"Sho! That hain't nothin'," said the other ; " I c'n blister that off in a week, smooth as the palm o' my hand. If you want my hoss bad 'nough tu gi' me a dollar, we 'll call it a trade."

"Oh, Harrum! Swappy de 'oss pour de 'oss," the little man pleaded.

"No, I got tu hev a dollar tu boot."

"'Ow Ah goin' give you more as Ah gat?" Joe asked piteously. "Ah geeve you half dollar, dat all Ah gat, me."

He held up the coin before the other, who took it with a sigh of resignation, saying, "Wal, seein' it's you, Joe, but I'm jest the same as givin' away my hoss," and each began unharnessing his horse amid the congratulations of friends.

The little group of Danvis people passed on to where a peddler mounted on a cart was auctioneering his wares.

"Oh, just look what I've found tucked away in a corner, an' I thought the last blessed pair was sold yesterday," he cried, stretching to arms' length a pair of puckery rubber suspenders that smelled infernally of sulphur. "Just look. Stretch like a deacon's conscience. Long enough for any man. Short enough for any boy. Oak-tanned luther ends an' gold buckles, I guess, but mebby they're brass. Don't let your women folks wear their fingers aout knittin' galluses for you, but walk right up an' buy a pair of these beautiful e-lastic suspenders, worth one dollar tu any man, but I sell 'em for half that money, an' tu-day, secin' you all want tu save a quarter to go int' the show, I'll let you have 'em for quart' of a dollar a pair, an' I'll say no more an' take no less."

Such a generous offer was not to be withstood,

and the new-fangled suspenders were passed out to
the crowding purchasers till it seemed as if the red
cart could have been laden with nothing else, yet
the enterprising proprietor was continually discovering some new article, and each more tempting
than the last. Now it was a ring or brooch, now
some cheap and tuneless instrument, now pocket-
combs, side - combs, and back - combs, jackknives,
distorting hand glasses, song books, lives and con-
fessions of criminals, and so on, changing as often
as interest flagged.

There were numerous booths where refreshments
of mead, spruce beer, and great cards of good old-
fashioned yellow gingerbread were temptingly displayed, and the familiar, obese, and blue-frocked
figure of Old Beedle was present, dispensing foam-
ing glasses of innocuous beer from a cask in the
tail of his wagon, and with them such kindly words
and genial smiles that it seemed to his juvenile
customers as if they were receiving a great deal
for a cent.

There were peripatetic venders of apples in baskets, and home-made molasses candy on boards,
both wares cried by the youthful Canadian dealers
at the usual price of "Two of it, one cen' 'piece."

Noisiest of all were the tooters, vociferously pro-
claiming the wonders of the side shows, the fat
woman and the strong man, the albino negroes and
the man without arms, and the waxworks of Mon-

sieur Jonsin from Paris, all of which were now on exhibition and each to be seen for the small sum of twelve and one half cents.

The twanging of the banjo, the thumping of the tambourine, the voices of the performers and the laughter of the audience sounded smothered and echoless as they beat against the canvas walls, yet were most attractive to the outsiders who crowded about the narrow entrances.

As Joseph Hill stood in rapt admiration of the colossal portrait of the fat woman, counting the coins in his pocket with his fingers, he was startled by hearing his name called in a familiarly imperative tone, and looking in the direction from whence it came saw the gaunt form of his father standing upright in a lumber wagon, brandishing his cane toward him with one hand and with the other restraining young Josiah from leaping to the ground. Maria, who with her daughter Ruby occupied a portion of the seat from which the patriarch had risen, was frantically shaking a handkerchief toward her husband, and Pelatiah, who as driver sat in front with two of the smaller children, had his breath indrawn and his mouth made up, to add his voice to the family call.

" Wal, if this don't pooty nigh beat Sam Hill," Joseph exclaimed, as he hastened over to them. " Seem 's 'ough I thought o' most ev'b'dy a-comin', but I swaow, I never thought o' you a-comin', father."

"You did n't, hey? An' you could n't hear me when I did come, a-gawpin' at that 'ere pictur'," Gran'ther Hill scolded in a cracked catarrhal voice. "What is 't a pictur' on, anyway? A elephant dressed up in women's clo's? I 'll bate they hain't got no sech a critter."

"It 's the fat lady, father," Joseph explained, " an' the white niggers. Haow come ye tu come, father ? "

"Fat lady and white niggers," the old man repeated scornfully. "By the Lord Harry, what is this cussed world a-comin' tu when *shes* 'at goes raound showin' their carkisses like hawgs tu a cattle show calls theirselves ladies, an' niggers calls theirselves white ! I come 'cause I was a mine tu ! Did n't you ? Did you s'pose the' wan't nob'dy but you a-comin'? Don't ye s'pose Josier wanted tu come, an' Ruby an' t' other young uns, an' du you s'pose I was goin' tu let 'em come daown here along wi' M'rier an' Peltier and git lost an' eat up ? That would be smart ! "

"Why, I 'm glad you come if you can stan' it," Joseph declared. " Be you middlin' well ? An' you, M'ri an' Ruby, an' 'mongst ye, an' you tew, Peltier ? Oh, M'ri, if I hain't got the almightedest snarl o' feathers ! Wal, not sech a turrible sight on 'em, but sech neat ones you never did see a'most."

"Yonder comes Lisher an' Jerushy an' Lovel

an' his wife an' young un, all comin' tu ask what I
come for, I 'll lay a guinea," said Gran'ther testily,
" an' if there hain't that 'ere cussed Pur'nt'n
woman an' her man. I hain't nothin' ag'in the
beasts, but I swear I wish 't they 'd eat her.
Young Gove, drive your hosses up tu the fence an'
hitch 'em! Sed daown, Josier, 'fore I knock ye
daown. G' 'long! "

The horses were driven to the nearest hitching
place and given a bundle of hay from the hinder
end of the wagon, whose occupants were by this
time overtaken by their townsfolk in spite of Gran'-
ther Hill's attempts to elude Mrs. Purington.

" Wal, I should think you 'd 'a' hed more regard
for your health, Capting Hill," the tired dame
panted, fanning her hot face with a folded handkerchief, " an' I don't see what you let him come
for, Marier. It 's jest flyin' in the face o' Provi-
dence."

" Damn my health, marm, it 's ol' 'nough tu ta'
keer of itself," the veteran declared, standing very
erect and looking fierce. " Haow d' ye s'pose
M'rier was goin' tu help herself? The' hain't
nob'dy flew yit; but I wish t' the Lord Harry they
would, higher 'n Gilderoy's kite, an' never light
this side o' glory halleuyer."

" I 'm dreatful glad you come, Cap'n Hill," said
Sam, shifting Bub to his left arm that he might
shake hands with the old man. " They say the' 's
a bustin' old painter an' some wolves."

" Yis," said Uncle Lisha, " an' some Injins ; but they won't le' ye kill 'em, 'cause they hain't got but a few."

" Hev they got all them ? " the veteran asked eagerly. " Come, let 's git aour keerds an' g'w'in t' the carryvan afore the young uns dies o' waitin'. Take a holt o' my hand, Bub. For'a'd, march."

As they approached the thronged precincts of the ticket wagon and Sam detached himself from his party to enter into the struggle for tickets, he was accosted by his impecunious youthful acquaintance of yesterday, who was now standing forlornly apart from the crowd with his little brother, looking with longing eyes at the blue and yellow cards as they were passed to the outstretched hands by the imperturbable ticket-seller.

" You wan't one of 'em, was ye ? " said the boy, with a melancholy smile of recognition.

" Hello ! " Sam responded cheerily. " Hain't you shavers goin' in ? "

The boy shook his head in sorrowful resignation.

" The big fellers got all the jobs, an' I hain't got no money."

" You wait here till I come back," said Sam, after a moment's hesitation, and then shouldered his way into the crowd, through which his tall, strong figure enabled him soon to reach the wagon. Presently emerging from the press somewhat flushed and rumpled, but smiling, he returned to the boys and handed the elder a couple of half tickets. " There, bub, you an' the little chap go in an' see the hull caboodle on 't," and Sam rejoined his friends before the boy could give audible expression to his thanks and astonishment.

Joining the drifting tide of mixed humanity, our Danvis friends were carried with it inside the great tent into a world of strange new sights, sounds, and atmosphere. If this was not the perfumed breath of Araby, these were the beasts and birds and reptiles of the tropics and far countries of the earth, this medley of discordant sounds that frightened children and startled their elders, — the natural everyday voices that had shaken the torpid air of Indian and African jungles.

The keepers, who walked unconcernedly in front of the cages and were the familiars of the uncouth elephants and camels, bore such impress of strange experience and wide travel as made them quite different from ordinary mortals, and speech with them an overwhelming honor.

" Yes, that 'ere is a boar constructor or animal condor," Solon Briggs explained to his neighbors, whom, with his wife, he had joined near the front of the cage in which a great serpent was coiled. " I s'pect that was the specie that onderminded the humern race of mankind by temptin' of Eve, 'cause you see he 's cal'lated by the dimensions of his len'th for reachin' arter apples. An' that 'ere is the rile tiger, so called on account of his allus bein' riled, an' that critter that's got stripes jus' like him is called zebray on account o' his resemblin' a jackass. An' anybody 'ould know them was licrns, only the female specie hain't got no mane. An' hain't them elephants the curisest freak o' humern natur'? It does appear 'at if they was pervided with another pair of visible organs in the behind of 'em they might perceed back'ards jest as well as for'ards, hevin' a tail on each end of 'em. That 'ere is called the backteryan camel on account o' his hump."

"Poor creetur's," said Aunt Jerusha, "I should think they'd git dre'f'l tired o' goin' humped up so all the time."

"Them is what they kerry water in when they cross the de-sart of Sary — she 't was Abram's wife," said Solon.

"Briggs must ha' made most o' these 'ere animals hisself, I consait, he 'pears tu know so much abaout 'em," Gran'ther Hill growled sarcastically. "Come, Josier, le''s go an' look o' the painter an' them wolves; I want tu see suthin' 'at I know suthin' abaout myself. There!" he continued, as, leading his grandson and followed by Sam and Pelatiah, he halted in front of the cages of these animals, "that's the sort o' pussycat an' dogs 'at used for tu be a-yaowlin' an' a-yollopin' raound yer gran'-

ser's campfire when he was on airth the fust time. Ah, ye ol' yaller cat! You sneakin' whelps! Yer gre't gran'marms knowed me."

He shook his cane at them, and the panther spat at him and the wolves slunk into a corner as if each recognized in him an ancient enemy of its kind.

Presently the attention of all was drawn to the performance of the elephants, when one huge beast made its majestic progress around the ring with a howdah full of delightedly frightened children, and the other walked with slow and ponderously careful steps over the prostrate form of the keeper.

Then a pony ridden by a monkey ran in the ring, at which time Antoine made his appearance. Having been entertained by many friends, he had arrived at a condition to fully enjoy the show. Now he was in a bellicose humor, thirsting for a hand-to-hand encounter with the bear, now he was affectionate, desiring to embrace every one, including the equestrian monkey.

"Say, Sam, Ah wan' kees dat leetly nigger. Ah luv heem more as Ah luv mah fam'ly, bah gosh! Ah 'll was nabolition mans, me, an' Ah 'll wan' stole dat leetly nigger. Sam, ant you wan' help me stole dat leetly nigger?" and so maundered on till, to Sam's great relief, his attention was directed to the band and he began to dance in front of it, dividing the attention of the audience with the clown, who, with the ring-master, made the nearest approach to a circus that was then permitted in our virtuous commonwealth.

The humor displayed by the clown in his ancient jokes and repartees was irresistible, and when after turning a succession of somersaults he ran his painted nose against a centre post of the tent Aunt Jerusha declared : —

"He's the quickest witted man I ever see, but the clumsiest creetur' for one 'at's so spry by spells. Eunice Pur'nt'n, if you've got your camphire bottle, you le' me hev it an' I'll go an' rub some on his nose, for it's painin' on him turribly, I know it is."

Mrs. Purington never ventured far from home without her bottle of camphor and smelling salts, and possessing herself of the first Aunt Jerusha hastened forth to offer a balm for the supposedly injured member, while audience and actors looked on in silent wonder.

"Here, you poor distressed wretch, le' me put some o' this sperits o' camphire on t' your nose. It'll take the soreness aout if it does make it smart some," she said, approaching the clown, who left off his lamentations to stare at her in dumb surprise. "Le' me rub some on 't right on," she urged, "or put it on yourself if you'd druther."

"Thank you," he said politely, "if you'd be so good, just a drop," and he soberly submitted to the

Danvis people were on their homeward way, and a
little after nightfall their own mountains closed
around them and again shut them in from the busy
world of which they had had such a brief but
memorable glimpse.

operation while the paint came off his nose on to the tips of her fingers. " Thank you, dear old lady," he said in a low voice, " and bless your kind heart.　It 's done me ever so much good."

He returned her to her place as politely as if she had been the finest and fairest lady in the land, and then tripping back to the centre of the ring he propounded another conundrum.

" Why is the old lady's heart like my nose ? "

" Wal, sir, why is it ? " the ring-master demanded.

" Because it 's tender, of course," was the answer, and there was tremendous applause.

" Oh, dear, it 's tew bad, it 's tew bad ! " Aunt Jerusha sobbed, almost in dismay at having attracted such general attention, " but if it done him a mite o' good, I hain't sorry."

Now the performers retired from the ring, the lively measure of the galop changed to a solemn andante, and the audience breathlessly awaited the grand event of the day.

There was a clang of bars and an opening door, and the lion tamer entered the den, driving the snarling beasts to one end of it, from whence they came one by one at his command and sullenly performed their parts.

" Oh, dear suz ! " Mrs. Purington wailed in a tearfully restrained voice, " they 're a-goin' tu eat him, I know they be, an' the show folks expex it.

That's what makes 'em play so solemn on the music, jus' for all the world like a fun'al hyme tune. Say, mister," she piteously appealed to a showman who stood near, " won't you go an' tell him tu go right aout o' there? It don't seem as if I could stan' it tu stan' here an' see him eat up right afore my face an' eyes."

" Don't be alarmed, ma'am," said the showman, "there's no danger. The last man they heat was so tough and disagreed with 'em so bad, they ain't 'ankered harter human flesh sence. More 'n hall that, 'Err Driesbach is a Dutchman, han' the beastises can't habide the smell o' saurkraout."

She only half believed this and kept her smelling bottle in hand till, greatly to her relief and that of most of the audience, the brave lion-tamer backed out from the royal presence, and the band burst forth in a jubilant strain so loud that it set the elephants to trumpeting and all the carnivora to roaring and howling.

Every one was glad that this part of the show was over, but alas, it was all over, and even now the shutters of the cages were going up and the canvas walls were going down, and the crowd dispersed except the few who lingered for a last look at the camels and elephants, and such as were fooled into parting with their money to see the hurried, final exhibitions of the side shows.

Before the afternoon was much further spent the

www.ingramcontent.com/pod-product-compliance
Lightning Source LLC
Chambersburg PA
CBHW031038120726
47905CB00007B/2233